·CASTLE RIDGE·

Small Town Romance

BOOK ONE

THE
Romance
DANCE

"Allie Burton writes fun, flirty, sexy romance.
I can't wait to head back to Castle Ridge!"
—Romance Author Addison Fox

BESTSELLING AUTHOR
ALLIE BURTON

THE ROMANCE DANCE
A Castle Ridge Small Town Romance Book 1

Copyright © 2016 by Alice Fairbanks-Burton

All Rights Reserved

Published by Alice Fairbanks-Burton
ISBN-13: 978-1-7326764-5-9
Cover by The Killion Group, Inc.
Interior Design by Author E.M.S.

Other Books in Castle Ridge Series
Where small town love takes you higher.

To Mom and Dad,
who demonstrated every day what real love means.

THE
Romance
DANCE

ALLIE BURTON

Chapter One

Reed O'Donnell's nemesis stood in the center of the room. His stomach clenched and every muscle and tendon in his body tightened, fighting off nausea and anxiety. "What the hell are you doing here?" Muttering to himself, Reed's voice quivered similar to a tenor carrying a final long note.

Without being aware, his feet shifted over the recently-sanded wooden floor, sidling toward his enemy as if being called by a siren's song. Even covered by a white tarp the shape was recognizable. His shaking limbs moved slowly—his brain fighting his body's desire.

"I knew there'd be dancing, but you?" His lungs shrunk and he couldn't breathe.

Since he'd be moving out of one of the apartments above the rented space, he believed he could put up with the torture of canned music from the new dance studio for a few weeks.

"What have I agreed to?" The annoying, taunting, tinkling sounds struck in his head like an old mistress, summoning him to return to the relationship. A relationship he'd cut ties to after the accident.

It must've come during his lunch break. An unexpected and unwanted arrival.

The concrete mound in his chest worked its way up his throat. He moved closer, narrowing his gaze at the enemy. The thing that had made his world and brought him down in a crash so ugly and destructive Reed was lucky to have survived.

He grazed his hand over the tarp, feeling the sharp angles underneath. The familiar object sent a cold shiver skittering across his skin. Glancing around, he checked to make sure no one was watching. Even though the new tenant had recently moved in, he hadn't met the dance studio owner yet.

It wouldn't hurt to take a peek. To face his enemy for the first time in years.

The crinkle-crinkle of the tarp lifting off the object sent his pulse racing. He took a step back.

The glare from the baby grand piano with its polished wood and shiny foot pedals afflicted his eyes. The richness of the antique surface placed the piano from the early 1900s. Old, or as some people would say, an antique. The question of whether the instrument sounded lyrical and pitch-perfect would be in the piano's inner workings. His trained ear could recognize the slightest bit out of tune. Not that he wanted to hear this piano. Or any piano.

He wanted nothing to do with anything or anyone associated with music.

As if a game show theme song ticked in his mind, curiosity and temptation had his fingers lifting the lid off the keys. An old habit, he placed his fingers in position. His hands no longer looked slim and manicured. Scars lined his palm and fingers, and calluses roughened his thumb. These hands, his hands, didn't belong to a concert pianist anymore, to a composer and lyricist. They belonged to an accident victim and a construction worker.

The horror of the accident returned. Pain struck through his head. He fisted his hands, fighting to regain his equilibrium. It had taken years, but he'd turned himself around and landed on his feet. He'd walked again. He'd found his place in this new life.

Pressing his index and middle fingers and holding down a couple of keys, the harsh mingling of notes carried from his fingertips to scrape along his spine. The muscles in his neck tightened, and he trembled. He yanked his finger away, as if he'd been scorched.

An image of his last concert flickered in his head. His adoring audiences, his clamoring fans, his fiancée's final kiss.

The shivers changed into quakes, rocking his body and his world. The rocking rushed through him, roasting his anger and his loss. Horrifying images flashed through his head, causing more agony and more anger. Images he didn't want to remember.

This instrument had destroyed him.

A crescendo of grief and anger and guilt crushed together—an *acciaccatura* of notes taking no space in time, and yet all the space in his chest. His lungs expanded with pain. Pain of knowing these fatal emotions were his own fault. Every muscle in his body wound tight—a wind-up toy ready to let loose. If only he hadn't...

He kicked the piano.

A loud bang echoed through the dance studio, followed by a discordant tone of the keys knocking together.

"Stop! What are you doing?" The shriek broke through his trance.

Reed wheeled around. A beautiful woman poised on the edge of the dance floor. Her beauty hit him like a percussion section, even with her narrowed, icy-blue eyes and scowl.

"That's an antique piano." Her long, tall, graceful frame sashayed forward. A dancer. Black tights under a swaying skirt moved back and forth with her hips. A light-pink sweater tied around her tiny waist emphasized her slender, straight shoulders. Her blonde hair pinned in a tight bun on her head, not a strand out of place. Anger and some other emotion made her skin glow and her gaze light with a royal blue. "Musical instruments should be treated with respect."

Just like people.

His heart squeezed and a burning sensation pricked his eyes. Kicking the piano had been wrong, but he'd done much worse.

She bent to inspect the spot where his foot had landed giving him a view of her nice backside. Two nice round mounds a man would love to—

He yanked his gaze away. He wasn't interested. Not now. Not ever. The attraction was as unwelcome as the piano. "What is *it* doing here?"

She stood tall and straight. Her shoulders pulled back and the glower on her beautiful face was sharp enough to cut. "The piano is for my dance studio."

A brick dropped in his gut. He was told the tenant was a retired ballet dancer. He'd expected a gray-haired woman with skin hanging from her thin frame. Not this toned and tall goddess. "You're Quinn Petrov?"

Reed hadn't wanted the dance studio in his building, fearful he'd hear the music in his apartment upstairs. But turning down the fully-paid lease didn't make sense, when he'd be moving into his own house when he got far enough in the renovations. Plus, the dancer had been pushy and determined with his leasing agent. He figured while he lived above the dance studio he'd work on other jobs during the day and only return to his apartment at night.

"Yes." The dancer ran a slender finger across the lid. Her expression appeared sad and sentimental, reminding him of an old love song. "This piano is special. Please don't touch, *or kick*, it again."

"Sorry. I won't go near the piano. Ever." He spoke with finality. Once he finished the studio construction, he wouldn't come near the downstairs floor of this building again. His leasing agent could take care of the details.

Her soft, pink-petal lips lifted into a grin. "What did the piano ever do to you?"

He hadn't expected a friendly tease. If only she knew what the piano had done. Knew who he used to be. And how the piano had changed his life for the better, and then for the worse.

"Are you one of the construction workers getting my dance studio ready?" She had a clipped New York accent. The one saying she was above him.

He remembered the accent from his years living in the city. New Yorkers found it hard to believe a man from the backwoods of Colorado could become a successful professional pianist and composer. They'd peered down their snooty noses at him, which had caused him to bury himself into the music even more. To work harder and become more successful. So, when he'd lost the music it had been devastating.

The dancer had paid cash for the lease deposit, and for remodeling the main floor of the old Victorian house on Main Street of Castle Ridge. Ballerinas had to make a decent salary, for her to suck this much cash into a new venture.

He'd struggled after the accident to pay his medical bills and find a new career for himself. A career where he wouldn't have much contact with women. A career far removed from the music industry.

Grumbling inside and knowing he should be polite, he shoved out his ugly, scarred hand. "Reed O'Donnell. Remodeler and your landlord."

Quinn Petrov sucked in a chilly breath, the air cold from the unwelcoming greeting. Her landlord was surly and sexy. Animal magnetism. She rarely encountered that kind of man in the world of ballet.

Instant attraction blasted her in a wave of heat. The exact opposite of his reception.

A big guy with a rough exterior. Hard, callused

hands and a sucky attitude. His curly, messy, black hair appeared not to have been cut in months. Unkempt facial hair, as if he'd been living in the mountains, not in town. Brawny and bad tempered. Not a good combination.

His bulk reminded her of her grandfather, the one who'd lived in Castle Ridge, who'd hated this piano, too. He'd loved her and her grandmother, though. Her grandfather might've been a rough and tumble guy, but he was a softie underneath.

Unlike Reed O'Donnell. He was hard everything and everywhere.

Hard hands. Hard face. Hard body.

The name tickled a memory. She stretched to the tips of her toes, trying to grab the thought. The only thought pounding through her head was she'd planned to make nice with her landlord of both the dance studio and the apartment she rented above, because while they had a signed contract, she was short on funds.

Her possessions were minimal, as well. She'd moved into the apartment last night with only a few suitcases. Her pulse tapped out a quick two-step. She couldn't wait to come down to see how *her* studio was progressing early this morning. And she'd been impressed.

Smooth and shiny wood floors across the entire dance area. Floor-to-ceiling mirrors on the long wall, and the shorter, back wall. The bars to be attached to the wall sat on the floor next to the portable bars she could move into any position. A reception area needing carpet and paint. And a curved counter for her to welcome students and keep her computer and files was almost finished.

"I expected somebody older." His velvety-deep voice brought her attention to him.

She studied his emerald-green eyes. Eyes she bet could smolder with passion. Her attraction at first sight shocked, rooted her in place. She didn't fall into lust. "Why older?"

"It said on your application you were retired. You're too young to be retired." The man was handsome and logical. Again, similar to her grandfather.

"In professional ballet, twenty-five is old." And she'd survived to the ripe old age of twenty-eight.

In silence, he scrutinized her, as if she was an enemy combatant. Her stomach twisted and *jetéd*. What was he trying to find? Besides her tenuous financial situation, she was an open book.

"I need to get back to work." He tugged the tight, white T-shirt over well-worn jeans. Shuffling toward the exit, he dragged his right leg.

"Did you hurt yourself?" She understood physical pain. Ballet looked graceful; in reality, your body was tortured to get into certain positions.

He swiveled and scowled. "What?"

"When you kicked the piano, did you hurt yourself?" She shouldn't feel sorry for him; he'd kicked one of the few things she had left of her grandmother.

"No." His harsh, unyielding tone was a big stop sign.

For her.

He didn't stop. Just dragged his leg and his ass out of the room.

Absently, she trailed her fingers over the piano keys. She didn't press hard enough to make a sound. She'd learned the basics of playing piano from her grandmother. Only too soon, her mom had dragged her off to New York and a prestigious ballet school. Once enrolled, Quinn didn't have time to play an instrument.

She swayed with melancholy. The piano was one of the few precious things she'd retrieved before putting her grandparents' house on the market. With no place else to put the instrument she'd requested it be moved to the dance studio. No one had probably touched the piano in years, not since her grandmother had died. No one had probably ever kicked it, either.

What was Reed O'Donnell's problem? She'd heard from the leasing agent he hadn't wanted to lease to her. The man must have a problem with music and dancing. She didn't remember Castle Ridge being so exclusive. Growing up, Quinn would visit her grandparents for school vacations. She'd loved the quaintness and friendliness of the town. A perfect place to put down roots and find a community. That's what she yearned to find.

A place where people knew your name. A place to be involved and part of a family again, even if not a biological one. A place to belong.

Quinn couldn't sleep. She paced back and forth in the small apartment above the dance studio. There were so many things for her to accomplish before the soft opening, might as well use the time efficiently. She tiptoed downstairs and used her key to unlock the dance studio's back door. Shuffling to her office, she heard a rushing noise coming from the back hallway.

She changed direction, and pushed open the bathroom door. Water shot from one of the faucets and flowed over the newly-installed tile counters. Water poured onto the floor.

Shock shredded through her. She charged toward the unexpected fountain the size of Bethesda Fountain in Central Park. Taking off her bathrobe, she pressed the cloth on the source of the shooting leak. The material was soaked in seconds. She stomped her foot and water soaked her socks. Panic fluttered in her chest. She didn't know what to do. If she let it go, the water would fill the tiled bathroom floors and seep into the main dance studio. The water would ruin the newly-smoothed and varnished floors.

Her panicked thoughts flew to Reed O'Donnell. The angry man had avoided her all day, as if she had a virus. When she worked in the storage room, he worked in the studio. When she was straightening or decorating the studio, he worked in the bathroom or small kitchen. When they did run into each other in the small space he avoided her, barely acknowledging her existence.

She knew he lived in the second apartment upstairs. She'd heard him clomping around earlier tonight, and wondered if he was alone. He'd know how to fix the plumbing. He was the only one who could help. After all, he was the landlord.

Abandoning her soaking bathrobe, she darted up the shared staircase, slipping on her wet socks. Instead of going left to her apartment, she went right. She banged on his wooden door with her palm. "Wake up! Wake up!"

Something fell to the ground. Another crash. And then, grumbling.

The door ripped open and a furious Reed stood on the other side. His green eyes were sharp emeralds traveling the length of her body, causing a quivering sensation on her skin. His mouth curled in an ugly snarl, not a lustful smirk. "Do you know what time it is?"

He wore only track shorts hanging halfway on his hips, as if they'd just been slipped on. As if he'd been naked until her knock on the door. Trembles traveled her body again. His wide waist led to a chiseled chest with a smattering of small, curly, dark hair. Her fingers itched to fondle the texture. Carved abs and pectorals showcased his extensive shoulders. Strong, thick arms hung at his sides.

Licking her lips, she swallowed. Was there a woman in his bed? Her body heated at the thought. "Are you alone?"

His dark eyebrows rose in an are-you-ridiculous arch. "Are you kidding me? That's why you're here?"

"Of course not." Her face flushed. He thought she wanted him. She'd never come knocking on his door in the middle of the night to ask for sex. Granted, he did have one incredible body.

He scowled. "What do you want in that sexy-as-sin nightie?"

She glanced at the silky peach camisole and short-shorts. The outfit didn't leave much to the imagination. Spirals of warmth curled around her spine and she couldn't respond.

"Well?" His presence distracted.

Finally, she remembered why she was there. Her pulse jumpstarted. "The studio bathroom is flooding."

Grabbing his cell phone, his expression went fully alert. "How bad?"

"Bad." The image punched in her stomach. "Come on."

She led the way down the stairs, trying to put his insinuation behind her, trying to forget the image of his half-naked body.

"How did you discover the leak in the middle of the night?" His bare feet pounded behind her, one step louder than the other.

"I couldn't sleep. I went down to work." He didn't understand how important the success of her studio was to her. He probably thought she was a total loser.

Quinn stopped at the entryway to the bathroom, while Reed pushed past her, slipping on the wet floor. He yanked her robe off the spraying faucet and tossed it to her. "I need my toolbox."

"I'll get it."

"It's out back in the storage shed in the garage." He scooted under the sink using abdominal muscles that appeared to be carved of rock. "I'll turn off the water."

Hurrying outside in the cold mid-November air, she crossed the backyard and ran into the garage. Her hand flipped the light switch, and she perused the room searching for the storage area. The garage wasn't part of her lease. Assuming he kept a car inside, she was surprised to see something covered by a large tarp. Maybe it was construction equipment, like one of those big sawblades.

She didn't have time to find out. She needed to find his toolbox and get back to the half-naked man lying under her sink. Her skin, which had cooled from the nighttime air, heated again. Her landlord was one sexy guy. So different from the male dancers she usually associated with. He was thick, firm muscle, while most dancers were thin, lanky muscles. Both strong, but oh, so different. And it hit her which kind of muscle she was most attracted to. Too bad her landlord hid his physique under a gruff exterior.

Opening the storage area, she spotted the large metal toolbox and grabbed it off the shelf. She hurried to the studio, praying the new dance floor wouldn't be ruined by water. She didn't have the money to cover damages. She'd spent her savings and the money from the sale of her grandparents' house to invest in this business.

Sliding to a halt at the entrance of the bathroom, her heart went *ba-boom*.

Reed lay on his back on the bathroom floor in the puddle. The upper half of his body was hidden. The lower half...

Wow, wow, wow. She fanned herself, unable to stop inspecting him.

His black track shorts were soaking wet, molding to his impressive bulge. His shorts had crept up, revealing muscular thighs. His calves were just as impressive. Even the long, jagged white scar on his right calf leading to his mottled and unevenly-shaped ankle made him rugged. As if he'd suffered and was tough enough to survive.

Tingles spread over her skin, sparking desire. She hadn't been attracted to a man in a long time, and never to someone so much larger than herself. The other men she'd dated were more on the slender side. She could imagine him carrying her across the dance floor and up the stairs to his apartment, ravishing her.

"What the hell are you staring at?" The furious tone cut her fantasy, killing any desirous dreams.

Reed had scooted out from under the sink to find Quinn staring at him, staring at his grotesque leg and mangled foot. An angry flush started in his toes and crept up his body. He wasn't a goddam model or a graceful dancer. "Didn't your mother teach you it's not polite to stare at a person's scars?"

"What?" Her eyes were confused for a second, and then her cheeks reddened. "No. I wasn't."

"Water's off, and I found the source of the problem." He sat up and snatched the toolbox. He didn't want her watching him, assessing *his* damage. Lucky for him, she couldn't see his scars on the inside. "I can handle the leak."

"You think you have an ugly foot?" She stripped the wet socks off her feet. "Look at my feet." She wiggled her toes and his gaze followed, fascinated by the large calluses on delicate feet. "Ballet dancers have the ugliest feet. We put our feet through torture with the wooden tips in the toe shoes when we go *en pointe*."

He leaned back, surprised she had an ugly body part. Even more surprised she'd show him. He certainly didn't go around displaying his scars. There were too many and they ran too deep.

"What happened to you?"

The innocent question shattered inside him. As if answering her question would be easy. He remembered the police interrogation and reporters' questions. "Accident."

"I'm sorry." The trill of her voice sounded like a vibrato adding warmth to her tone.

No. He wouldn't think of music. He wouldn't think of her. "While you were getting the toolbox, I called my brother to help. You can go to bed."

The word conjured images of him taking her to bed. Electrical charges arced between them giving him the urge to do exactly that. Laying in water wasn't a smart thing with electricity hanging in the air.

"I'll help until your brother arrives." She crouched down, exhibiting her muscular calves and thighs. Strong and flexible legs. "What do you need?"

Her. His heart throbbed and he licked his lips. His cock stirred. Impossible. He hadn't been attracted to anyone since the accident. That part of his body had shut down, and he wasn't willing to turn it on again.

"Wrench." Scooting back under the sink, he held out his hand. He didn't want her help or need her help. Except she was there, and he didn't know how to get her to leave.

Metal clattered upon metal, the noise reminding him of a percussion jam. She must be searching for the tool. Maybe she didn't know what a wrench was.

Then, he'd have no guilt at sending her back to her bed — apartment.

Cold metal slapped into his palm. He pulled the tool in and realized it was the correct one. Darn.

"How long have you been a handyman?" Another innocent question slashing in his lungs.

The wrench slipped from his hand and hit his abs. "Remodel construction specialist and landlord."

The title was so different from his last position. Concert pianist and composer. Not that he wasn't proud of how he'd pulled himself together and created a new career for himself. Something completely different from his old life. With his old job, he'd never be laying in a puddle of water in the middle of the night, unless it was a hot tub.

He picked up the wrench and loosened the compression nut. "Slip joint pliers."

She slapped the correct tool in his hand.

The woman knew her tools.

Pointing the emergency flashlight he'd gotten from the storage closet, he focused the beam on the leak. What he needed was another hand. He should wait for his brother, but she was here and the sooner they got the job done the sooner he could be alone. "Can you give me a hand?"

"A hand?"

"Yeah, you know, the thing connected to your wrist." Maybe it was a mistake to ask for help. "Never mind."

"No, I'll help." Her nightie swished, as if she moved between silk sheets. "What do you need?"

"I need you to hold the flashlight, so I can see."

Sounding grumpy because he shouldn't be thinking about her between the sheets, he scooted far to the left. There wasn't much room under the sink.

"I need to crawl under there?" Trepidation tripped in her tone.

"If you don't mind, Blonde-Swan." The second the moniker slipped out, he regretted it. He didn't know her well enough to give her a nickname.

"Blonde-Swan?"

"Just a nickname." He should leave her alone, instead he pushed wanting to be done with this wet job. "You said you wanted to help."

"I do." The sexy swishing got louder, closer.

She lay on her back and scooted farther under the sink. The warmth from her body slid along his skin, sending tingles of attraction to his loins. Her long leg lay next to his damaged one. Perfection next to destruction. He was a grotesque monster next to her doll-like body.

"What do you need me to do?" The soft lilt at the end of her question sent a shiver up his spine.

"Point the light at this joint." He handed her the flashlight and the beam swung around. He'd have to show her the joint. Reluctantly, he took her hand and guided it into position. Locked together, her delicate hand hid the scars on his. He didn't appear so hideous.

"Is this good?" Again, the sexy lilt playing to his lust.

"That's what she said." His brother Dax chimed in, and pounded on the top of the sink. "Ba-dum-bum."

Fever flushed through Reed at his brother's lame

joke. He hadn't heard his brother come in. He dropped the wrench again.

The tool fell and smacked Quinn on the forehead.

"Ouch." She held her other hand at the spot.

"Oh, shit. I'm sorry. Are you okay?" He stroked her forehead where the angry bruise formed. "Dax! What're you doing messing around? I wanted your help, not a comedian."

"I'm fine." Lifting her arm, she rubbed her forehead. Her upper arm smashed against her breasts, making them jiggle and pushing them higher in the low-cut camisole.

His cock noticed, hardening into a bigger shaft. He tightened his muscles, trying to control the anger surging inside him. As well as other things. He didn't want this attraction, and he certainly didn't deserve a woman so beautiful. And he'd hurt her. "I'm sorry. My idiot brother surprised me."

"You asked me to come. What's going on down there?" His brother peered under the sink. "Is this a new, kinky way to—"

"Dax, dammit." Reed shoved himself out from underneath the sink. Reaching back around, he held his hands out for Quinn. She placed her slim hands in his. Like a monster, his ugly, scarred hand swallowed her tiny one. The earlier image of her hand making his look better slipped away. He had too much ugliness to cover up.

He helped Quinn out. "Thanks."

"You called me." Dax took her elbows and helped her to her feet. A knight helping an injured princess being held captive by a monster. His sexy smirk enhanced his handsome face. "Who is this beautiful—" His gaze traveled the length of her body. "—and wet woman?"

Reed stiffened and clenched his hands into fists. His little brother shouldn't be ogling her. Not with her perky breasts sticking out of the soft silk material, not with the way the wet cloth clung to her slight curves and hugged her hips. He grabbed Quinn's wet robe and held it in front, covering most of her. "Here."

Her relaxed, answering grin showed she wasn't concerned with how much of her body was displayed. As a dancer, she was probably used to people staring at her. "I'm Quinn Petrov."

His brother's charm was already working. Annoyance pulsed at Reed's temples.

Besides their green eyes, it was hard to tell Dax was his brother. Dax had longer, blond hair while Reed's was dark and curly. Dax's lanky and able body was the opposite of Reed's thick trunk exterior and his limp. Dax's fun attitude toward life contrasted with Reed's darker views.

"Bro, why didn't you tell me about your new woman?" His brother gave an exaggerated wink, trying to embarrass Reed.

If Dax stayed in town longer than his ski patrol shift, he'd know who Quinn was. "She's not my woman." He sounded grouchy and short, and he hated himself for it. This woman didn't matter to him. Not what skimpy clothes she wore, or who she dated. "She's my tenant."

"Interesting." His brother's eyebrows rose and lowered in a more-than-interested action.

"I should get changed." Quinn's soft smile had his insides twisting. "Nice meeting you, Dax."

"I'll be seeing you around." The suggestiveness said more than his words.

The twisting inside Reed's gut pulled tighter, watching Quinn's wet backside sway out of the bathroom. He couldn't pull his gaze away from the mesmerizing move.

"Getting out of bed was worth it for the view." His brother's face took on a wolfish expression. "I want to be a landlord, if I can have hot tenants like her."

"Stick to blowing avalanches up." He wanted to blow up. At his brother, at Quinn, at the situation. He never should've called Dax. "Help me finish fixing the leak."

Dax crouched down by the sink and picked up the flashlight. "So what's going on between you two?"

"Nothing." Reed climbed back under the sink, with a caulk gun in hand.

Why would his brother think he'd have anything going on with a woman as beautiful as Quinn? He hadn't dated anyone since his fiancée. He only socialized with his family, rarely talked to anyone else except his construction clients.

"It's the middle of the night." Using a suggestive tone, his brother pointed the light at the pipe connection. "You're dressed in only shorts. She's in a sexy nightie."

He strangled the caulk gun like he wanted to strangle his brother. "Shut up, Dax. Nothing is going on between Quinn and I."

Dax wiggled his eyebrows. "Then, you won't mind if I ask her out."

Chapter Two

Quinn didn't see Reed until late the next afternoon. First thing in the morning, she'd checked the bathroom, and the mess had been cleaned up. While she'd worked in the studio, deciding on posters and scheduling classes, he never came by. When she'd returned from lunch, the tools and equipment left lying in the bathroom were gone. He was avoiding her.

The empty spot in her chest grew. Her goal was to meet people, and so far, Reed was her only contact with the rest of the town.

Using the remote for the stereo system, she turned music on and twirled across the newly-finished and undamaged floors. The smoothness grazed her bare toes, reminding her of the grandest of stages. Reed put a lot of effort into making the floors perfect. She appreciated the perfection.

Losing herself, she twirled from the mirrored wall to the windows on the far side and back. Her enthusiasm bubbled. It felt good to dance again.

Without pressure and without admonishments. In her head, she vaguely heard the corrections from her mother, the ballet teachers, and the ballet director. Now, she was free to ignore the voices, and dance with inner joy.

Twirling, she plowed into a hard wall that hadn't been there earlier.

"Uff." A hard masculine wall.

Surprise tangoed with embarrassment. "I'm sorry. I didn't see—"

Reed.

He stood solid as a brick. His muscular arms wrapped around her, making her feel protected. A new feeling, a nice feeling. Through his ripped T-shirt, she felt the carved muscles of his chest, and the width of his shoulders, and her entire body tingled.

"Sorry." His voice was raw and edgy. "You twirled at me so fast I couldn't move out of the way quick enough. Stupid leg."

"I should've been watching where I was dancing." She didn't move. Stayed in the circle of his arms, enjoying the sensation.

His expression softened with what appeared to be concern. "You have a bruise."

"A bruise?" *From bumping into him?*

His finger brushed a hair across her forehead. "Here. From last night."

From him dropping the wrench.

Her hand floated to the slight bump, knowing her body was pretty indestructible. Ballerinas might appear delicate and slim, but they were strong and unbreakable. Through training—or torture, as she'd called the triple daily workouts—she'd grown used to pain. "It's nothing."

"I should've called you Black-and-Blue-Swan, instead of Blonde-Swan." He dropped his other arm from around her and took a step back. "I'm sorry."

"It's okay." The loss of his touch wasn't. Which was weird. She wasn't a touchy-feely person. It wasn't how she was brought up. "What was the damage from last night? I mean, besides my forehead." Her laugh sounded stilted and forced. Between the unusual sensation of loss when he'd dropped his arms and her lack of funds to pay for repairs, every bone in her body tensed.

Glancing back at her piano, he flashed a short smile. "The pipe connection needed to be sweat-soldered."

She stretched on her toes. "Is that going to cost me?"

"No. It was the plumber's mistake. He'll take care of the cost of fixing it." He peered at the piano again.

"You've already handled it?" An odd sensation at not having to fight for every little thing burgeoned inside her. Oddly nice. "What about your time? Helping me last night?" Her skin flared, remembering their intimate position lying on the floor next to each other.

Reed's cheeks reddened. Was he remembering the exact same thing? Her body heated more. "No worries. I'm the landlord. It's expected."

"Thank you. I appreciate it." Her bank account appreciated it, too. She still owed a debt. And she was intrigued by this man. Who better to take to dinner than a local involved in the business community? "Let me at least buy you dinner."

"No." He backed away, as if she'd offered to castrate him, not feed him.

The heat flowed out of her body leaving her cold. But you didn't survive in the cutthroat ballet world without learning determination.

"I insist." She'd eaten enough lonely meals in her lifetime, and her landlord seemed interesting, unusual, layered. "You were really helpful last night. If the water had leaked until morning, this beautiful dance floor would be ruined."

"And I would've had twice the work." Did he believe if he didn't look at her it would be easier to say no? "I should be thanking you."

"Thank me by letting me buy you dinner." She grabbed his forearm, and the thick muscles tightened beneath her hold. The proof of his strength spiraled to her core, and again, the thought of being protected grew. "One of my goals to get this studio going is to meet townspeople. You're from Castle Ridge. If I take you to dinner, you can introduce me to people."

His face scrunched in a grumpy expression. "I don't do people."

She captured his gaze, unwilling to let him win by avoidance. "What does that mean?"

"I don't socialize. I don't go out."

His don't-argue-with-me tone had her scoffing. "Ridiculous. You talk to me."

His frown deepened, making his scowl more menacing. She'd seen worse scowls from choreographers and fellow dancers. The expression didn't scare.

She pushed. "You talk to your brother."

His menacing expression went darker. His frown resembled a U-turn sign, except his face flashed *No*. The mention of his brother made his attitude worse. Why? They got along last night.

She wasn't going to give up, even if she had to play the sympathy card. "Please. I need to get out and meet people, and you're the only one in town I know."

Reed should've said no.

The negative response had perched at the tip of his tongue. And then Quinn had widened her Colorado-sky-blue eyes, never letting go of his gaze, and said please. She'd sounded lonely.

Lonely, he could relate to.

Not that he was lonely. He had his job, and the house he'd bought to work on. He had his brother and sister. That was all he needed.

The second he entered the Castle Ridge Lodge and was greeted by Danielle Marstrand, he should've left. His sister's best friend's expression of shock registered, and his feet twitched, wanting to head back in the other direction. Except, Quinn was standing by his side. She'd wonder why he turned tail and ran like a coward.

"Reed!" Danielle moved around the desk and opened her arms wide. Her short, brown hair swung with the movement. Her small stature didn't impede the quickness of her stride. "What're you doing here?"

Quinn would also wonder why he was the town's hermit.

There were things he didn't explain and didn't talk about. "Can't a guy go out for dinner, Dainty Danielle?"

"Stop with the nicknames." She hugged him like she always did. She'd been his sister's best friend since middle school, and was considered part of his family. "I'm only questioning you going out for dinner." She took a step back and stared at his new tenant. "Who's this?"

Quinn held out a delicate hand. "I'm Quinn Petrov. I'm opening a dance studio in town."

A ball bounced in his stomach, the rhythm one of disappointment. That's right. His new tenant was here to meet people, not to be with him. He quickly punctured the ball with his will, not planning to analyze the emotion or the beat.

"I've heard about the dance studio." Shaking the dancer's hand, Danielle appeared more than curious. "I'm trying to convince my teenage daughter to give ballet a try."

Quinn unzipped her jacket, revealing a fuzzy sweater. "I'll be teaching other classes besides ballet. Your daughter might enjoy hip hop or tap dance."

He snorted. "Her daughter is a serious skier. That's all she wants to do."

Danielle frowned and angled her head in consideration. "I want my daughter to try other things. Skiing isn't a serious pursuit."

She had been on the ski team with him, and his sister, and several other people. She'd declared her hatred for the sport after giving birth to her daughter, but his sister had babbled on about another local skier who'd broken her heart. At least she could ski if she wanted to, unlike Reed.

"I'm offering adult classes too." Quinn took a business card out of her purse. "In fact, the first two weeks I'm offering free classes for people to come in and try a dance out."

"Why would you give away your services?" He didn't think the idea was a good business decision.

"To get people interested." Her expression grew determined. As determined as when she'd decided she needed to buy him dinner. She reminded him of a concerto where the singer's voice basically argued with the orchestra. He usually went along with things, never arguing or yelling. If he didn't like something, he avoided it. "There's never been a dance studio in town before. I want to teach people what it involves, how fun learning to dance can be."

"Sounds like torture."

She smacked his arm in a too-familiar way. "Then, I'll make you my first victim."

The playful interchange seemed so normal, so happy, and for second he wished.... He noticed Danielle watching them. His entire body stiffened. His life was his life and he wouldn't be altering for anybody. "No."

"It does sound fun. I'll try a class, if I can fit it in between work and school." She waved at her desk. "I need to get back to work. I'll tell Isabel you're here."

"Great. Just great." More people to observe him out of his element.

"Isabel, your wife?" Quinn's tone was stiff.

Jealous or curious? Probably the latter.

"Sister. She's the sous chef." A gossipy sister, who would spread the word he was out with a woman and bug him until she got the details about Quinn. He sighed. This was going to be long night.

The hostess of The Heights restaurant led them to their table. A teenage girl whose parents owned a flower shop. A man he'd remodeled a kitchen for waved from a corner booth. Reed jerked his head in slight acknowledgement. He didn't want the man approaching. A family sat at a long table. He'd gone to high school with both parents, and now they had an entire brood of children.

The restaurant crowded in on him with people he knew and people he didn't. People he recognized, and people he didn't want to acknowledge. He hunched his shoulders, remembering one visit where he'd closed down the bar, playing tune after tune on the beat-up piano in the corner. He hadn't eaten here since his return to town several years ago.

He scanned past the large picture window showing the town's main street leading to the mountain slope. Wishing he could escape from notice by swooshing down the mountain, he stumbled on his bum leg.

"You okay?" Was graceful Quinn embarrassed to be with a cripple?

This was a mistake. "We should order something to go." That's how he usually did things. Or his sister would bring leftovers to his apartment.

"No." Her firm voice matched her expression. "I want to meet people."

Not hide away like he did. They were opposites. Opposites in where they came from, and how they lived. Opposites about what they wanted for the future.

"You should've gone out with my brother." Solving the problem.

Dax wanted to ask her out, while Reed didn't want to go out with anyone. He didn't.

"We're here now." She laid a hand on his arm, her touch already becoming familiar and making him uncomfortable. "Your sister knows you're here. Let's stay."

The hostess stopped at a table in the center of the room. "Is this okay?"

"Don't you have a booth?"

"I don't want to hide in a booth." Quinn nailed his plan.

She was obviously becoming familiar with his habits, too.

After settling at the table and placing their orders, Reed kept his head down. She might want to be seen, he did not. He never should've let her talk him into eating out and coming to The Heights. The lodge and restaurant belonged to a local family for generations, and while there were lots of tourists in the winter and summer, they were in the in-between season, when locals came to socialize.

He noted the curious glances and sly looks. They recognized him and knew his reputation. The monster had come out of his cave, and not to complete a job. Izzy told him he was being ridiculous when he spoke the sentiment out loud. He didn't think so.

"Do you know anyone in the restaurant?" Quinn sat straight in her chair, a grin glued on her face.

The clatter of cutlery mixed in his head with the clink of glasses. The noises blurred and separated, creating a tune in his head. Angling his head, he listened. He heard nothing now. Must be his imagination.

"Some." He might know them, but he felt like an outsider. He'd grown up with many of these people, and yet he was uncomfortable with them. Chit-chat wasn't his forte. He'd been gone so long, and when he'd returned, he was nothing like his former self.

"Anyone who might be interested in dance lessons?" She sounded so hopeful.

She shouldn't have picked him to introduce her around town. "Many of the guests are from out of town."

"A little early for skiing." Her common sense put him in his place.

Caught again.

His sister Izzy, and Dax, didn't push him to go out and be social. They enjoyed quiet dinners, at either Izzy's house or Reed's apartment. He let his siblings enjoy their party lifestyles. He was satisfied being home alone.

Shifting uncomfortably, he lifted his head to check and see if anyone observed them. "There's a couple over there who are married and have kids." More people he'd gone to school with.

"Will you introduce me?"

"Let's wait until after dinner."

"You're right. We wouldn't want to be rude and interrupt." Her regal chin dipped, and her capitulation made him believe he'd won a battle. "I'm anxious about meeting people, them liking me, them being interested in the studio."

He pulled back in his seat. Insecurity from Quinn? She'd been a steamroller from the moment she'd decided to rent his property for her dance studio. He'd told his leasing agent not to rent to her because the music would drive him crazy. She'd persisted. Persisted on the renovations for her studio. Persisted on helping with the leak in her barely-there pajamas. Persisted about dinner.

Their emailed communications had gone back and forth, with Reed finally caving. He knew he'd be moving into his house soon. Of course, that was before he'd met her piano. A piano drawing his attention while he'd worked in the studio.

His own determination to stay apart weakened, and he gave in. "We'll go to the bar after dinner. It will be easier to meet people."

Her lush lips lifted into an angelic smile. "That would be lovely."

The smile, her smile, shot through him like cupid's arrow. His muscles tightened and his cock sprung. This wasn't going to be good. With Quinn being his tenant and temporary neighbor, she was going to mess up the nice, quiet life he'd carved out since his accident. And he wasn't ready for it to change. He never wanted his life to change. He was happy. Satisfied. Content.

Her expression glowed before she bit a tempting lower lip. His twitching cock contradicted his satisfaction claim.

"I don't want to give a hard sell, but I need people

to sign up for classes." She bit her lower lip again. "I don't know how informed you were during the negotiations I had with your leasing agent. I ran into a sticky financial situation."

He paused with his water glass halfway to his mouth. He wasn't worried about her personally, he wasn't. She was his tenant, and shouldn't be sharing her financial details. The waiter brought their meals to the table and he decided not to return to that particular conversation.

His steak had a strip of bacon shaped into a smiling mouth and two eyes made from tomatoes. One of the tomatoes had been cut into the shape of a wink.

"So cute." Quinn pointed with her fork.

His sister's teasing greeting. And a warning that when she was less busy in the kitchen, she'd be out to visit. He lost his appetite. "How's your dinner?"

Quinn had ordered the pasta special. She twirled the strings of spaghetti onto her fork similar to how she'd been twirling across her dance floor earlier, when she'd bumped into him and he'd held her close, inhaling her scent of roses.

He eased his legs apart to lower the constriction. He couldn't let this woman affect him. He had to avoid her until he finished the studio. He had to go back into his cave.

"Wonderful." She spun more pasta onto her fork and he stared entranced. Her long, slender fingers lifted the fork to her mouth. Her lips came around the fork and pasta, and he fantasized about something else in her mouth. Who ever thought eating pasta could be a sexual act? "Tell your sister the meal is fantastic."

"You can tell her yourself. I'm sure she'll come say hi." He was positive.

"Would she be interested in a dance class?"

"Izzy would love it." He knew this for a fact, because his sister was the life of the party. Always laughing and dancing and flirting. She'd been the only light in his life since the accident.

"How did you get started with your construction business?"

He froze mid-saw of his steak. He couldn't tell Quinn the truth. Didn't want her sympathy. "I did construction in college."

"That must've been a lot of work. Studying and working construction." She continued to eat her pasta and he continued to salivate watching her. "Are you part of the Main Street Business Association?"

"No."

"Why not? I thought it would be a great way to meet other business people and get involved in town." Her eyes lit up like a candelabra, excited about the prospect.

He didn't mind making business contacts, it was the socializing part he hated. Planning meetings and happy hours. He'd done plenty of charity events and parties in his past. "It will be good for you."

"But not you?" She challenged.

He scrambled for an acceptable answer. "I grew up here and know most of the people."

"Great." Leaning forward, her cleavage pushed out in the tight sweater she wore. She emphasized with her fork, pointing at him. "You're the perfect person to introduce me around."

He felt as if her fork stabbed him in the lungs. All the air leaked out of him. "I don't want—"

"The town's grown quite a bit. A lot has changed since I visited my grandparents as a kid."

He didn't need to be around her or anyone else. "Where do your grandparents live?"

The spark in her gaze dimmed. Her expression became strained. "They had a house on Pearl Street."

His gut clenched. The same street where he'd bought a fixer-upper house. He hoped she didn't visit them often. "I'm sure your grandparents could introduce you to people."

"They died several years ago." Sniffling, her voice went raw.

His weakening worsened. Cracks formed in his wall of self-imposed exile. He wanted to hold her close and take away her pain.

"Reed." Two arms wrapped around his neck.

Cinnamon and other kitchen scents told him who it was. "Hello, Izzy."

"Danielle said you'd come here for dinner?" His sister sounded happy-surprised as she took an empty seat at the table. Her wide smirk displayed one emotion, the question in her green orbs displayed another. "And I heard you weren't alone." Izzy's tone nudged. Her inquisitive gaze landed on Quinn.

"This is my sister, Isabel. Sous chef and gossip extraordinaire." He wasn't sure how to describe Quinn. Beautiful. Determined. A pain in his ass. "This is Quinn Petrov. She's my new tenant at the old Victorian house on Main Street."

"The dancer from New York." Izzy took off the

white chef's hat and tucked away reddish-blonde strands of hair escaping her topknot. She took a seat. "You two should have a lot in common."

His pulse jumped, not wanting his sister to reveal his past. "What would a construction worker and a ballet dancer have in common?" He formed the sentence as a question, but the warning should be clear.

"What indeed?" His sister wiggled her eyebrows.

Of course, his sister didn't take the hint. She never took hints.

He glanced at Quinn and back to Izzy. Before she caused more trouble, he asked, "How are the remodel plans for the restaurant and kitchen?"

"I don't know." She huffed. "The hotel owner is keeping it a secret."

"You're not doing the remodel, Reed?" Quinn's sharp blue gaze went between them. "He's done such a fabulous job on my dance studio."

Her praise puffed up his chest. "Wasn't even asked. Brought in a firm from California."

Another big secret of Parker Williamson's, the hotel owner. The man had been acting strange for the past few months, but who was Reed to judge?

"What brings you to our little ski town?" Izzy leaned her elbows on the table, ready to listen to a good story. "Do you ski?"

"Not since I was a child." His tenant shook her head, and a strand of hair escaped from its severe bun. The urge to tug on the hair and paw the softness itched in his fingers. "My grandparents lived in Castle Ridge, and I had fond memories of my visits." Quinn's voice tinged with renewed sadness he hated to hear. "I'd planned to live there. At the last minute, I needed to sell their house to fund my studio. A long and sad story."

He wanted to hear. He wanted to know everything about this intriguing woman. His heart slammed against his ribcage. *No.* He would walk her home, say goodnight, and avoid her.

"Do you enjoy dancing, Izzy?" His new tenant's determination sprang forward.

He admired how Quinn went after what she wanted. He used to be like that. Until the accident. Now, he wasn't interested in anything except work.

"Only my brothers call me Izzy. Reed has this thing with nicknames." His sister messed his hair. "And I love to dance."

While he was the exact opposite. Now. He used to love music and dancing and socializing in a crowd. When he'd been injured and lost his fiancée, none of that mattered anymore. Surviving was his only goal.

"You have to take my free adult sample classes at the studio."

"I will." Izzy stood and plopped her hat back on her head. "I need to get back to work."

After she left, Quinn asked, "I've met your sister and your brother. Any other family members around?"

"My parents moved to Florida."

She scrunched her face into a questioning expression. "Why would they move when their kids live here?"

"None of us were living here when they made the

decision." *Oops*. He didn't want to talk about where he'd lived. That would only lead to other questions. "What about you? Any annoying siblings?"

"Only child, although I always wished I had a brother or sister. My mother was a single parent and died when I turned eighteen." Quinn didn't seem as sorrowful about her mother's death as her grandparents.

"I'm sorry." Sympathy flickered through him, imagining never seeing his parents again. He didn't visit them often enough because his parents fussed and nagged him to be more social.

He'd never return to his old ways. His real career had ended. His fiancée gone. He'd never play in front of large audiences again. He'd never hear sweet music in his head. He'd never love a woman.

Dax strutted into the restaurant like a model for an outdoorsman advertisement. Tight jeans, nice sweatshirt, stylish jacket. When they'd been younger, Reed had always strutted beside him, not realizing how it appeared or the effect it had on the local girls.

Envy buzzed and he tried to squash it. Dax was more handsome, more social, and more able-bodied. The slight curls of his brother's too-long blond hair bounced with the movement. He waved to a couple of the townspeople Reed had ignored.

"Speaking of annoying siblings."

Quinn's eyes widened when she spotted his brother, and her mouth moved into a welcoming smile. The two of them would look good together. Reed hardened his lips, trying not to snarl.

His brother gripped his shoulders and rubbed.

"Hey, big brother." Dax swiveled toward Quinn and winked. "Hello, beautiful. You danced through my dreams last night."

What a corny line.

Her winsome chuckle showed she appreciated his remark.

Reed's stomach soured. "What do you want?"

His brother quirked his head and examined him, as if he were a competitor. "Is that any way to welcome your much younger and handsomer brother?" Dax took the seat Izzy had vacated.

Quinn picked up her purse and stood. Maybe she was trying to escape his brother, too. "If you two will excuse me for a moment. I'll be back."

"Dax will be gone." Reed's tone came out too fast and too hard. He shouldn't be angry at the interruption. He should leave and let his brother take his place.

Her smile slipped. "Oh."

His bones cracked with her disappointment about not spending time with his little brother.

"I will await your return." His brother bowed his head in a flourish.

Reed waited for Quinn to get out of hearing range, then smacked his younger brother on the arm. "You look like an idiot."

"You act like a caveman." Dax analyzed him. "Why? If you're not interested in Quinn?"

"I'm not interested in her." Reed's cock protested. Even so, he wouldn't let himself become interested. He wasn't the right kind of man for her. A principal ballerina was too good for him. Any woman was too good for him.

"If you have no personal interest in her, you can help me win her."

The request cut across his chest. "You don't need any help with the ladies, Romeo." Reed knew how Dax operated. He was a love-them-and-leave-them type of guy.

"I've been off my game lately." His tone lowered into a defeated whisper.

"What happened with Flirty Phoebe?" Reed couldn't keep the ill-will out of his voice. His brother had been dating the woman for several months. Dax's first long-term relationship, ever. She'd been the female version of a rake, flirting with everyone in sight, even going after Reed.

"She moved away." Dax's serious expression morphed into a joking tilt of his lips. He slammed his chest with his fist. "I'm trying to heal a broken heart here. The least you can do is help me get a date with Quinn."

What about Reed's heart? The organ was finally coming back to life with Quinn's presence, and he hated the vulnerability.

Chapter Three

After dinner, Reed strolled with Quinn back to the dance studio. She didn't seem to mind his slow pace because of his limp. He did. On the way to the restaurant, he'd been too nervous to think about the drag of his foot. Now, with the quietness of the evening, the long scratch of foot on pavement scratched similar to chalk on a blackboard.

The entire way home, his brother's request drummed in his brain. *Help win her?* Like she was a prize at the annual Snow Festival. Dax and Isabel were much better at flirtations than him, nowadays. Reed had been a player in high school and college. Once he'd become involved with the symphony, he didn't have time for such nonsense. He'd had one serious girlfriend who'd become his fiancée. Elizabeth was now dead because of him.

A deadness invaded his soul. He felt nothing. Which was wrong.

"I'm not tired, and would love to get some work done on the studio. Would you mind if I showed you where I want to hang a couple of posters on the wall?" Quinn asked when they arrived. There was nothing romantic in her question. She didn't want to prolong the evening, she wanted help. "Unless you have other plans?"

"No. No plans." He never had plans. His new life consisted of work, sometimes visiting his sister or brother, and more work. If he didn't have a major project, he'd go to the Craftsman house he'd bought and work on the renovations. Using a hammer in his scarred hand was the exact opposite of playing a piano, and took him away from his tortured thoughts of his past life. Constructing and renovating had probably saved him. If he wanted to be out of the apartment before the dance studio opened, he needed to work hard on his house the next few weeks. "What's the scheduled opening date for the dance studio?"

"The free sample classes will start a week from Monday, and we'll have a fun recital for the grand-opening ceremony. Regular classes will start after the showcase." Quinn pulled a few rolled up posters from behind the desk. She flattened them across the counter, bending over the surface, giving him a glimpse down her sweater and the small globes of her breasts.

The lust rose again. His fiancée's breasts had been large, a full mound in his hand. Quinn's resembled small plums. He didn't understand why his pants tightened. Forcing himself to glance away, irritation ground in his gut.

She picked up one of the posters and twirled

toward the front door. Keeping one hand at the top of the poster and one on the bottom, she squinted and stretched to the tips of her toes. "What do you think about here?"

In his mind, she could stand there all night and he'd never get tired of the view. "You need to flatten the posters out first."

"You're right." She let the poster roll back up and waltzed to him. Her grace and light-footedness made him feel like a clumsy bear, causing his irritation with himself to increase. "I'm hoping you, and your brother and sister, will sign up for free lessons."

"I can't dance." Pain shredded from his gimp leg to his heart, as if the request alone had made the agony return.

He'd enjoyed dancing in the past at parties and symphony galas. Holding Quinn would be so different than Elizabeth. Quinn was tall and slender, small breasts and tiny waist. Elizabeth had been shorter and rounder.

"Everyone can dance." She clicked a remote and music filled the studio.

He jolted wanting to cover his ears or demand she turn the noise off. The jarring sound whirred. He noticed the way her hips sashayed back and forth in a dance of temptation and desire. A movement that had him imagining sex with her. Now, the music didn't seem so bad.

Except he hated music and he hated this unwanted desire.

Moving behind the counter, he did not want to exhibit evidence of his rising attraction through his jeans. He did not want to be attracted, and he did not want to dance. He'd never been Fred Astaire, but he used to have fun on the dance floor. Not anymore.

"Have you seen my limp?" Reed was lucky he could walk.

Her smile faltered and her expression became serious. She wiggled toward him and kneaded his upper arm gently, and he imagined her hands all over his body. "What happened to your leg?"

"Nothing adventurous or exciting." Renewed pain shot from his ankle. The scars across his entire body, seen and unseen, throbbed. He didn't know if the torment was real or imaginary. He never talked about his injuries. Not with anyone.

"So you haven't had the limp for life." Her gaze scoured his face, searching for clues. "Is it a recent injury?"

He didn't want to think about that dark night. The night his world had changed, his career had ended, and he'd killed his fiancée.

"A few years ago." Fisting his hands at his sides, he stepped away from her and pivoted toward the far wall.

"Did you dance before the injury?" Her cajoling tried to dig deeper, resembling the psychiatrist he'd been forced to visit.

"Not professionally."

She laughed, tinkling like certain keys on a piano and echoing around the dance studio in chorus. The melody struck a cacophony in the center of his chest and reverberated in his head. His entire body stilled. He wasn't going to tell her any more. He wasn't going to be attracted to her anymore. *He wasn't.* "When do you want these posters hung?"

"When you have the chance." She waved to a spot near the front door, stretching on her toes again. "My goal with this studio is to make dancing fun again." She sounded more passionate about the fun than the dancing.

He'd loved everything about his career until he'd lost the music in his head. Chords and notes and melodies had become his enemy.

"What do you mean, make it fun again? It wasn't fun before?" He estimated the size of the poster as he estimated her changing expressions.

Her eyes dimmed and her hands fluttered in the air. Her focus narrowed on a target. Her mouth pursed in determination. "I want people to know anyone can dance." She twirled toward him again and took hold of his hand. "Even people with a limp."

His hand in hers sent a stream of warmth through his veins. He relished the feel of their hands entwined, and yet disbelief made him dizzy. "Even people like me?" He put a sneer in his voice.

She placed her hand on his shoulder and pushed him back and pulled him forward. Her touch lighted a spark inside him. Her words put the spark out. "Come on."

The music thundered, hurting his ears, reminding him of his other loss. A bigger loss than his fiancée. Glancing at the piano, he stumbled, and heat engulfed his face. "No."

"Please." She begged, and her sapphire gaze beseeched. "I plan to teach disabled kids and adults to dance."

His midsection erupted in flames and scorched up his throat. For a second he'd thought she wanted to dance with him. "So I'm a charity case."

"No!" Her sharp rejection didn't make him less annoyed. "I want to prove you can dance. That anyone can dance. Would you deny disabled kids the opportunity to dance, even if it's not perfect?"

"Of course not." Offended, he understood their struggles.

"Then, you can dance."

Possibly. He'd look stupid doing it. No woman would want to dance with him, except for Quinn, who was trying to make a point. She'd be using him for an example or a guinea pig.

"Try." She squeezed his shoulder to guide him forward and the pinch went straight to his toes. "Two steps forward. One step back."

"No."

She frowned and angled her head, studying him. The disappointment in her bright eyes caused him to rethink his rejection.

"Okay." She removed her hands from his body and crossed her arms. Her expression hardened with the determination he'd experienced before. "If we're not going to dance, I'm going to continue asking questions about your injury until you answer." She tapped her foot on the wooden floor.

The noise set off an explosion in his head. The tapping combined into a rhythm of torment. He could hear the music from her stereo overlaid with the tapping of her foot. The direct stare cut his will and the discordant notes threw his own tempo in disarray.

He should stomp out of the room and never speak with her again. She had no right to demand answers. He hadn't even told his family the entire truth about the night of the accident so long ago. "Stop."

"Stop what?"

"Stop harassing me." He acted the prima donna, and he never had been. He'd only been given the reputation because of Elizabeth.

"Dance with me, then." Quinn continued to tap her foot.

The *tap, tap, tap* was torture.

"Dance?" She held her hands in position.

His body tilted toward her, wanting to go into her arms, wanting her hand on his shoulder, wanting the tapping to stop.

"Fine." He obeyed only because he didn't want to argue, and he didn't want to talk, and he didn't want to hear her foot tapping.

"Wonderful." She enthused, as if he'd given her a great gift, and his tempo evened out. "One, two, three."

She glided across the dance floor with a flowy-ness to her body. His awkward shuffling didn't compare to her light steps. He was a weight holding her back. She moved with the music, becoming part of the dance itself. He understood the sensation, remembered. That's how it had been when he played the piano. He'd become lost in the rhythm and harmony. His fingers had moved across the keys of their own accord, blurring the lines between playing and being.

He couldn't become one with the music anymore. Couldn't hear the music in his mind.

"Good." Her praise relaxed his frame.

Maybe he could dance. Though since he didn't date, he wouldn't need dancing skills. He should tell her to stop, this lesson was a waste of time, but her hand on his shoulder sent shockwaves of awareness through him. Awareness he hadn't felt in a long time. His hand on her waist vibrated through the thin material of her shirt. Their joined hands seemed to merge.

He'd never been this in sync with his fiancée, Elizabeth. She'd jammed when he'd flowed. She'd zigged when he'd zagged. She'd drank when he'd...

She'd drank and she'd died.

He stumbled and fell against Quinn's body, the strength of her slender frame keeping them both upright. Their harmony halted. Their simpatico movements shut off.

"Sorry." He dropped his hold on her and stepped back. Away. What had he been thinking? He couldn't dance with Quinn, couldn't hold her in his arms, couldn't make this into more than it could ever be.

"Are you all right?" No tone of disgust, only concern. She moved toward him to touch him again.

He moved back in a dance of avoidance. "I told you, I can't dance."

"You were doing fine."

"You need to find someone else to teach." His muscles tightened with the image of someone else in her arms.

"You're perfect."

He was anything but perfect. He was big and ugly and scarred.

"What about Dax?" The question slipped out of Reed's mouth like a glissando—the musical equivalent of stepping on a banana peel. "He wanted to ask you out."

He held his breath, waiting for her response. Half hoping she'd say no. Half dreading she'd say yes.

Dax?

Quinn's stomach dipped with disappointment. Reed's brother was too gorgeous and he knew it. Dax appeared to be about living in the moment, while her plans were about building a foundation, a family, a home.

She studied Reed in his jeans and nice, plain sweater that didn't draw attention. He seemed the more-steady type. The type she was attracted to.

"Well, what about Dax?" Reed's expression tightened as if he was having a difficult time breathing.

She'd enjoyed being in his large arms. Had enjoyed his company. Was intrigued by his moodiness and surly attitude. His no-trespassing sign had her wanting to uncover the truth. But he obviously wasn't interested in her, if he was asking her out for his brother. Maybe Reed had a girlfriend, which meant she shouldn't become too attached or too friendly.

Her disappointment double-stepped. She needed someone to help her make friends and contacts in town. She needed to consider Dax. He would be fun to hang out with, and he'd know as many people as Reed. "Sure."

His shoulders slumped, and he glared at the ground. "Great." He didn't sound great. "I'll give my brother your number."

She'd given the answer he wanted, and yet he seemed dissatisfied. As if her answer was wrong. Scrunching her brow, she sorted through her confusion.

"Put the posters where you want them on the floor, and I'll hang them tomorrow." He turned away from her, concluding their dance session and the conversation.

"Wait." She didn't want to lose the friendship they'd established tonight. *Didn't want to lose him,* a small voice taunted in her head. He reminded her of her grandfather, with his surly exterior and soft heart. Reed made her feel protected and safe. She wanted him on her side. "About the opening night showcase to get publicity for my dance studio."

"Great idea." Walking backwards and away from her, his expression was downcast, unreadable. Shuffling stiffly, his limp was more pronounced.

Empathy tugged at her. She'd been injured many times, and tried not to show pain. She wasn't allowed to show pain. Professional ballet dancers did not cry. She stretched to the tips of her toes and dropped on her flat feet. She knew dancing could be therapeutic for his limp and his attitude. "I'll need a partner."

"I'm sure Dancing Dax will be willing." Reed's terse statement cut through the air.

Cut through her nerves. She stepped boldly forward. "I don't want Dax. I want you."

The last sentence struck through her chest. The

truth flashed like lightning. She'd never said that to a man before. There'd never been a deeper meaning when she'd had sex in the past. She was attracted to Reed, but he wasn't interested. She needed to focus on her business. The home and the family would come later. "If I dance with you, if I make you look good, that will impress everyone."

His expression darkened. He thundered toward her. "Sure, ask the gimp."

His words stabbed. Her head bonged and her bloodstream rushed. "No. That's not what I meant. I can teach you how to dance, and I think it will improve your limp. I want to teach you to dance." *I want to hold him in my arms again.* She forced the thought away. "Your girlfriend would love it if you could dance again."

"I don't have a girlfriend."

His bitter tone made her chest burn. Having a girlfriend wasn't the reason for his rejection. He just didn't want to date or dance with her. She continued to push, wanting more explanation or anguish. Her grandmother always said she pushed too hard. Her mother always said she didn't push hard enough. At some point she'd find the right balance. "Dancing is a great way to win a woman's heart."

"According to my sister, cooking is the way to win someone's heart." His eyes glazed and his mouth dipped into a frown. His expression appeared a little lost, pulling on Quinn's heartstrings even more. "I always believed it was music."

"Music and dancing. A winning combination." She had to keep on track. His resistance wasn't personal.

This was about business. If she could show the town Reed could dance, she could persuade others she was a good teacher.

A deeper reason, a more important reason rose to the surface. Dancing would make him happy. She knew it in her soul. She'd seen dancing change a mood or attitude. She only had to prove it to him. "Will you dance with me?"

Stretching on her toes, she waited for his answer. His expression didn't change. His gaze darted around, searching for an escape. An escape from her, from the room, or from answering the question.

"No."

The negative answer had her internally doing a grand plié. Not swayed, she needed Reed to dance with her. Wanted him to dance. Instinctively, she understood he'd accept a challenge. "Because you don't want to, or because you don't think you can?"

His entire body seemed to tighten. His mouth bowed into a taut shape. The music in the background crescendoed, as if understanding his tension.

And hers. Had she pushed him too far?

"I can do anything I put my mind to." He spoke with authority. He must've faced many challenges in his lifetime and succeeded.

She liked a man who believed in himself. "Good. Then, you'll be my partner."

Later that night, Reed entered the pub with only one thing on his mind: find Dax. He'd called, interrupting the hockey game Reed had been watching. Spotting his brother at the bar, he stomped over, anger racing to be let loose.

His brother had both elbows on the counter and slouched on top of the bar. His long hair covered most of his face. He wasn't having a good time. Not anything resembling the happy-go-lucky guy he used to be. Flirty Phoebe had done a number on him, and Reed's involvement hadn't helped.

"Hey bro." Dax slurred his words.

It wasn't the slurring that caught Reed's attention. It was the sorrow underneath the drunkenness. He understood and sympathized, and his anger lessened. "Aren't you a little old to be calling your big brother to pick you up?"

When they both came home from college, together they'd close the bars down and take a different girl home every night. They partied and danced and flirted. A woman had changed both of them for the worse.

"I didn't want you to pick me up. I wanted you to have a beer and hang out." Dax raised his head and pierced him with cloudy green eyes. "It's something you never do anymore."

"I don't want to go out and get drunk." Images crashed in Reed's head. Of another night and another drunk and the accident that ruined his life. Drinking didn't achieve anything, and it certainly didn't make a man feel better.

"I'm not going to do something stupid like drive. That's why I called you." Dax reached for his glass and put it to his mouth. Realizing it was empty, he signaled for another.

"How much has he had to drink, Joe?" They'd attended high school with the bartender.

"Too many. You should take him home."

"I don't want to go home." His brother slammed the mug onto the bar. "I bet Phoebe isn't home." He slapped a hand on Reed's shoulder and tried to stand. "I want to talk to Quinn."

Similar to an altered chord, the wrong note twanged in his chest. "You're not in any shape to talk to Quinn."

"You're going to talk to her for me." His brother's stupid, sloppy, big-brother-worshipping grin lit his face. "What's her number?"

"I can't give out her number." His knee-jerk answer was to lie. She'd given permission. Her number had been in the paperwork and emails between her and his leasing agent.

The smile slipped off his brother's face, his defeated expression yanking at Reed's conscience. "Please. I need to have success with a woman."

He didn't need to ask why. His brother hadn't been the same since his ex-girlfriend broke up with him, took him back, and dumped him again. She'd been dragging Dax along for months now. "How about I take you home?"

"I don't want to be alone." His voice cracked.

Reed hated seeing his brother this way, and he didn't want to dump him at the ski patrol lodgings. "I'll take you to my place."

"Let's roll." Grabbing his coat, his brother almost fell to the ground.

He put his arm around his brother's waist, and

helped him out of the bar and around the corner, back to his Victorian. They staggered around the back to access the private apartments on the upper level. The light was on in Quinn's rented apartment, and the window open.

His brother stumbled forward out of his grip. "Quinn! Wherefore art thou, Quinn!"

He hadn't expected his brother to embarrass himself. He grabbed for him.

A shadow moved toward the open window. Quinn's silhouette backlighted by the light behind her. Was she wearing the same little silk nightie she'd worn the other night? Not that he wanted her to display herself for his drunk brother.

She opened the window more. "Hello? Is somebody out there?"

"It's Dax!" He fell.

She leaned over the windowsill. Her hair, which she usually wore in a bun, was down. The light from the room shone on its silky softness. "Dax? What're you doing out there?"

Reed's pulse pumped, creating an increased blood flow. He bent down to check on his brother. The idiot had passed out.

"Dax? Are you still there?"

Reed didn't want his brother to look stupid. He couldn't *not* say anything. He also didn't want her to realize it was him standing beneath the window. His brother had started with a poor imitation of Shakespeare. Reed would continue in that direction. The increased blood flow swelled both his heads.

"I needed to see your fair face." He made his voice

a little higher and slurred, feeling dumber with each word he spoke.

Her giggle wafted to him. "How can you see me in the dark? Are you drunk?"

"Only drunk on your beauty." He stomped his foot. Continuing this charade was madness. He should step into the light and tell her Dax had passed out. *Just* passed out. Would she recognize Reed had delivered the last two lines? Then, he'd look even more foolish.

"Sweet, but unbelievable." Her skepticism told him she wasn't buying. "What do you want, Dax?"

She believed it was his brother.

Hurt spiraled in Reed's stomach. Even though they'd spent hours together, she didn't recognize his voice. Did he want her to?

Remembering their earlier conversation about music and dancing being a winning combination, he said, "To dance with you to beautiful music in the light of the moon."

"There is no moon tonight." Her tone held an edge of amusement. "And no music."

He regarded the cloudy sky. "Who needs moonlight when your beauty is a light to behold." Did he really say that? "There's always music between us."

Music was a black hole to him. They'd never share music.

"How poetic, seeing as we've only met twice." Her sweet laughter haunted.

She spoke of Dax, not him. Believed he was Dax.

Reed's face flared and his body weakened. He was acting a bigger fool than his brother. If she ever discovered the truth they'd both be in trouble. His brother had started the conversation and Reed needed to finish.

"You bring out the poet in me." Which was true. He'd never spoken to his fiancée with such fanciful language. Maybe it was because he was pretending to be someone else.

"Thank you?" She sounded unsure. "It's late. Why don't you call me tomorrow, so we can make plans?"

He pulled his fist down in celebration. Reed had gotten a date with Quinn.

Too bad she believed he was his brother.

Chapter Four

After their initial greetings, Reed and Quinn worked in compatible silence the next morning. He'd wanted to work in the studio when she wasn't around, except she was always around. He needed to finish painting the remaining walls, hang her posters, and take care of several other details.

She focused on her computer behind the front counter. The situation was the exact opposite of working beside Elizabeth. She'd always had a need to chatter, even though she knew he was concentrating on the music in his head.

That wasn't a problem anymore. A sadness drifted through him.

Except thinking back to his and Quinn's first meeting, he'd noticed sounds in his head, and the urge to play the damn piano. Anxiety had the sad song picking up tempo. He glanced at the instrument across the room. Every once in a while, he'd hear a tinkling or a synchronized clatter in his brain. As if the music he'd lost was trying to be heard. The tempo raced, making his head spin. Her tapping foot last night before they'd attempted to dance had established a repeating pattern. The cutlery at the restaurant had tinkled into a symphonic noise. And last night his even breathing had set a tempo to a personal soundtrack.

Sweat formed on his brow.

The paint brush swished against concrete. The clock on the wall *tick, tick, ticked*. Quinn's fingers clicked on the computer keyboard. The racket combined in a rhythm. A rhythm playing in his mind. He swished the brush in between the ticking of the clock. Quinn's tapping overlaid on top, pulling the sounds together, creating a melody.

He felt dizzy. Each noise vibrated in his head like scales on the piano. The notes played in his mind in a twisted confusion of a one-instrument concerto.

Oh my Bach! He heard new music again.

Shock stung his brain, sending tremors to his limbs. He dropped the paint brush.

"Are you okay?" Quinn's lilting tone brought him out of his funk.

"Yes." His voice was raw, because he really wasn't sure. His arms and legs continued to shake. Music had returned to his mind with force. He couldn't shut it off.

"Are you sure you're okay? You're pale and sweaty."

His knees trembled, and he wanted to sink to the ground. He couldn't show his fear and anxiety. She'd already noticed a difference in him. Could she tell chords played in his brain like a symphony? He wasn't ready to tell her. He wasn't ready to tell anyone. What if the music disappeared?

Trying to calm himself, he focused on her.

Her hair was back in the tight bun. The band holding the luscious hair in place must give her a headache. He wanted to rip the band out and run his fingers through the loose strands. He didn't know what was worse, lusting after a woman he couldn't have, or hearing music again, knowing it would probably disappear. A darkness descended around him. He'd lose both.

Forcing himself to peer in the other direction, his gaze fell on the piano. Another type of urge thrummed in his hands. Ever since he'd kicked the piano, he couldn't kick out his desire to play. Every time he'd walked into the room, he'd noted the instrument.

Two wants calling to him in the same room.

Two desires he didn't deserve.

"Is your brother okay this morning?" Her question startled him, rearranging his thoughts resembling notes of an unwritten song.

His hand froze mid-stroke of the paint brush. He'd tricked her last night. Better to focus on that situation than his mind. "Yeah. Why?"

"Dax was drunk and came to my window." She sounded more amused than pleased, lifting Reed's spirits. Maybe she didn't like his brother as much as he believed, except it would be better for her to like Dax. "I hope he's okay." Obviously, she cared if he was better.

"I'm sure he's fine." Reed's terse tone held no

sympathy, because he had no sympathy. He hated seeing his brother upset. That was no excuse to get drunk.

The flowery language he used beneath the window taunted. And yet, he'd felt like his much younger self last night, enjoying their conversation, being free.

"I was expecting Dax to call." Her disappointment speared through Reed's lungs.

She wanted his brother to call, wanted to go out with him. With little enthusiasm, he said, "My brother asked me for your number."

Dax hadn't known to ask for her number, because he'd been passed out on the ground. Reed hated the idea of giving out the contact information.

The chime on the door went off and a young girl and her mother came into the studio. A sign out front invited anyone inside to visit and ask questions. The girl appeared to be around ten, with her hair tied back in a long, brown braid. She scanned the studio with wide-eyed wonder.

The mother frowned with suspicion, her coat buttoned up to the neck.

"Can I help you?" Quinn moved around the counter, eagerness showing in every step. The short skirt she wore over dark tights clung to her hips.

The mother put her arm around the girl, tugging her close, as if afraid someone might hurt the child.

"Are you here to sign up for dance class?" Quinn grabbed a brochure and held it out to the mother.

Quinn might be too determined, although he found it refreshing when not directed toward him. Elizabeth always tried to pass off the work.

"I don't know." The woman was reluctant. Her expression remained tight and fearful.

He didn't recognize the woman or the child. The urge to make everyone more comfortable had him setting the wet brush on the edge of the paint can. "Quinn is an excellent dance teacher. You and your daughter could watch a class first."

Quinn beamed and he warmed inside. He wanted to help her succeed. *Only* because she was his tenant and getting a new tenant would be more work, and the town needed a dance studio.

"The website said she'd have classes for me, Mom." The girl slipped from her mother's grip and wandered with a slight limp to the edge of the wooden floor. Her face lit with the possibilities. She held her right arm close to her body at a weird angle. Her hand fell limp from the wrist.

Uh oh. Sympathy for the girl swarmed him.

"I'm offering free lessons so students can try classes." Quinn spoke to the mother using her sales-pitch voice. "What kind of dance would your daughter be interested in learning?"

"I'd love to learn hip hop…" The girl held up her limp hand. "I'll probably need to start with something simple."

The mother rushed to take her daughter's hand, as if to hide the offending limb. "Sara would really love to dance. I'm not sure she can physically handle the class."

Reed quivered, trying to hold back his fury. The mother didn't believe in her daughter's capabilities. He clenched his hands into fists. People hadn't eved in him after the accident. Didn't think he could ever walk or take care of himself. He'd proved them wrong. He'd completed extra hours of physical therapy. He'd pushed himself.

He might not be able to ski, but he started his own construction business. A successful business where he labored hard. People had been right about him not returning to the symphony, but he'd made something of himself. He didn't care for small talk or gossip, so he chose not to go out. Sure, he hid from aspects of his life—out of choice, not capability.

"As I told Mr. O'Donnell here." Quinn danced to his side and gripped his arm with both hands. "Everyone can dance."

He stiffened. While he felt sympathy for the girl, he didn't want his own disability displayed.

"I'm sure Mr. O'Donnell doesn't have the same limitations Sara does." The mother sounded insulted and afraid. She clutched her daughter's hand tighter. Afraid for her daughter.

Afraid Sara couldn't keep up or would embarrass herself. Or embarrass the mother.

The trembling returned. Justified anger for this child raced through him. He hated how the mother placed limits on the child's abilities. The doctors and nurses had tried to stop him from doing the extra physical therapy, and if they had, he wouldn't be standing here today.

Sara needed to discover her own limitations. She should try everything possible. Even dancing. Even if it embarrassed her mother.

He limped forward. "Actually, I do." Bending

down, pain slashed through his ankle and he didn't care. He wanted to be at the same level as the girl.

The mother pulled Sara back. The girl snuck from under her mother's over-protective arm and came toward him. "Do you have an owie?"

If only. "Yes, I do. Miss Quinn has promised she can teach me to dance. So if I can dance with a bad leg, you can dance."

"That's right." Quinn's eyes shone with unshed tears.

A glow spread inside him. He enjoyed helping her and this young girl.

Quinn rubbed his back and he let himself enjoy the contact. "I've asked Mr. O'Donnell to dance in the grand opening showcase with me."

He jerked to a stand, letting the jagged agony of his injury slice across any good feelings. Turning to gape, his eyebrows practically flew off his face. He forced himself to not scream a big, fat, no-way-in-hell.

She took hold of his hand and the torment slid away. "Do you think he should do it, Sara?"

"Yes. Yes." Sara jumped and clapped her strong hand against her weak one.

The tepid noise went straight to his heart. The girl believed in him, and he believed in her. He wanted Sara to try to dance, but he didn't want to be roped in to the showcase. An unrecognized yearning slid through his system, and stopped at his unease.

"So if he can learn to dance and participate in my show, you can try out a dance class. And if you like it, you can sign up for more." Quinn's tone was solid. Her gaze pleaded with the mother.

So did Sara's. Her big, brown eyes begged.

"I guess it won't hurt to try." The mother snatched the brochure out of Quinn's hand and opened it to the sign-up page.

After the mother finished the paperwork, Sara waved to him. "I can't wait to see you in the showcase."

He couldn't back out now. His wild thoughts spiraled into tunnel vision focusing on his betrayer.

Once Sara and her mother left the studio and the door chime went silent, he pivoted toward Quinn. "Why did you set me up?"

"I'm sorry." Her voice went higher. Guilt flashed across her face, and color stained her cheeks, embarrassed at what she'd done. "When you told them I'd promised to teach you to dance, I thought—"

"I. Didn't. Agree." He leaned in toward her, only a hairsbreadth distance. "Push-Quinn."

"What?"

"Push-Quinn, like pushpin. Because you're pushy," he mumbled, because he really didn't want her thinking he gave her much thought.

"You were so inspiring talking about your injury and how it didn't stop you. So sweet." Her sapphire eyes widened like pools and his annoyance drowned in them. She placed her hand on his chest, not pushing him away.

"I'm not sweet." He'd done his best to stay away from people. To be reclusive. That wasn't going to end because of Quinn and her stupid show. Because of her hand on his thumping chest making him feel alive again.

"You'll break the girl's heart if you don't dance." The disappointment on her face, disappointment in him, caused the thumping to stutter and stop.

"My pride will break if I do." The admittance slipped out with his own failed expectations. He'd never be the man she thought.

"So the inspirational talk was just that? Talk?" She pushed against him, disgust curling on her mouth.

He didn't move back. Thoughts tangled and swirled, similar to *aleatoric* music relying on elements of chance. He'd overcome so many physical challenges since the accident. Pushed and pushed and pushed some more. It was the mental challenges that brought the most anguish. He could deal with the pain of physical therapy, but the internal pain of misguided emotions put his entire body in a twist.

This was why he'd gone along with Elizabeth's plans and machinations. It was why he'd holed himself up in Castle Ridge and chosen a new profession where you didn't need social skills and grace. It was why he chose to work with tools and not people.

A thrill went up his spine. He wanted to dance with Quinn. The main thought excited and scared him. Spending hours in her arms learning the steps, getting closer. He was also afraid and he hated the fear. "I'll do it."

"Don't sound so terrified." She placed her hand back on his chest and his heart beat again. He felt alive again. "You'll be fine, I promise."

"How are you going to guarantee that?" His shaky voice was unsure about his promise and his capability.

"Because I'm going to teach you how to dance with your limp. It won't even be noticeable." Her deep-blue eyes pinned him down. Her determination drilled into him, making him believe maybe he could dance.

Maybe he could do more with Quinn.

He leaned closer, wanting to test the theory out. Wanting a kiss.

She didn't move back or object. Her tongue darted out and licked her upper lip.

More thrills cruised up his spine, one after the other. His pulse pounded, rushing blood to where it was needed most. Catching his breath, he tilted even closer.

The door chimed.

She jerked back, breaking his trance. He glowered at the open door and the person standing there, watching, in his designer jeans and stylish jacket.

His shoulders drooped and he took a step away from Quinn and temptation. Frustration curled in his midsection. "What're you doing here?" He wasn't welcoming.

Dax rubbed his eyes as if trying to understand what he'd seen. "I came to see you."

"Me?" Both Reed and Quinn said at the same time, then scrutinized each other.

Her red cheeks displayed guilt and surprise. But what she felt guilty about, the almost-kiss or the interruption, he wasn't sure. He hoped it was the interruption.

"Quinn, I think." His brother ran fingers through his hair. "My head's not totally clear. I thought..." Dax skimmed between Reed and Quinn again, confusion on his face. "I thought I was supposed to ask you out."

His brother hadn't been as passed out as he'd thought last night. Dax must remember some of the conversation. Reed's cheeks torched, remembering the words he'd spoken.

"Maybe I only dreamed last night." His brother dropped his hand and went to turn around.

"No, you didn't dream it." Glancing at Reed, she stepped around the counter. "We did talk last night. And I did say you could call to make plans." She shot Reed another glance looking to him for guidance.

He shifted on his feet. What could he do? Even though Reed had been attracted to Quinn, he hadn't planned to do anything about it. He'd promised to help his heartbroken brother ask Quinn out. Mutual desire wasn't supposed to happen.

He took another step back.

That's what he needed to do. Step away. He didn't want or deserve a relationship with Quinn. His happy-go-lucky brother would be better for her. Dax would take her out on the town and introduce her to people.

Reed had created a certain type of life for himself. A hermit life. He wasn't expecting to find love, and he shouldn't mess things up for his brother because his male needs had suddenly made themselves known. He'd only hurt Dax and Quinn in the end. And if Reed stepped away now, no one would realize his attraction to Quinn. He'd deny desire even to himself.

That evening, Reed returned to the empty studio to finish hanging the pictures. He'd left minutes after

Dax arrived, and hadn't returned until now. Seeing him ask Quinn on a date wasn't Reed's form of entertainment.

Holding the nail between thumb and forefinger, he banged the nail into the wall with extra force. The thought of his brother holding Quinn in his arms, of them kissing, twisted inside his belly. Eventually, he might end up witnessing their togetherness, their happiness, and bear it as his own form of torture.

The studio doors chimed and Izzy breezed in. She unbuttoned her light jacket and tossed him a casual smile. "Where's Quinn?"

"Hello to you, too." The un-acknowledgement stung. Did both his siblings like Quinn better than him?

"Grumpy, much?" Another woman who also wore her hair up most of the time because of her chef's job. Tonight the reddish-blonde locks fell free. "I'm normally working the dinner shift so since I have tonight off, Quinn and I are going out for dinner. Did you want to join us?"

The offer tempted. Being with Quinn and his sister would be an interesting revelation. Izzy was about over-the-top fun and flirting, and while Quinn seemed fun, she appeared to have a more serious demeanor. But he needed to stay away from her. She was dating his brother.

The woman of his thoughts waltzed into the room, making everything brighter. Her eyes lit with excitement when she noticed him hanging her pictures. She graced a smile toward him, and hugged his sister.

After saying their hellos, she asked, "Are you ready to go?"

"I was asking Reed if he wanted to join. Do you mind?" His sister's glance strayed between them, putting two and two together.

As if putting them together.

His muscles tensed. They weren't together and never could be, no matter how close they came to a kiss.

"Great idea." Quinn's rapid agreement had his pulse quickening. "I mentioned to Dax where we were going. He might join us as well."

Reed's pulse slowed to a deliberate lento beat. He didn't want to be in competition against his brother, because there'd be no competition. Dax was a ladies' man, and the only reason he'd asked for Reed's help was because his brother had hit a low point.

"No, thanks." Good thing Reed hadn't answered quickly. "I already have plans." Frozen dinner, beer, and television. Doesn't get much better. The thought fell flat in his mind and his gut for the first time.

"Good for you." Izzy sounded super-positive, because she knew he never had any real plans, and maybe this time she believed he did. She kissed him on the cheek and said goodbye.

Quinn gave him a wave. The two women left, talking rapidly to each other, a final female laugh lingering in the air.

He wanted to reach out and catch the laughter to save for later when he'd be alone.

Smashing the nail into the wall, he continued to work finishing hanging the pictures. He had nothing else to do. Swiveling around to check on his work, the piano caught his attention. He'd tried to ignore the instrument whenever he was in the dance studio. It was always a looming presence. Taunting him.

Ignoring the instrument was easier when Quinn was present. He'd much rather watch and think about her than some stupid piano.

Except Quinn wasn't here. The piano was. And it called to him in his loneliness.

In the old days, pre-accident, the piano provided solace whenever he was lonely and upset. While he loved being on the ski team with his siblings, he didn't put in the extra hours they did. He put in extra hours at the piano. He'd written volumes of music while in his relationship with Elizabeth, most of it tempestuous or sad. The thought of her usually shredded through his mind. Now, the pain seemed less intense.

In a daze, he found himself standing beside the instrument. The piano had called to him every time he'd been in the room. Tonight, he couldn't ignore its siren call.

Probably because of the almost-kiss.

He sat at the bench and the warm wood felt right.

Lifting the lid, his fingers thrummed, anticipating the playing. The sound. The joy. He brushed his fingers across the ivories without making a noise. Each key calling to him, *play me*.

He glanced around. No one was present. No one could hear him cheat on the vow he'd sworn to never play again. Just this one time. He wanted to forget himself in the music.

Placing his scarred fingers in position on the

keyboard, he took a deep breath and blew the air out again. The scars were ugly, not painful. He'd used his hands to hammer and to paint and to carve. He'd worked hard on his physical therapy to make his hands able and flexible. It was his musical mind that had stopped working.

That didn't appear to be the case anymore. He wanted to play, and the music in his head wanted to be heard. His shoulders relaxed. His mind focused. And he played.

Played as if he'd never stopped.

The music returned to him filling the room with melodious tunes. Filled his mind with chords and notes and even the dreaded scales. Filled his heart with wonder.

He ran through old pieces he used to play. He wasn't perfect, the rhythm a bit off. He didn't care. Throwing his mind and body and spirit into it, he swayed with the playing. With it came the memories. The joyous concerts, the applause and accolades, the discovery while writing new music. His music. He used to play because his creative spirit wouldn't let him not play and create. Now, he played again with the same passion, if not the same practice.

His fingers moved over the black and white keys of their own accord, picking out new chords and arrangements. Something haunting and beautiful. Something new.

The rhythm in his soul soared. His body hummed with the new composition. He hadn't been able to write music since the accident. He'd been blocked, and assumed it was punishment for his sins.

His fingers stalled and the keys clattered together.

Sins. His sins. Sins that still existed.

Elizabeth was dead. While he was alive, but not really living.

Chapter Five

Quinn paused at the front door to the studio, listening to the piano. The first note stopped her, the chords flowing together in perfect harmony. She'd returned to the studio because she'd forgotten her business cards and brochures to hand out to people. Peering through the glass, she spotted Reed hunched over her piano. His fingers flew across the keyboard like a champion dancer flew across the stage. Shock and the music wove around, tying her up and keeping her in place. She'd thought he'd hated the piano. He'd kicked the instrument the day they'd met.

His handsome profile stood out from the shadows of the darkened studio. His dark hair flopped in front of his face in an adorable, little-boy way. His eyes were closed, as he played from memory. His mouth set in a line of concentration as if the music tortured him. His chin dipped and swayed with the tune. Passion branded his expression, and sent tingles of awareness through her bones.

So much passion. Passion she imagined turned toward her.

Stretching on her toes, she remembered their closeness this morning. He'd been about to kiss her, until Dax arrived. She'd wanted that kiss. Felt the attraction arc between her and Reed. He'd backed away and backed off, letting his brother have free rein to ask her out. The let-down had her saying yes to Dax.

Oh, but the feelings Reed poured into the piano had her knees weakening. She wanted him to play her like he played the piano. The way he ran his fingers across the keys, she imagined him running across her skin. His intensity for the music she wanted directed toward her. And his passion—she wanted to experience his passion.

The intense melody shifted into something more dramatic and haunting and lonely. He picked the keys out, as if he was making the song up. The eerie chords floated in her body and settled in her chest. He poured real emotions into his music.

This common construction worker wasn't so common.

The music stopped, and he slammed his fingers onto a bunch of keys. The harsh din jerked her out of the haunting fantasy and back to reality. Lifting his hands, he punched his elbows onto the keyboard and dropped his head.

This man was tormented. Why?

She tilted forward, wanting to soothe and comfort him. To run her fingers through his hair and massage his temples. She wanted to know what had caused his anguish.

Not now, though. He wouldn't be pleased to know she'd seen his raw emotions. They didn't know each other well. Turning, she hurried back to the restaurant, trying to push the image of his sorrow aside.

"Did you get the cards?" Izzy asked when Quinn returned to the table at the pub around the corner.

She came to a standstill. The question hit her dazed senses. "No, I…forgot." She wouldn't tattle on Reed to his sister. The moment had seemed private for him.

"Forgot?" Her friend raised an eyebrow, amusement written on her face. "That's why you went to the studio."

"I don't really need them." Handing out business cards and brochures wasn't as important. Reed and his feelings were important.

"Did you see Reed?" Izzy's curious tone prodded, asking more than the mere question.

The angle of him hunched over the piano, despair in his body language, had sympathy pounding in Quinn's head. "Yes."

"Did you talk to him?"

"No."

"He was in the studio and you saw him, yet you didn't talk to him?" Her friend took a sip of wine from her glass, considering Quinn over the rim. "I guess that's not odd for Reed. My brother has a way of pushing people away."

Her muscles tightened, and she shifted in the opposite seat wanting to know him, yet knowing she shouldn't ask because Reed would hate to learn they'd talked about him. Yet, the urge to know more pushed her. "Why does he turn people away?"

His sister slouched. "I shouldn't really share his secrets."

"I think it's more sorrow than secrets." She'd felt his anguish pouring out of his music.

"Maybe you should've been a psychologist instead of a dancer." Her friend raised her glass in a toast.

"So there is something wrong."

Izzy set her glass down. Her sharp, green gaze assessed, resembling Reed's in so many ways. "You care about him."

Quinn froze and held her breath. Reed's sister had realized the truth. She cared about him, and she cared about his emotions. Except realizing her feelings didn't mean she wanted to broadcast them. Plus, she cared about everybody. It was part of her nature. Just because Reed tugged at her heart didn't mean he was special. She didn't even know him very well. And she didn't know the extent of his emotional scars.

"Of course I care about him. Like I care about you and Dax and everyone else I've met in town." She rushed through the sentence, trying to make her lie plausible.

Her friend continued to study her. Quinn's cheeks heated, flaring to the top of her head. She swallowed a big gulp of ice water trying to cool her skin.

Izzy leaned forward eager to hear everything. "Are you attracted to my brother?"

"Thanks for coming to repair the oven so quickly." Parker Williamson patted Reed on the back. He wore his normal suit and tie, appearing slick with perfect hair and white-toothed grin. "We just need to keep this equipment up and running through New Year's Eve."

"Thank Izzy for begging me." Glancing at his sister standing nearby, he let the sourness come out in his tone. If the lodge owner had called, he wouldn't have helped. "Unlike *you* asking me to put a bid in on the kitchen remodel, Mr. Hotel."

Reed didn't expect his high school friend to give him the job, but he'd expected a chance. He'd been making repairs and installing items in the lodge's professional kitchen since he first started his business. A complete kitchen remodel would've been a challenge, and would've been great for his company's resume.

Parker's gaze darted around, looking anywhere else. "I didn't have a choice. The kitchen remodel is tied up with other contracts I've signed."

"Whatever." He tilted over the stainless steel oven door and stuck his head inside to find the source of the problem.

"Send me the invoice, and bill at your highest rate because of the short notice." The hotel owner's false breezy tone didn't make Reed okay with the situation. "Talk to you both later."

"Parker's been acting strange." Izzy conspiratorial voice got closer.

"Parker's always been strange." They'd been acquaintances in high school. Danielle's older brother had been Parker's best friend, until all of sudden they weren't. Not that it was any of Reed's business.

"Speaking of strange…"

But everything was Izzy's business. He didn't respond.

"Quinn said something interesting last night."

He jerked and bumped his head on the inside of the oven. His mind tingled, wondering what she'd said, but he didn't want to lead the queen of gossip on. Biting his tongue, he stayed silent.

"Don't you want to know what?" Izzy's tone went higher, trying to hook him. She enjoyed when people begged her to share news.

He wasn't playing the game. Even if he really wanted to. "Not really."

"Even if it was about you?"

His lungs whooshed with air, dropping his heart straight to his midsection. His head beat like kettle drums. Quinn had talked about him? Good or bad? And did he really want to know? He tried to imagine what she might say. The only thing he could think of was how she regretted their almost-kiss.

He poked his head out of the oven. Although if he left it inside and turned it on, he wouldn't ever need to learn what she thought. "What?"

Izzy studied him as if trying to read his mind, unnerving him. She'd always had a way of reading people and usually being right. Standing, he fiddled in the toolbox, pretending to search for a tool, trying to play it cool, probably looking like a fool.

The rhyming words jarred. The words could be used for lyrics in a song. A sad love song. His mind jolted. He hadn't been able to think of lyrics in forever, his guilty mind unable to string two musical words together.

Now he heard music in his mind and words imprinted on his brain. Rhyming words, lyrical words. Words for a song about love.

His ribcage squeezed tight when Quinn's image flashed before him. He closed his eyes and reopened them to find his sister watching him with a narrowed, shrewd gaze. He hated when she analyzed people, especially him. She'd done it as a kid and had told him he should play more piano and ski less. She'd been right.

He lifted a wrench and throttled the handle. "Are you going to tell me or not?"

Her lips slipped into a slow, satisfied smile annoying him. "Quinn said she was attracted to my brother."

His heart jumped back into his chest with an increased tempo, then it slowed into the tune of the sad love song he'd been creating in his mind. "Which one?"

"What?"

"Which brother?" He clenched the wrench tighter. "You do have two brothers, you know."

"I know, but..." Izzy's brow scrunched. "Quinn hasn't met Dax. He never came last night."

Typical Dax. Only thinking about himself and his interests. Didn't he realize Quinn had probably been waiting for him as she'd been waiting for his first call? Reed curled his lips in distaste.

"Why would you think she'd be interested in Dax?" Izzy didn't dismiss the idea outright. She didn't know about their water leak meeting, or about the Cyrano moment.

Reed's shoulders slumped and he wanted to kick himself. He never should've continued the window conversation pretending to be his brother. "Probably because Dax asked Quinn out and she said yes."

His sister's mouth dropped open. She appeared disappointed, as if she wanted Quinn to like him. This conversation resembled middle-schoolers talking about who was crushing on whom. Except this wasn't some teenage crush. This was something more. He firmed his lips in rejection. Probably only lust. He was a man.

With his sister's words ringing in his head, he worked later that day in the dance studio, attaching the wooden poles to the wall. Aware of another presence, Quinn's presence, he turned his head.

She floated into the studio from the back, wearing tights and a long sweatshirt. She studied him similar to how his sister had done earlier. "I heard you playing the piano last night."

He stilled and his throat strangled at her statement. His gaze flew to her face. The slight smile kicked in his gut. She knew one of his secrets.

As if the piano had been dropped on his head, he was stunned. He didn't know how to react or what to say. He wasn't ready to tell her about his other life, his pre-accident life, where he'd traveled the world playing concerts in front of hundreds of people. How in his downtime he'd composed music and written lyrics. When he'd lived life to the fullest.

She stared, expecting a response.

"I'm sorry. I know the piano is special to you." His tone was stilted and formal. He picked up the long wooden pole for the ballet barre, wanting to stab himself to get out of this conversation.

"At least you weren't kicking it." Her tease ruffled his pride, because he held instruments to the highest respect.

He straightened his shoulders and clenched his hands around the pole. "I do know how to play."

"I'd say you could do more than just play." She sounded breathless with anticipation, expecting him to tell more.

Share more of himself and more of his secrets.

He slammed the end of the pole on the ground. He couldn't do that. He should never have sat at the piano, never given in to temptation. Lesson learned. He wouldn't be tempted again. Not by the piano and not by her. "I guess."

She sashayed toward him, her hips moving up and down in a hypnotic rhythm. "The song you played was beautiful. Haunting. Magical." Her magic was more powerful. She wound a spell around him. "What was it?"

The tune wouldn't leave his mind; it teased and taunted him every minute of the day. In the past, when he'd been composing, this was how it had always been. He'd need to put pen to paper and transcribe the chords from his brain. If he tried to ignore the sounds, the chords would jangle and jumble and crescendo until he heard nothing else. If he didn't write the tune down, his head would explode.

But he wasn't writing music. Sure, there'd been melodies pulsing with increasing amplification in his brain. Last night without realizing, he'd combined notes in an original way. His hands trembled and his grip around the pole slackened. His entire body wavered. Would he be able to write music again? A full composition? Did he even want to?

"What was the song?" Her reminder brought him out of his head and into the studio.

"Nothing." He positioned the pole on the brackets he'd screwed into the wall. "Something I was fiddling with."

Something new. And because of the fact he heard notes combining in his head made it something wonderful, and terrifying. The conflicting mixture made him sick. His stomach roiled and churned. He wasn't only hearing music in his head, it was new music, his music. His to compose and play. The roiling exploded shaking through his limbs. What if the new music teased him and left him again?

"Can you play it for me now?" She placed her delicate fingers on his arm, creating tension in the muscle.

He dropped the pole into position and took a step away, letting her hand fall from him. "I've got a lot of work to do."

She twirled around, taking in the studio. "We're almost ready."

"I've got a punch list of items to complete." He snatched the upper brackets. The metal clanged together. He didn't play piano for people anymore. He'd say he didn't play period, except she'd heard him, and he still clamored to tickle the ivories.

Maybe when she was gone or upstairs with both doors closed he could chance a second sitting. The sickness twisted in his stomach from his wavering. Did he or did he not want to play? The indecision paralyzed.

"Pretty please." She twirled and *pliéd* with the request. "For me?"

Her words tugged. Tugged him toward the piano and wanting to play. He wanted to please her. What if he froze? What if he couldn't remember the tune, or even how to move his hands? What if she stared at his scarred fingers and was disgusted? Sure, she'd seen his ugly hands before, but playing piano the scarred skin would be a focus.

He dropped the metal brackets back into his toolbox. "I've got another job to get to."

"It's after five."

His panicked gaze flew to the clock showing the lateness of the day, switched to the piano, and to the door. "I didn't realize it was so late. I should go."

"No." She touched his arm, and he focused on her long, slender fingers. "Please play."

Every muscle and tendon and ligament stiffened. He wasn't ready to share his music knowing she was listening. He needed a distraction, something that would guarantee she wouldn't ask him to play again. Only one thing came to mind. Something he didn't want to do almost as much. Almost.

"Dance with me instead."

Her eyes lit and her smile grew. At least he'd pleased her in another way. "You want to dance?"

"If I'm going to be featured in the showcase I'll need lots of practice." Or torture.

He'd be in her arms, knowing she planned to date

his brother. So close and yet so far. Really far. The original score beat in his brain with his thoughts. More lyrics to harass him. At least she'd forget about her request for him to play.

She clicked on a slow waltz instrumental. Stepping toward him, she positioned his hand on her waist and placed her hand on his shoulder. His fingers quivered. Their opposite hands held and his palm went instantly clammy. She'd be so grossed out by his nerves she wouldn't want to dance with him.

Giving him a few instructions, they took their first steps in silence. He knew the dance. Dragging his limp foot was agonizing.

"Everything okay?" She sounded tentative.

"Just dandy." He stumbled, coming in late on the step. His body tensed and scorched. He never should have suggested dancing.

"Don't think about the steps. Let the music move you like it does when you're playing piano." Her suggestion buzzed through his veins, making him hyper-aware.

They both moved to music in different ways. They both appreciated music.

She used her leading hand to indicate their direction. "Speaking of music, I'd love to dance to the piece you played. Do you know who wrote it?"

So much for her forgetting. "No."

"The melody reminded me of a piece played by the New York Symphony." Her gaze burrowed, shafting deep into his soul. She was digging for information. "I can't forget the piece, and don't remember who composed it."

He grunted, pretending to not understand the real question.

"It's funny, almost coincidental. The song I remember was as haunting as what you played."

The comparison struck a clanging chord. She probably thought they were similar, because they'd been composed by the same man. He stumbled again. He couldn't allow her to get any closer, to dig any deeper, to discover more. Discover his past.

Chapter Six

"Don't know." And by Reed's tone, he didn't care.

Quinn's bullshit meter went off the charts. Maybe he cared too much. He certainly didn't want to discuss the song. *Interesting.* She needed to try a different tack.

She guided him into a quarter turn, maneuvering with steps and questions. "Where did you learn to play the piano?" This wasn't only curiosity on her part, she wanted to know more about him.

As a people person, she'd always loved to learn everything about everyone. It helped her imagine doing something different as she practiced her fiftieth *plié* or stretched her legs to breaking point. Although, she admitted to herself, this man made her more curious than anyone ever.

"Where did you learn to dance?" His question was choreographed in the perfect counter-move. He didn't want to answer questions.

"I started dancing as a toddler and loved it. My mom said I had a natural ability." Her mom had been a professional ballet dancer who always ended up in the chorus. She'd wanted more for her daughter, especially after Quinn's father left them when she was two.

"You are a natural dancer."

"I enrolled at a full-time ballet school when I was ten." A chill chased up her spine. She'd been a child, unaware of the commitment she'd made. Her mother knew exactly what documents she'd signed. "I hated it."

The long hours, the dormitory quarters, the sparse food. And the competition. The girls had fought for first position, fought for the best roles in the dance recitals. They'd short-sheeted beds so you'd get to sleep late. They'd tattle if you overate. They'd purposely tried to get you in trouble.

For Quinn it was being in a family of one. She'd wanted to become friends with her schoolmates and fellow dancers. She'd wanted to learn about their backgrounds and hobbies. Not that any of them had time for hobbies. Loneliness drifted through her, but didn't linger. The emptiness didn't feel so empty.

"Why did you hate ballet school?" He slid his foot along the floor, knowing the next step.

"I rarely saw my mother." Her lungs hitched. The woman only visited on show days to critique her performance, always finding it lacking. "Once in New York, I never saw my grandparents, who lived in Castle Ridge." The hitch in her lungs grew stronger, as if she was out of breath. She wasn't. She was in perfect physical condition. "I sold the house to a broker. That's where the piano came from." *And my back up financial reserves.*

"I understand now why the piano is special to you." Reed's voice hummed with emotion. He must've connected to the piano, too.

"My grandmother played. She tried to teach me. I couldn't sit still long enough."

"You were meant to be a dancer."

She knew she had the body type and the grace. She loved the joy of dancing. Being a professional dancer had wreaked havoc on her muscles and tendons. And on her nerves. The daily double or triple workouts. The strict diet. The competition's mind games.

She'd been strong and determined, but she wasn't mean, which is what it took to make it in the competitive ballet world. She sighed. "That's what my mother told me."

She swallowed the bitter thought like she'd swallowed the diuretics. She had been a good dancer, and yet she'd begun dreading getting up in the morning. Nausea had built throughout the day leading to a performance. On stage, she'd plastered a smile on her face. She didn't hate performing, she hated the pressure from the choreographer and other dancers, hated she was being judged, hated she always had to watch her back. "Did your mother want you to build things?"

His arm jerked, pulling her closer. His broad chest rubbed against her and his body warmed her to her toes.

"My mother never imagined this is what I'd end up doing, Curious Quinn." His stilted answer made her wonder. His too-blank expression told her he was hiding something.

She ignored the new nickname. "You said your parents moved to Florida before you and your brother and sister moved back to Castle Ridge." The three siblings appeared to be close. She couldn't imagine the parents not being part of it. "Where did you move back from?"

He didn't answer right away. The music played on and she was content being in his arms. Very content.

"New York." He spat.

She leaned back to see his expression. Why hadn't he mentioned this before? "New York City?"

His lips puckered, as if tasting something sour. His eyes darkened. He twirled her around in a flourish. "Yes."

The answer was as surprising as the advanced dance move.

"We might've met or passed each other on the street." She studied his tall frame and broad shoulders in flannel shirt and jeans. In her New York world, most of the men were thin and lanky, strong. Not big like Reed, though. Dancers, not construction workers.

"I don't think we ran in the same circles." Sounding offended, his movements stiffened.

She wanted to bring the more easygoing Reed back. The one who'd offered to dance and agreed to perform in her showcase. "Were you in real estate and construction there?"

His movements halted altogether. "Which reminds me, I have work to do." He removed his hand from around her waist.

A chill ran from her waist up her spine. He didn't

want to answer her questions. He wasn't an open book. He'd allowed her to read the first few pages, but because of her insistent questioning, he'd slammed the book closed.

He tugged his other hand out of hers and she slid her hand off his shoulder, releasing him. For now.

While she'd been asking questions, he'd been dancing without instruction. He knew how to dance. The puzzle of Reed grew deeper. She wanted to dig down and figure him out, put the pieces together.

Why? The internal question shook her, trembling traveled from her head to her toes. None of the other men she'd dated ever had her so intrigued. Why did Reed?

Reed was almost finished attaching the barres to the walls in front of the floor-to-ceiling mirrors in the dance studio. Good. Because he was tired of looking at himself. He couldn't help noticing how much he'd changed from the accident. The limp was pronounced, but he'd adapted his walk to make it less noticeable. The scars hadn't faded, but the skin around the scars had gotten tanned, and less attention was called to the disfigurement. It was his body that had changed the most. He used to be long and lanky, toned but not muscular. Now, his shoulders were broader, his arms were thicker, and because he'd done so much physical therapy both of his legs belonged on a steroid-filled bodybuilder.

The new shape had made him appear a hulking monster. Studying himself now he didn't look terrible.

Did Quinn prefer her men skinny or thicker? Not that it mattered.

The door chimed and Dax trotted in. "Done admiring yourself, brother?"

Reed's cheeks heated at being caught studying his body in the mirror. "What're you doing here?"

His brother had his long hair tied back. His ski jacket flapped open, revealing a fluorescent sweatshirt matching his ski pants. Not his ski patrol attire. "Thanks to your poetic words from the other night..."

He didn't speak poetically much anymore. Another way he'd changed. He spoke in a grouchy voice with short sentences, while his brother spoke in hurried words as if there was a party he always had to get to. Except for the other night under Quinn's window, when Reed had new lyrics tapping at his brain.

"...I'm taking Quinn skiing."

A shaft of green struck his middle, an anguishing, powerful ooze. Turning away, he tried to school his features to his normal indifferent expression. The man staring back at him in the mirror had a thundercloud imprinted on his face. Guess she preferred lanky over bulky.

He had to respond with some comment. "That's progress."

Dax strutted next to him and checked himself out in the mirror. "This is where Quinn will spend her days, while she spends her nights with me."

His egotistical strut and his machismo claim roused Reed's protective instincts. His little brother needed to treat Quinn with respect. "Be good to her." He jerked back. His protective instincts usually covered his siblings first, not a woman he'd only met a few days ago.

His brother flashed the reflection his famous pick-up-line smile. "Maybe I should put mirrors on my ceiling. You'd do that for me, right?"

Jealousy flared, incinerating the green ooze into a major fire inside his body. Every muscle in his body stiffened. His hands shaped into sharp claws. Trying to control his streak of envy, he took a deep breath. This was his little brother. "Glad to see your confidence is back. Guess you don't need my help anymore."

His brother's confidence melted, as if touched by his internal heat. Dax's jaw dropped. His cocky expression turned scared. He grabbed the collar of Reed's shirt. "You can't abandon me. Let's see how today goes."

"You're on ski patrol and an expert skier. I'm sure today will go great." He'd always helped his little brother. He hated he'd knocked him down a peg with a few words. Obviously, Dax's confidence was shaky.

Hatred for this ex-girlfriend drilled Reed. He'd never known his brother to be so confused and unsure. The cocky demeanor was lovable, but he wondered if it was a pretense.

"On the slopes I'm an expert. What about après-ski?" Dax's panic was comical.

Reed didn't laugh.

"Après-ski?" Quinn floated into the studio wearing a decorative knit hat, her long hair streaming from beneath. Pink ski jacket and ski pants, and black snow boots lined with fur completed the outfit. She resembled a fashion model with her thin, athletic frame and perfect, gleaming smile.

Reed swallowed, trying to control his rushing pulse. Rushing from his heart to his cock.

Dax's fake grin returned. He stepped toward her. "You're hot."

That wouldn't have been Reed's choice of words. Gorgeous. Amazing. Worshipful.

Her smile grew wider. "I haven't skied since I was ten. Let me get through the skiing part first, before we talk about après-ski."

His brother took her gloved fingers. "You're with a professional. You're in good hands."

More like fast hands.

Half of Reed cheered him on. He wanted the fun and happy version of his brother back. The other half, the one that cared about Quinn, wanted to kick Dax's ass.

As if she'd read Reed's mind, she slipped her hand away. "Do you want to go skiing with us, Reed?"

The offer shot his spirits in the sky, cooling the jealousy. Even though the actual question was an arrow to his heart. "I can't ski." He studied the ground. The bright shine off the wooden dance floor made his eyes sting.

"That's what you said about dancing." Her determined tone made the arrow sticking from his chest quiver.

The two things were completely different.

For the most part, dancing was slow and steady, performed on a flat surface and in comfortable shoes. He glanced at her again. And in the arms of someone you were attracted to. Skiing was off-balanced and downhill, reckless. The hard boots wouldn't conform to his misshapen ankle, making the entire experience painful.

"I didn't *want* to dance. I can't ski." He kept his voice short and rough. He didn't want her feeling sorry for him. He could walk and the doctors told him he'd never do that again. He could play the piano, although he hadn't wanted to until recently.

She opened her mouth to push the point.

He became a rock, impenetrable. "Go. I've got work to finish." He picked up the drill from his toolbox not sure what exactly he was going to do with it, he just needed something in his hands. Something to distract.

"Are you sure?" Dax must've seen something on Reed's face. His wish to ski, or his wish to ski with Quinn. "You know, there's adaptive skiing—"

"No." He didn't want someone guiding him around a mountain he knew like the back of his scarred hand. He didn't want help. Revving the drill, he wanted them to leave. "Go and have fun."

The last part was the hardest sentiment. He didn't want them to have fun, yet he did. Dax was his brother and Quinn was...was a friend. Possibly his brother's future girlfriend.

The athletic couple left the studio side by side. Their fast paces and smiling faces were proof they should be together. Same abilities, same socialization skills.

He slapped his forehead. *More lyrics. Fast paces and smiling faces.* The rhyming words and the new melody wouldn't leave him alone.

Staring out the window, he watched the couple dash across the street laughing at something. Together.

A gloom descended. Any hope of being with Quinn wilted inside, knowing he hadn't had any real chance. He'd always known. With his disabilities, he missed too much of regular life. He couldn't get involved with a woman and have her miss part of life, too.

Better for his brother to be with Quinn. Someone Reed knew and trusted, not a complete stranger. As long as Dax behaved himself and didn't continue his wild playboy ways.

Chapter Seven

Reed sat at the piano with his hands poised above the keys. Nerves flitted in his stomach, making him ill. The song, his song, buzzed through his brain. The one whittling away at his conscious. A song wanting to be written, heard, completed. Sharp notes of doubt punctured through the music. Could he really have a new song inside him? His fingers itched to play each new note, to hear them slide together in musical harmony, to put them together with the words dancing in his head.

Dancing because the lyrics were about one specific person.

He slammed his hands on the piano. A person he shouldn't be attracted to and shouldn't be writing songs about, ever. Quinn was on a date with his brother. She'd never see him as a strong, virile male. Dax might be heartbroken, but Reed was broken. His brother's heart would mend, while Reed's body was unrepairable.

His cell phone rang, taking him out of his confused thoughts. He answered automatically.

"This is the Castle Ridge Hospital Emergency Room," the calm voice on the other end of the line was the opposite of the news it would convey. Hospitals rarely called with good news.

His heart stuttered. Had his risk-taking brother finally gone too far? "What happened?"

"Quinn Petrov—"

His stuttering heart swelled and spasmed. He immediately assumed the worst because he'd been through the worse. He tamped down on his trembling lips. "Is she okay?"

"She's fine." If she was fine, the hospital wouldn't be calling. "She had an accident on the slopes."

"Where's Dax? She was skiing with him. Is he hurt, too?" Reed's pulse skyrocketed. His worry and fear spiked into anger at his brother.

The crinkling of papers came across the line. "She was brought in by the ski patrol."

"Dax is ski patrol." *Dammit.* Reed wanted the entire story. "He's not injured? Or there? How bad is she?"

"She's hurt her ankle and hit her head."

"Concussion?" He'd been a skier his entire life. He knew the risks and the common injuries.

"We don't know yet." The tone on the other side remained calm. "She asked for you."

Calm was the last thing he was experiencing. His swelling heart beat to a hopeful song. She'd asked for him. Not his brother. Where the hell was his brother?

He needed to get to Quinn's side. She shouldn't be alone. "On my way."

He bolted out the door as fast as his stupid limp would carry him. He thought about driving, but between holiday visitors and parking at the base of the mountain, it would be faster to walk. For most people.

Where was Dax?

He'd been skiing with Quinn. He was a ski accident expert. Why hadn't the clinic called him? Why wasn't he at her side when she'd fallen? The unanswered questions whipped around in Reed's head like the swirling wind. He took out his phone and dialed his brother.

"I can't talk right now." Dax sounded breathless when he answered. "I lost Quinn on the mountain and I'm trying to find her."

Reed's head pounded with a bass note. "She's not on the mountain." He clenched the phone in his hand trying to control his anger at his brother's irresponsibility. "She's in the emergency room."

"What?"

"She's hurt." His chest constricted.

"How hurt?" Dax's voice squeaked.

Reed pushed harder and faster, not caring about the pain shooting from his ankle to his calf. The hospital said head injury. Any accident with the head was serious. He knew. Shuffling past the ticket booth and restaurant, he spotted the red cross of the small emergency hospital. The ski patrol headquarters were located next door.

"I don't know. I'm almost there." The bass in Reed's head hit harder. How could his brother not take better care of Quinn? She was a precious package to be protected. "How did you lose track of her?"

"She skied real slow."

"You should've stayed with her." He couldn't stop the censure. His brother had always been reckless. And Reed had always been around to clean up the mess. Who had helped his little brother when he'd been in New York? They were both too old for this.

"I'm not used to skiing with beginners, big brother." Not exactly an explanation, and certainly not an apology.

Reed should've lectured his brother before the start of the day. "She told you she hadn't skied since she was a kid. She doesn't know the mountain." He strangled the phone in his hand, wishing it was his brother's neck. "What were you thinking?"

"Don't get your panties in a twist," Dax fired back. "I deal with these kind of emergencies every day. I'm sure she'll be fine."

This wasn't about any old emergency. This was about Quinn. Reed's worry grew bigger, pushing out the air in his lungs. He was suffocating.

"She better be." He put a threat in his tone. Or his little brother would have to deal with him.

Quinn's eyelids were glued shut. Her head thumped, and every part of her body ached. Her left ankle throbbed. Images returned. Hurrying down the hill, crossing her skis, falling...and crashing. She remembered the soft voice of the female ski patrol member, and the swishing of the snow beneath the basket carrying her down the slope. Where was she now?

She lay on a cushy surface, and something soft covered her. An antiseptic smell stung her nose. A beeping filled her ears. She tried to move her legs.

Her belly clenched and nausea burned. Her heart charged. Her legs wouldn't move. Struggling to open her eyes, she took short, shallow, gasping breaths.

The world was fuzzy. Two large figures loomed. Dax wearing his ski helmet. And Reed.

The burning cooled and some of her panic receded, knowing he was close.

His face was etched with lines of concern. He held his chin between white-knuckled fingers. Staring, his gaze never left her face. The burning returned to her cheeks this time. He studied her as if she was a piece of art, not a big mess.

"She's awake." Sounding relieved, Dax sent a flirty smile toward the door.

Not at her. She focused out and noticed a cute nurse exiting the room. Quinn felt nothing. No jealousy about the man she was on a date with smiling at someone else. Someone probably much prettier at the moment. Her warm cheeks scorched higher. Reed must think she looked terrible. She tried to raise her hand. Tubes and cords slowed her movement. "How do I look?"

"More importantly, how do you feel?" He leaned forward, possibly wanting to examine inside her head. Her body overheated from his closeness and his concern. "When I got the call, I was so worried."

Dax nudged his brother's shoulder, pushing him aside. "I'm so sorry, babe. I lost you. One moment you were behind me and then you were gone."

She didn't remember the day the same way. A quick lesson, a single easy run, and Dax had led her toward the back of the mountain. The entire day she'd been playing catch up, trying to follow the speck of his green coat racing ahead. Dax had pushed her to the edge of her abilities. That's how she taught, so how could she complain?

Except she hadn't let go of Reed when they'd danced. She hadn't wanted to let go. Her hand on his shoulder had quivered with attraction. Their joined hands had connected them on a deeper level. She'd peered into his green eyes with tiny flecks and been lost in their depths.

She never should've said yes to skiing or yes to Dax. Her gaze strayed to his older brother.

"Reed called me when he got the call from ski patrol. I got here as fast as I could." Dax plopped on the edge of the bed.

Pain sliced through her foot and ankle, and she grimaced.

"Get off the bed." Reed's sharp voice had her examining him. She could see his concern. "You're jostling her."

"Sorry, sorry. I'm not very good in hospitals." Dax's cheeks flamed red. He shot an uneasy glance at his brother.

She sensed the tension between the two men. "I thought you were on ski patrol." The statement accused. He'd been too fast all day. Fast talker, fast teacher, and way-too-fast skier. She couldn't keep up.

"Avalanche expert." Standing, Dax stuck out his chest. "I know how to deal with emergencies and accidents on the mountain. Once they get to the ER, I'm outta there."

"And you've obviously never been a ski instructor." She huffed, too exhausted to show much anger, even though he was the reason she was in the hospital.

Reed cleared his throat and shifted on his feet. "People from Castle Ridge practically ski before they walk." His explanation didn't make up for his brother's impatience, but she liked that he tried to protect him.

Dax moved back toward her, grabbed her hand, and squeezed too tight. "I'm really sorry. When you get out we'll do something you want to do."

His awkward apology soothed her temper. She didn't have the strength to argue. "Okay." She tugged her hand out of his.

"Maybe you should leave while she's in a forgiving mood." Reed used the older-brother-knows-best tone.

Dax's focus shifted between the two of them, showing his indecision. "I don't know. Quinn?"

If he was uncomfortable and didn't want to be here, that was fine with her. He was a distraction from Reed's attention. "Don't stay on my account."

His eyes widened, and his mouth lifted in a semblance of an awkward grin. "You're sure?" His hopeful expression included a sheen of perspiration. He kept glancing at the medical equipment. He was truly anxious about being in a hospital.

Softening toward him, she didn't need him here as long as she had Reed. "I'm sure once they check the X-rays they'll release me."

A woman shuffled into the room in ski patrol pants and jacket. Her long hair was tied in pigtails. She seemed vaguely familiar. "I'm Lexi." She said to the room in general. "I brought you off of the mountain and wanted to see how you were doing." Her quizzical perusal encompassed the three of them, stopping at Dax.

She must know him. They both were on ski patrol. "I'm doing okay."

"You were the one who brought Quinn in?" Dax's question accused. "Why didn't you call me? She was skiing with me."

Lexi's eyebrows arched. "I didn't see you anywhere around." She spoke slowly with a question mark at the end. Like, where the heck were you?

The answer Quinn wanted. "He skied too fast for me."

"Give me a break." He scowled at Reed. "I was born into a family of skiers. I don't remember how to slow down and teach someone."

Which might've given her a break—a break in her ankle. Her muscles tensed, trying to control an ugly retort. "I told you I hadn't skied in years."

"Yeah, but you're athletic, babe." The compliment didn't appease. "I thought you'd be fine."

"And..." the ski patrol member's cheeks reddened. She glared at Dax, as if knowing his irresponsible ways. "Not only weren't you around, Quinn *asked* us to call your brother."

Her pulse pounded, beating out her mortification. She remembered saying Reed's name. She'd been thinking about how his life must've changed after his accident. Had she bothered him while he was working?

He flattened his lips together, hiding a smile. Did he find this amusing, or was he glad she'd asked for him?

Dax glowered at his brother, as if noticing the slight smile, too. He fisted his hands together and inclined toward Reed in a menacing way. "What."

Not a question. More of a demand.

The air in the room went frigid. Tension radiated between the brothers.

Lexi swung her arms, trying to break the awkwardness. "Well, it doesn't appear to be anything serious. Let me know how the patient is doing, Dax."

"I'll follow you out. Text you later." He bussed Quinn on the cheek, waved, and hurried out of the room. "Later, Reed."

Shaking her head, she watched Dax's retreating back. He was a fun guy, but not responsible, and not for her.

"Don't take it personally. He's got a phobia of hospitals." Reed crossed his arms in front of his broad chest. He seemed to have run his fingers through his disheveled hair several times. Had he been worried about her? "You should've seen him when I was in the hospital. He only visited a couple of times, and I was there for months."

His words sent a stream of sorrow through her. She couldn't imagine being in a hospital for months. "I hope I'm not here for even a few days." She couldn't afford to not open her dance studio on time.

"You should know if anything is broken soon." He

paced to the edge of the room and back again, resembling a caged-in tiger, a limping-unsure tiger. Plunking down on a chair near her bed, he ran fingers through his hair. His stared at the ceiling, as if trying to decide what to say. "I'm sorry this happened. My brother doesn't understand everyone can't keep up with him physically."

Soothed, she relaxed against the small bed. Reed knew the right thing to say. He didn't lie to make things sound better. He didn't panic. She liked that about him. He was a pillar of strength in an emergency. She'd never had that before. The ballet doctors treated the dancers as commodities, trying to fix whatever was wrong with minimum days of dancing missed and minimum fuss.

"Is that what happened to you? A skiing accident?" If he'd been in the hospital for months his accident must've been horrific.

His facial muscles ticked. His eyes dimmed with sorrow. He shifted in the hard chair and avoided her gaze. The memories must be torturous and she wanted to reach out and hold his hand. "Your accident was nothing like mine."

"What kind of accident was it?" Her question came out slow and careful. She didn't want to scare him away, yet she wanted to know.

"Car accident." His Adam's apple moved up and down. The answer had been difficult.

A bittersweetness flowed through her. He'd told her. The precious honor scared and drew her closer. She wanted to be his confidant, someone he shared his painful past with, someone he trusted.

She didn't want him remembering bad memories, but sometimes talking helped release the horror. "In Castle Ridge?" The wintry roads must be treacherous.

His lips pursed in a mutinous expression. "New York City."

"You had a car in New York?"

"No." Back to one-word answers.

Sorrow sailed through her bloodstream. They were going backwards, and she wanted to move forward. "With the city's crawling traffic, most accidents are fender-benders."

"This one wasn't." The words sounded as if they were being ripped from his soul. "Someone died."

His expression blanked. Thinking about it must be too harsh a memory. His skin turned an ashen color. He closed his eyes tight, forming small wrinkles.

She placed her hand over his. The simple touch meant to calm, instead the contact ignited a spark deep inside. A spark of rightness. Holding his hand felt true. Like she belonged with him.

Rubbing his cold skin, she caressed the ridges of the scars, trying to comfort. He was obviously tortured by the accident. Not the noticeable wounds on his hand or his limp, but inside. She wanted to help him with the internal scars, too. The urge to heal him overwhelmed, and she found joy in this need. "Whose fault?"

The hospital machines beeped. The wall heater whined. The clock on the wall ticked.

His breathing grew heavier and heavier. He gasped.

Without him speaking, she knew. Knew the ugly truth.

"Mine."

The word thumped in her chest and echoed, getting deeper and deeper, and sadder and sadder. "I'm sure it wasn—"

"My fault." His tone brooked no argument. His face seemed to age in seconds.

Squeezing his hand tighter, she wanted to comfort him, to say the right words as he often did. She didn't know how to react to his confession. Internally, she floundered. Her lips flapped, yet nothing came out. Here, she'd been honored with his blunt honesty, and she didn't know how to respond. Holding his hand, they sat in silence, each of them stewing in their thoughts.

"Good news." The cute nurse breezed into the room holding a chart, not realizing the morose mood in the room or the important discussion Quinn wanted to finish, but didn't know how. "You've only got a sprain. No concussion."

"Thank you so much." Relief whooshed out in her voice. She'd been lucky. What if she'd broken a bone and it took weeks to heal? She wouldn't be able to open her dance studio on time, which meant she couldn't pay the rent on time.

"Great." Reed's eyes lightened, as if he'd been worried about her. He used his free hand to rub down her arm in a soft caress.

Tingles of attraction spiked off contact, sending a trail of shimmering desire through her. She noted the lightness of his expression and the intensity of his gaze. The morose mood had vanished, but the meaning of their conversation lingered in her mind.

"We need to finish up the paperwork and get you your release instructions. It shouldn't take long." The cute nurse scanned Reed similar to how she'd scanned Dax, earlier.

Every unbroken bone in Quinn's body tensed. She didn't like the nurse inspecting Reed as if he was there for the woman's pleasure. He was there for her.

"Will you be driving the patient home?" The nurse hinted she wanted him to drive her home and right into bed.

The pain in Quinn's ankle traveled to her heart. She lolled forward, waiting to hear his response.

"Of course." No hesitation on his part. No flirty smile at the nurse. Reed didn't even notice the woman flirting with him. The exact opposite of his brother. A hum of satisfaction danced inside Quinn.

"I'll need to run to the studio and pick up my car. I walked, because parking is so difficult."

Had he left the studio in a hurry to get to her? Her head swooned and she felt faint, except then she wouldn't get to go home with Reed.

The nurse held up the chart. "I'll get the paperwork started, and by the time you get back she'll have care instructions and be ready to go."

After the nurse left the room, Quinn grabbed his hand again. "Thanks so much, Reed. I don't know what I would've done without you."

"No worries." His gaze shifted and he tugged his hand out of hers. Now they were alone, he acted nervous again. Could it be because he thought she wanted to return to their discussion?

Not at this moment. She'd wait until they weren't

in a hospital room and could be interrupted at any minute. Beaming, she couldn't wait to be alone with him for more than discussing his past.

Wanting to put him at ease, she switched the focus to her problems. "I was so worried about hurting myself and I wouldn't be able to open the dance studio on time. Which would mean begging you to let me pay the rent late." She wasn't worried anymore. She'd had sprains before. A little rest and she'd be fine.

In the meantime, Reed had come to her rescue, so he must care. She sensed the attraction between them, and couldn't wait to discover where it would lead. From what she'd seen, he was so reserved with women, she'd have to take the lead in this relationship just as she led in their dance. A tingle of excitement boogied down her spine.

Another smile flitted onto her face, a flirty smile. A come-and-get-me smile. "Or bribing you with my body."

Reed scurried out of the hospital. Quinn's words tempted and teased. Except when she learned the truth about him, about what he'd done, she'd be running away from him. He might be the one bribing her to keep his secrets.

He shoved the gear of his truck too hard and it grinded, scratching across his back and making him shiver. Parking outside the hospital, he couldn't believe he'd confessed about the accident to a virtual stranger. He'd never told his family the details, and he'd only known Quinn for a week. Not that he'd shared everything. Loud music buzzed in his head. What had he done? He was surprised she was talking to him. Then again, he slammed the truck door shut, she needed a ride home from the hospital.

Quinn sat in the lobby in a wheelchair, with crutches at her side. Her skin appeared paler, and there were deep shadows under her eyes. His chest tightened, feeling her pain. No matter how lucky she was at not having broken anything, she'd been through a traumatic incident. His anger toward himself lessened. She wasn't the type of woman who would tell tales.

After hospital aides helped her into his truck, he turned on the ignition and drove toward Main Street. "What are your release instructions?" Worry swirled in his gut. She was on her own and had no one. Except him.

"The usual." This must be old-hat for her. "Rest. Ice. Compression. Elevation."

"You've done this before." He turned into the driveway on the side of the Victorian house and pulled between the garage and the back entrance.

"Ballet dancer is a hard career on your body." She sounded tough, but there was a shakiness, as if she wasn't as cavalier as she pretended. She opened the truck door, and swung her crutches around.

"Hold on." He opened his door, jumped out, and ran around to her side. He wasn't going to be like his brother by wishing her luck and leaving. "Let me carry you."

"Ridiculous. I'm going to have to get around on my own."

"Not today." He wasn't taking no for an answer. He swept her into his arms and headed for the back door.

The strands of her hair swept across his face in a tease. The scent of roses tickled his nose. Trembling, he wanted to bury his face in her neck and get both sensations at the same time. He restrained himself.

He finally had her in his arms again, and this time he was leading her. When they danced, she was in control. Now, he carried her up the stairs, resembling the caveman he'd been accused of being. Except he wasn't carrying her away to be ravished. He was carrying her to keep her safe.

And this turned him on all the more. His legs weakened. Not from her weight, but from the thought. He wanted to protect her, and cherish her, and hold her close. Yet, he'd pushed her into dating his brother. Mistake or self-preservation?

Her blue gaze captured his. The sapphire color deepened into pools of what appeared to be desire. He wanted to dive in. He didn't even notice her weight, because he was floating on air. Did she feel this same tug of attraction? Was it possible?

Hope and disbelief intermingled like the wrong chords in a song.

Crossing the apartment door threshold—the symbolic act of newlyweds—he stumbled, almost dropping his precious package.

"I can't believe you carried me up the stairs." Her expression held awe.

He became more powerful with her arms wrapped around his neck. "Just because I limp doesn't mean I'm not strong." He kept his tone light and teasing.

"I didn't mean it that way." She ran slender fingers across his chest. Similar to static electricity in the winter, each touch sparked inside him. "I'm a full-grown woman, and those were steep stairs."

His body reacted to her statement with a twitch of his cock. He knew she was a full-grown woman. A very attractive full-grown woman, who was currently in his arms. "I'm fine. Where do you want to go?"

"My bed."

Me too. His cock twitched again, and he hoped she didn't notice his reaction. He wanted to take her to bed. His hope sprung like his manhood. She'd definitely been friendly. Maybe…

Passing the small living space with the cozy kitchen, he noted a few of her womanly possessions, and how they made the space homier. A vase with flowers. A ballet-slipper-shaped teapot. A Degas print of ballet dancers hanging on the wall.

He carried her into the small bedroom and settled her on top of the flowered comforter. Reposing against the large decorative pillows, she twisted her long hair into a messy topknot. He wanted to untwist it again. His pulse thrummed. The tight stretchy fabric she'd worn under her ski clothes clung to her slender frame, highlighting her perky breasts and tiny waist. Her long limbs spread across the bed, one foot and ankle wrapped tight in a brace, reminding him of the real reason he was in her bedroom.

Stretching his back, he glanced around to see the changes she'd made to the room. The apartment had been sparsely furnished. She'd added feminine touches of perfume bottles on the dresser and flowered throw pillows on the bed. A photograph of an older couple sat on the bedside table next to a couple of romance novels.

Nothing like his sparse digs. He'd left so many of his things in New York. He didn't need the trophies or accolades or musical knick-knacks he'd collected. He didn't need reminders.

"I haven't had time to do much decorating."

He jerked at her comment having been caught staring. What would she think of his curiosity? "Can I get you something to drink? TV remote?"

"I'm not an invalid." She repositioned herself higher on the pillows, drawing attention to those perky breasts. "I'll be back on my feet in a few days."

"Baby yourself for a while. Do what the doctor said. You're lucky it wasn't worse." If it had been worse, he would've wrung his brother's neck.

"I will. I promise."

Reed raised a skeptical brow, knowing her casual attitude about injuries. He understood the need to push boundaries, but he'd make sure she didn't overdo things.

"I hate being injured." She lifted her bad ankle and dropped it on the bed. She cringed.

"Do you know what I asked when I woke up after my accident?" He wasn't really going to tell her anything serious, wanting to keep the mood light. Sitting carefully on the edge of the bed, he wiggled his brows dramatically. "Will I ever dance again?"

A laugh burst out of her. Her entire body moved with joy, sending a wave of happiness in his direction. He glowed with her response.

"I can't believe I'm laughing when I should be upset." Her brightness drew him closer.

"You're going to be fine." He glared at the wrapped ankle. "You will dance again. And I'll be around to help with what you need."

The offer slipped out. He didn't really have a choice. She didn't know many people in town, and he didn't want his idiot brother taking care of her.

She reached up and ran a hand under his jaw. "That's so sweet."

He wanted to melt. Instead, he stood and straightened, letting her hand fall. He was too unsure, and wasn't ready to deal with rejection. "What are neighbors for?"

Her cheeks flamed red. "I would like to slip into something more comfortable."

Which made him more uncomfortable. He forced a teasing smirk on his lips, trying to keep this light. "That's what all the women say to me."

She laughed again, and the sound filled his chest. No one's laughter had ever made him this happy.

He had to focus on her request and not let his thoughts go deeper into the gutter. Would she be wearing the sexy peach outfit she'd had on the other night? Or maybe he could convince her to wear nothing at all. "What do you need?"

She pointed at the dresser with the perfume bottles and other womanly paraphernalia. "The sweats in the bottom drawer."

He moved to the dresser and opened the drawer to be confronted with tiny, silky concoctions that weren't sweats and wouldn't cover much of her body. The pink and red and black slips of fabric teased his groin into a reaction, imagining how she'd look wearing the black thong and only the black thong. He stared into the drawer unable to lift his head, afraid his face would be red. "Um...um...where exactly are the sweats?"

He didn't want to paw through her underwear. Well, maybe he did, but wasn't willing to let her watch him.

"Toward the back."

Shoving his hand back, he dug around with his fingers through the silkiness until he felt plain cotton under the tips. He held the sweatpants up and shoved the drawer shut, hoping his mind would follow.

He handed her the sweats and realized a problem. Was he going to have to dress her? His hands shook. "Um, do you need help?"

Her head shot up, and a slow, teasing smile settled on her mouth. She licked her lips. "I've got good balance. I think I can handle it."

"Okay, then." He bounced on his feet, nerves causing his entire body to twitch. He wanted to stay, all the time knowing he should leave. "Water?"

"Yes, thanks."

He came back with a filled glass. "Once you're changed, you should rest. You've got my cell phone number. Do you need anything else before I go?"

She angled her head, considering. "No. Thank you so much for your help."

"No worries." Except he had plenty of worries. How was he going to control this attraction to his tenant, neighbor, and the woman his brother had dated? "Call me for anything."

Forcing himself to turn around, he marched across the bedroom floor, and out of her apartment. He closed the door and slumped his back against the wood. He wanted to bang his head. She might think he was knocking. He picked up his feet and trudged to his apartment and entered. Surveying his private space, he noted he didn't have any decorations and he'd lived there for several years. The apartment resembled a low-end rental unit. He was a guest in his own home.

Not that he'd be living here much longer. Once he finished the remodel on the Craftsman house he'd bought a couple of blocks over, he'd move in and spend time decorating the house to his specifications.

He headed to the kitchen and opened a beer.

His door flew open. "I've been so worried about Quinn." Dax rushed inside with a furrowed brow.

Reed didn't buy it. "Why didn't you stay at the hospital then?"

"I don't do very well at hospitals. You know that." His brother yanked open the fridge and took out a beer for himself. "How is she?"

"Sprained ankle." He slouched against the counter and watched Dax.

"I should go see her." He nodded several times in between taking sips of beer.

"She's probably sleeping."

"It's early." He blew off any concern.

"Not for someone on pain medication, party-boy."

Dax's life was carefree and filled with adventure. Until this last girlfriend, he'd bedded one girl after the next, and none of the women minded. Maybe he wasn't good enough for Quinn. Not now that Reed was getting to know her better, getting to like her, getting to…

"Got to make up for lost time." His brother leered—a wolf proving he was only out for a good time.

With jerky movements, Reed snatched the beer from his brother's hand. "Is that what Quinn is to you? Someone to have fun with to heal your broken heart?"

"She's beautiful and fun, at least when she's not mad at me."

He emptied his beer and started drinking his brother's. She was more than beautiful and fun. She was extraordinary. With her passion for teaching dance, her love of life, her enthusiasm for everything.

"I should text her, see if she's awake." Dax pulled out his phone. "What should I say?"

"First, I'd apologize for causing her accident."

"Her falling wasn't my fault. She was doing fine."

"You don't realize all people aren't naturally athletic." Like Reed. He'd been an athletic child, as good of a skier as his brother and sister, even though he'd spent hours sitting in front of a piano.

"Quinn is athletic. She's a dancer."

"A dancer, not a skier." He gripped the beer bottle tighter. Why couldn't his brother understand?

"So, what should I say?" Dax was obtuse. He hadn't always been this way. Ever since Phoebe, he'd been running from anything serious. He'd always enjoyed himself and partied, but he'd also been considerate of other people's feelings.

Running a hand through his hair, Reed couldn't believe he was helping again. He didn't want Quinn hating anyone in the family so he'd make his brother apologize. "Say you're sorry she's hurt and you called the hospital and found out she'd been released."

"Can you say it more poetically?" The charmer used a winsome smile.

"No."

Dax texted. "I told her I was at your place and wanted to see her if she's awake."

"No!"

He pulled his chin back in surprise. His head tilted in a questioning glance.

Stunned at his vehemence, Reed didn't want his brother being with her while she was vulnerable and in bed. "She's probably tired and doesn't want company."

Dax's phone buzzed. "She responded so she's awake. I'm going over."

His brother's huge grin struck Reed, morphing him into a jealous lover. She must not be attracted to Reed, if she welcomed his brother into her apartment.

Chapter Eight

Quinn wrangled her crutches to the bathroom, debating taking the sleeping pills the doctor provided. The throbbing in her ankle made it difficult to sleep, and she'd been dozing on and off since Dax left. He'd texted to ask if she was awake, and when she'd said yes, he'd surprised her by knocking on the door. Surprise at his visit had become shock when he'd been extra considerate. Asking her what she needed, if he could massage her neck, and if she was tired.

Nothing, no, and yes had been her answers.

When she'd talked about how her grandfather's old car was a stick shift and she needed to run errands the next day, he'd offered the use of his car. That had been nice. Dax was a nice guy, he just wasn't the guy for her. He was fun and social, and also immature.

A tinkling caught her attention. Squinting at the clock, she noted it was past midnight, and yet Reed played the piano. Her restlessness mellowed. She liked someone using the instrument, because it reminded her of happier times with her grandmother.

During the holidays her grandmother would play, and they'd sing Christmas carols together. Her grandfather pretended to read the paper, except she'd noticed the long glances and his pleased expression. Grandmother would play classical music, too, and Quinn would dance and spin pretending to be a principal ballerina. She smiled with the happy memories.

She hobbled to the apartment door and opened it. The music grew stronger, and pulled her forward. Resting against the doorframe, she listened. The ethereal melody entered her being, lifting her spirits. The tune played to her emotions. Longing, sad, hopeful.

The music hit a chord inside her with its depth and passion. She sensed Reed's agony as he played and she sympathized, wanting to make his sorrow go away. There was so much more to his story than he'd told her. She sensed it. This man who was so passionate and caring and wouldn't harm anyone on purpose. How could the accident have been his fault?

She wanted to go downstairs and watch him play. The way his large hands danced across the keys, the way his body swayed with the music, the way he closed his eyes partway, as if in the midst of desire.

Her body hummed, and she forgot about her aches and pains.

He'd been so helpful and sweet and caring. He'd come to the emergency clinic and waited with her until she'd been released. He'd driven her home and carried her up the stairs. Her skin scalded. She waved a hand in front of her face.

So strong. So manly. So kind.

Even though he'd been nice and funny and comforting, he didn't want to be with her. He wanted her to date his brother. Her lips quirked into a devilish grin. Too bad. She didn't want his brother, she wanted him.

Sometimes, he'd look at her in a way sending her pulse spiraling high. He'd touch her arm, or say something sweet or funny, and she'd want to melt into him. She needed to show him the two of them would be great together.

Placing the crutches on the top step, she swung her legs forward and landed a step down. The clunk of the crutches on wood sounded loud. She froze, hoping Reed wouldn't hear her approach. She took another step, and another.

Her ankle throbbed. Her temples pounded. Her body felt weak. She shouldn't be attempting stairs on her own, yet.

The music, his music, lured her.

Just as Reed lured.

Decision made. Time to go after what she wanted. Just not tonight.

Up early the next day, Reed couldn't stop the music playing in his head. He'd spent several hours sitting at the piano last night, pouring out his passions. Between Quinn's apartment door and the back door to the studio, the noise shouldn't have bothered her. In his past, that was how he always dealt with feelings, striking the keys and creating melodies meshing with his emotions. That's how his music was born.

Until his music died with his fiancée.

He'd been numb for a long time afterward. And when the music didn't come back, and he'd had to deal with the survivor's remorse and guilt, he'd pushed himself physically. He'd tripled his physical therapy exercises. He'd gotten a physical job in construction, before starting his own company and working twice as hard.

Thinking and worrying and fretting about Dax being in Quinn's apartment had caused Reed to pace back and forth last night. He'd needed more space, and had ended up going downstairs into the dance studio. The piano had been waiting.

He'd already resisted the temptation of Quinn, he couldn't resist another. So, he'd played.

His dashed hopes had emptied into an uplifting melody. Thinking about the way she'd stared, how she'd clung to him as he'd carried her up the stairs, how she'd laughed, had changed the music from sad and sorrowful to optimistic.

Music was no longer his enemy. Music had given him reason to hope.

Humming the tune from last night, he went downstairs, glad when Quinn wasn't working in the studio. With his emotions roiling inside, he couldn't face her this morning. The thought of writing down the chords and lyrics pressed against him. Another pressure he didn't need. If he wrote down the notes it might actually be considered composing, and he wasn't ready to commit. Didn't know if he'd ever be.

He'd go out to the garage and gather a few tools before knocking on her door to see if she was awake and needed assistance. That's what a good neighbor did. It was not because he needed to see her again.

Heading out the backdoor, he skidded to a halt. Dax's car was in the driveway.

The music in his head crashed into a tone cluster. The off-key chords rang and rattled. The tune clattered to a halt and stopped. His brother had spent the night with Quinn.

His heart, which had been beating in time with the melody in his head, sputtered fast and then slow. Cold air hit his face and scarred hands. He clenched his fists, not feeling the biting wind, only feeling devastation.

Hope that Quinn might be interested in him had actually begun to bloom. The small spurt of optimism had brought the music back into his mind and soul. But she didn't see him as a man, she saw him as a helper. The big, friendly giant, or a servant.

Dumb, dumb, dumb.

That rhythm would play in his head forever. Unless the music stopped again. An emptiness opened inside him, so vast and so dark he couldn't fully comprehend. He'd been an idiot believing for one second a woman would be interested in a lame man.

Jumping in his truck, he revved the engine and sped away. Dax could make her breakfast and help her get dressed as he'd helped her get undressed. The tires squealed against the pavement. The windshield wipers came on and made a scratching noise. Reed needed to get out of here. Away from the sounds, away from the piano he'd poured his emotions into, away from his brother and Quinn sleeping in the same bed.

He screeched around a corner and headed out of town, higher, farther away. The lane narrowed and curved, climbing the mountain road. Evergreen trees rushed past in a blur. For someone who'd been involved in a major car accident he drove more recklessly than normal.

Realization battered. Not getting a girl wasn't a reason to endanger himself. He really never expected to win Quinn's love. The anger inside him quieted to a dull roar. Slowing down, he pulled over at a scenic outlook. He got out and slammed the door shut. Breathing heavily, he paced to the edge and leaned against the stone wall viewing the dramatic drop.

The cliff went straight down. Rocks and boulders and plants covered the side. Small piles of snow stood in the shady areas. The slopes of the ski resort gleamed brightly in the sun. The town of Castle Ridge snuggled against the mountain.

Snuggled like Dax and Quinn were probably doing right now.

Reed's blood turned green and charged in his veins. He pounded the stone wall with his fist, not caring about injuring himself, or re-scarring his already grotesque hands. He needed to shut down whatever attraction he felt for Quinn. He needed to control his emotions. He needed to act blasé when he saw Dax and Quinn together.

"Not thinking about jumping, are you, O'Donnell?"

The man's sarcasm pulled him back to the surroundings. He jerked his head around and spotted the person who spoke.

Luke Logan. A friend from high school who had aged well. Perfectly-styled blond hair, sharp eyes, athletic build. He'd become a famous ski racer and traveled around the world. He hadn't kept in touch.

"What're you doing here?" Reed's body flared and he rubbed his hands against his old jeans. His old friend had witnessed his anguish. He had to pull himself together and try to be social. "Hadn't heard you were back in town. It's been a long time."

The two of them shook hands, both dressed similarly in jeans.

"Not long enough." Luke's dark voice edged with anger.

"You hate Castle Ridge that much?" Reed understood the desire to leave and pursue your dreams. He'd done it. And now he was back. And while he hated the reason for his return, he'd grown to love the small town again.

"Not the place. The memories."

"I saw your ski accident on the sports channel." The image of his friend being tossed down the side of a steep mountain, his body crumpled and unmoving when he'd finally stopped sliding down the hill, brought a shudder to Reed. "Was it as bad as it looked?"

"Worse." The professional skier clamped his mouth shut and narrowed his gaze. "You've got an injury of your own."

Blowing out a short breath, he glanced away and

back. He'd not even tried to hide his limp when he'd gotten out of the car in a hurry. "Yeah. Guess we're just two lame asses. We should hang out together, Crash."

He was only half-joking. He needed a male friend to talk to, someone who wasn't Dax.

"I'll be back on the slopes in no time." Luke's defiant-determined tone reminded him of Quinn. "I'm only here for a day to check out a rehab facility."

"Good luck to you." Reed patted his bum leg. Melancholy thoughts made his calf and ankle throb. He hoped physical therapy worked for his friend.

Rehabilitation had helped him to walk again. He'd never get rid of the limp. Never ski. And knowing his brother spent the night with Quinn, he'd never dance again, either.

After taking Dax's car to the office supply store, Quinn sat at her computer working, with her ankle propped on a chair. She needed the sprain to heal before she started her free classes, and before the grand opening showcase. If she took care of the injury she'd be dancing sooner.

Reed sidled into the studio, carrying brushes and a can of paint. He wore an old jacket and splattered jeans. Now she had even more empathy for him, imagining his suffering while he healed. Her pain would only last days, a week at the most; his would last forever. He halted when he spotted her behind the counter, his eyes wide as if he'd seen a ghost. His face became an inscrutable mask.

She jerked back, the expression hitting her like a poorly-performed *brisé* jump.

After the first kick of her piano, to experiencing his kindness and nursing skills, to hearing him play piano, she wanted to get to know him better and peel away the layers. And his clothes.

"Good morning, Reed." She sat up straighter.

"Is it?" His snippy voice added to her curiosity.

Had playing the piano half the night made him grumpy? "You were up late."

"Not as late as you, I bet." The accusation confused her. He set the paint can on the counter with a heavy thud.

"It was hard to sleep with all the noise." *Hint, hint.* She'd heard him play and wanted him to admit it. Wanted him to play for her.

His eyes widened in shock, and then narrowed. He crinkled his nose and his mouth pursed into a disgusted frown. His knuckles whitened around the paintbrush. He wanted to strangle someone.

Her?

What was wrong with him? When he'd left her last night she'd dreamed of him. When she'd heard him play she'd decided to go after what she wanted. Go after him.

He bent his head to open the paint can. "Don't complain to me."

She grabbed her crutches and slammed them onto the ground, refusing to take his bad attitude. "You were the one playing the piano until past two in the morning." What did he *think* she was talking about?

His head rose with a snap. "You heard? I thought

the apartment walls and closed doors would be thick enough so I wouldn't bother you." He smushed his lips together, and his cheeks turned a slight red. "You hated it."

"I loved it. You play with such passion and grace." She wanted him to play the tune she hadn't recognized, the one calling to her. She crutched toward him.

"I'm sorry I played your piano again." Lifting the lid, he dipped the brush in the paint. Every line on his face was tight. His lips formed a flat line.

"Don't be." Her chest swelled, remembering his passion. She moved close enough to touch. Placing her hand on his pecs, her own pulse raced, picking out a frantic beat. "I enjoyed every second."

He swiped her hand away and brushed the counter. "Did Dax?"

Confusion had her angling her head and studying Reed. "I assume your brother knows how well you play."

"Never mind." His disgust returned, crinkling his nose and forehead. He stroked the counter with the paint.

She jutted out her hip and decided to make her voice low and sexy. "You can play my piano anytime." Did that sound flirtatious enough for him to get a hint? "I'd love for you to play now."

"I'm busy." He ran a jerky hand over a spot on the counter checking for smoothness. His body acted like a wall of rejection to her suggestiveness.

Bristling, she kept calm and determined. She trailed a finger across his muscled arm. Maybe she needed to be more obvious. "I bet your hands are excellent for...playing."

He knocked her hand away. "Where's Dax?"

Back to Dax again.

She huffed. "I don't know." Why should she? He'd only stayed for about half an hour last night. "Dax is an interesting guy."

Almost bipolar. Last night he'd been so solicitous, and yet, when they'd skied, he didn't worry about her or wait for her. He usually rushed when he spoke, but some of his texts were rhythmic and poetic. He was considerate one moment, and conceited the next.

"Too interesting." Grumbling, Reed spilled a little too much paint.

"Dax can be thoughtful and sweet one moment."

Reed paused in the middle of a stroke. He slapped the brush onto the counter splattering the paint into globs. Yet, he didn't say anything.

"And so self-centered the next. Why?" She used her crutches to tilt toward him wanting to see his expression in detail. Reed had pushed her toward his brother and now seemed upset about an innocent visit last night.

His eyebrows gathered together like a storm. His mouth pursed, and his expression darkened. He smoothed the globs of paint with the brush. Back and forth. Back and forth. He was using the action to have time to think of a good answer.

His lips pursed and he blew out a breath. "You should give Dax a chance." The words came out in a struggle.

Her back stiffened and cold shivered across her skin. Reed had no right to tell her who to date. "A chance?"

She wanted to hear Reed say the words, that he wanted her to date his brother, confirm he really didn't find her attractive.

"A chance at a relationship." He choked.

No way was she interested in a relationship with his brother. "I don't think Dax is looking for a relationship."

Reed lifted the brush and turned to face her. His green gaze grabbed her with its intensity. "Are you?"

Certainly not a relationship with Dax. He was fun and could help her meet people in town, which was one of her major goals. Eventually, she wanted to settle down, and didn't see it happening with him.

Staring at Reed, her heart quivered. "Eventually."

A quaint house. Working and playing together. A family.

With Reed, she could imagine all sorts of possibilities.

Chapter Nine

Saturday morning on Main Street in the small town of Castle Ridge was exactly how Quinn remembered. Her last visit had been when she was around ten years old. Strolling along the street, she'd held her grandmother's hand, peering into shop windows and buying ice cream from an old fashioned ice cream parlor. Her grandmother's favorite had been mint chocolate chip, and it had become Quinn's favorite, too.

Today, she sat at a table outside her dance studio bundled in a jacket and flowered knit cap against the chilly mid-November morning. She was handing out flyers about her free classes and dance background. The friendly townspeople stopped to listen to her pitch.

Reed stood on a ladder hanging Quinn's sign. *Quinn's Social Dance Club.* She straightened her shoulders and let satisfaction fill her lungs. Not exactly what her mother always wanted, but she was finally seeing her name in lights. Except she was doing it on her terms.

She'd had an opportunity to be the principal ballerina for the ballet company. In order to achieve the position, she would've had to backstab and lie. The current principal couldn't be replaced unless she was injured and couldn't dance. The director had wanted her to purposely hurt the other dancer. Quinn refused to surrender her values. She'd known it was time to quit.

The name of her studio meant more than dance classes. It meant fun and being social. It meant the classes were open for everyone, not only people with certain builds or athletic abilities.

Reed must've sensed her glance because he looked at her and grinned. "Look good?"

Her heart ba-bumped. *He looked good.* He wore a knit cap with short curls sticking out. His unshaven face had that hard and sexy appearance. His jeans fit snugly around his nicely-shaped butt. He'd been standoffish for a couple of days, and she'd slowly wheedled and teased to get him out of his funk. He never told her what had caused his dark mood. "Yes. I love it."

"Great name."

"Thanks. I hope it gets across dancing is about fun and exercise." Not grueling hours of torture, not mind games, not destroying your body so you become an invalid by the age of thirty.

A group of girls stopped to watch the video of her dancing on the New York stage showing on her tablet.

"Are you girls interested in dancing?" Quinn pointed at the video.

The three middle-school-aged girls regarded each other and giggled.

"I'm giving free lessons the first two weeks. Here's the schedule of the different types of dance." She handed them a flyer. Knowing middle school girls, she added, "You could come together."

"I'd have to ask my mom," the girl with bright-red hair said.

"I know your mom, Lena." Reed's butt muscles flexed, climbing down the ladder with ease, his limp didn't seem to bother him doing certain activities. In bed his limp wouldn't be noticeable at all. "She'd love for you to try dancing."

Quinn couldn't stop a smile from blooming.

"Hi, Mr. O'Donnell," the three girls chimed.

He greeted each of them by name. Quinn warmed at the existential small-town moment. This was why she'd moved here. A place where people cared and everyone knew your name.

"I've seen Miss Quinn dance in person, and she's the best." His words lifted her spirits.

He'd been so helpful with making her studio perfect. Since her accident, he'd cooked meals, carried her laundry basket up the stairs, and checked on her constantly. Now, he was helping sell her business.

How did she pay him back? Guilt had her leg twitching. By sneaking onto the stairway at night to listen to him play the piano, knowing he didn't want her to hear. She couldn't help herself. The music spoke to her and heated her body. She'd thought about hobbling down the stairs, wrapping her arms around him, and giving him a kiss. She couldn't be more obvious than that. But she wanted everything to be perfect when they got together. She wanted to win him over slowly, not attack him from behind. For now, she'd settle for sending him scorching glances and sexual innuendos.

A couple boys of similar age moved in behind the girls, pretending not to be interested. By the gleam in their eyes, she knew they were. Getting boys to participate in class would be wonderful. More students and less chauvinism.

Lena pulled back her shoulders, noticing the boys, too. "My soccer coach said doing and teaching are two different things."

"Miss Quinn has taught me a little dancing, and if she can teach me," Reed patted his bad leg, "she can teach anyone."

Gratefulness caused her to melt and push forward. "Plus, certain types of dance help with body movement and coordination for other sports."

One of the boys put a hand on his head and his other hand on his hip and twirled. He fell into the other boy and they both tumbled to the ground laughing.

Reed sent a secretive smirk her way and she wanted to kiss him.

"Professional football players take ballet to help stretch and strengthen their muscles so there's less possibility of injury." He helped each of the boys to their feet.

"It also helps coordination." Quinn tapped a key on her tablet and brought up a male dance class. Her stomach swished, hoping they'd be interested. "I was thinking of starting a flexibility and strength dancing class for men, if I can find a few brave guys to sign up." She stared at both boys. "You two would be perfect."

"They both ski and play baseball." Reed nodded, understanding her selling point. "They'd be great, and it would be great for them."

She pushed a form toward them with nervous fingers. "What do you guys think?"

The three girls giggled.

"Brett in a dance class?" Lena pointed at the boy who'd attempted a twirl.

"He'd be an excellent date for school dances." Middle schools must still hold dances, right? Quinn loved dancing with a man who knew the steps.

And the score. She winked at Reed.

All five of the kids laughed. The boys hit each other. The girls blushed.

"I don't want to dance with Brett," Lena sounded as if she really did want to dance with him.

"Did you ever take a dance class, Mr. O'Donnell?" Brett's eyes widened. "You know, before your accident?"

Quinn held her breath. She'd stated twice now he was going to dance in the showcase. He'd practically promised Sara.

"I loved to dance." Sorrow flickered in his gaze. Past tense. He patted his leg again.

"Mr. O'Donnell is going to dance with me in the grand opening showcase." Quinn flashed a stiff smile, knowing he probably didn't want the world to know. Probably didn't want to be used. She needed his support, though. "And this same all-male class would help his limp."

His quick, angry glare sliced across her. He didn't like her giving him advice about his injury. Too bad. She knew she was right about dancing being able to help his limp, and besides, she wanted to hold him in her arms again.

"Are you going to sign up for the guy dance class, Mr. O'Donnell?" Brett's hopeful expression mirrored the other boy's.

Reed frowned sending her hopes into a dive. He studied her and she knew a pleading expression was on her face.

His shoulders slumped in defeat. "I'm doing the showcase. I'll decide on a class after."

The kids started talking at once. He gave her a you-owe-me look. A thrill spiraled down her spine wondering what type of payment he'd expect. She'd teach him to waltz and help him with his limp. When the time was right, she'd seduce him and do a more intimate dance.

Getting to her feet, she gave him a quick kiss on the cheek. Nothing too forward. His cheeks reddened, and he inspected the ground. Sweet.

"Ooh, Mr. O'Donnell has a girlfriend," Lena's tease brought Quinn's attention back to the kids.

The five kids filled out forms, so she could follow up with their parents. They rushed away, talking and joking and making plans to meet later in the afternoon.

She wanted her children to grow up free to run around town, not fearing muggers and gangs. "I hope they tell their friends about the classes."

Reed's expression hadn't changed. He stared, not saying anything.

She stretched her toes under the table and licked her lips. "Are you mad?"

At the kiss or her pushiness?

"You keep volunteering me for things." He kept his gaze glued to hers.

She couldn't tell what thoughts were processing through his mind. Staring back, she asked again, "Are you mad?"

Tiny flecks of gold glistened in his green eyes, pulling her in. Deeper and deeper.

"I haven't decided yet." His voice rumbled through her.

His gaze tugged her further. In to him. People passed, cars drove by. All she saw was Reed. Sparks shot through her, lighting every inch of her skin on fire. Her attraction to him distracted her from what she was supposed to be doing, distracted her from her goals. She didn't care.

Another shock. Her goals had always been at the forefront of her mind. First, for dancing and now, for her business.

"Hey, babe." Dax's friendly and overly-intimate tone jerked her out of her fantasy.

"Don't call me babe." His eyes were the same color as Reed's, except they didn't hold the same depth—at least, not while looking at her. Dax didn't arouse the same emotions.

He picked up a brochure. "How's the sidewalk-dancing sales pitch going?"

Offended, she asked, "Sales pitch?" This was important, her business was important.

"Do you remember Lexi?" He placed a hand on the

woman's lower back who'd been standing behind him. "The one who rescued you. She's interested in dance class." He sounded amused.

She squirmed in her seat. He believed her business a joke. "There's nothing wrong with dancing. Your brother is taking a class."

"Reed?" Dax's loud snort caused her to squirm more.

Reed's expression grew dark and stormy. He turned toward the ladder, wanting to avoid this discussion.

She was offended for him. "Yes, Reed. Why do you think that's funny?"

"He's such a...a..."

Reed swiveled back around. "A what?" His forceful voice ground out.

The tension between the brothers thickened like a sword fight from the Nutcracker.

"Hermit." Dax held up his hands in a no-foul motion. "My brother doesn't get out much, and won't have a lot of use for dancing."

Reed's strong mouth pursed and he wheeled around. He wasn't going to defend himself.

"I've gotten him to go out before, and I will again." So, she defended him. After the shared glances, she wouldn't hold her tongue any longer. "We'll go out, and he'll dance with me."

Reed's heart constricted, as if a fist had wrapped around and pinched. He couldn't believe Quinn defended him. It seemed like she was claiming him, too. How could that be possible?

His little brother appeared confused and unsure. Dax gaped between him and Quinn, calculating. Did he see more than what was there? Did he notice Reed's infatuation with his tenant?

There'd been the wink and the kiss on the cheek. The soft touches when he'd helped her with a task. Honestly, Reed was so confused he didn't know what to think. Why would she be interested in him, if she'd slept with his brother? Was she trying to make Dax jealous? If so, she'd picked the wrong guy. Reed wouldn't hurt his little brother.

Lifting the ladder, he squeezed the metal between his scarred hands. "She wants to prove gimps can dance."

Her face paled and her eyes went round. "No." She sounded horrified. "That's not what I meant."

His guilt weighted. He hadn't meant to insult her, only himself.

"What did you mean?" Glaring, Dax braced himself against her table.

"We'll talk about this later." Her gaze switched between the two brothers and the potential customers strolling by. "I'm busy right now." Quinn turned to Lexi and started talking about the various classes.

Reed grabbed the ladder and headed inside, avoiding a confrontation on the street.

Following, his brother yanked on his sleeve. "You were supposed to help me date Quinn, not go after her yourself."

Guilt, because Reed was attracted, had him blurting out. "I'm not the one sleeping with her." Gripping the sides of the ladder tighter, he sucked in a deep breath.

"What're you—"

"There's nothing between us." Reed didn't need his brother playing the role of jealous lover, when there was nothing to be jealous of. And he didn't want to talk about what his brother and Quinn had done together.

"Good. I want to ask Quinn out again." His brother stomped his foot, resembling a spoiled child, and Quinn was the toy being taken away.

His outlook blackened. He didn't have the ability to steal Quinn. "Go ahead. Ask her."

"You're dancing with her. Where are you dancing?" Dax's petulant tone grated on Reed's nerves, as he moved toward the back of the studio.

"Dancing, not dating." How he wished.

"I don't know what to say to her after the ski incident." His brother followed him, his voice going quiet. "I spoke with Phoebe."

The evil woman's name sent sympathy through Reed. He set down the ladder and watched his brother's expression. "What did she say?" He was the only one who knew the extent of his brother's pain, who'd added to his pain.

"She didn't want to see me or hear from me." Dax's voice cracked. "Which is why I want to go out with Quinn again. She's hot, and she'll take my mind off my ex."

Reed's temper spiked. He didn't want her hurt. "You can't use Quinn."

"I'm not using her. It's just a date." His brother winked, his earlier sadness evaporating. "Besides, she wants to get out and meet people in town."

The statement hit him as if Quinn's sign had fallen on his head. That was one of her goals, and his brother was the guy to help accomplish it. Sure, he'd been fine for cooking and helping with laundry. Now, she was ready to get out and meet more people from Castle Ridge. Dax was the right man for the job.

"Ask her, then." Reed ran fingers through his hair, staring at the shelved walls of the storage area.

Quinn had filled it with snacks and office supplies and an emergency blanket. She was stamping the place with her own personality, as she'd done to the apartment upstairs.

"She's busy right now. I'll text her." Dax pulled out his phone. "What should I say?"

"Where are you going to go?"

"Dancing." His tone rubbed in the fact he'd slept with Quinn.

Agony spasmed in Reed's chest. He didn't want to think about Quinn being in his brother's arms. "Her ankle is better, but she shouldn't push herself."

"Right." His brother jerked his head down, his thumbs poised above the keyboard. "I'll take her to dinner. What should I text?"

He ran fingers through his hair again. "Just ask her to dinner."

Dax's head jerked up. He assessed Reed. "I can't just ask her to dinner. Too boring." His brother whipped his phone around. "She's from New York. I need to make the ask good. Flashy."

"Whatever." He was done with this conversation. He shoved the ladder into place and headed out of the storage area.

"You're good with words. You're a lyricist." His brother held out his phone. "You text her."

Realization pulsed behind his temples. "That's the only reason you didn't go outside and ask her out to her face, Lazy Dax. You wanted me to do it." He'd thought the Cyrano game was finished. "I won't help."

"Come on, Reed." Dax knocked his upper arm with the cellphone. "I know how well you spoke to her the night by the window. She mentioned how eloquent she thought I was."

"You mean *I* was." The pulsing picked up tempo. Reed was tired of being used by both of them. Dax to help ask her out and Quinn putting him on display.

"It's a text. You'd be helping my broken heart and Quinn's need to meet people in town." His brother's cajoling nudged. "Please."

The pulsing slowed as his resistance waned. Taking Quinn out on the town wasn't something Reed would do anyhow. He didn't do socializing. Sure, he'd gone out to dinner with her once, but he enjoyed quiet nights alone. All alone. Freaking-quiet alone.

He snatched the phone. "Fine."

"What're you going to say?" His brother peered over his shoulder.

The music playing in his head tapped out through his fingers and onto the phone. Lyrics from the same song hummed in his head. Lyrics he'd created. Hitting send with a trembling finger, he shoved the phone at his brother. "She might say no."

The phone buzzed.

Dax's face lit. "She said yes!" He danced around, doing a poor imitation of an Irish jig.

Each step stomped on Reed's chest. Glad his texting had been effective, yet mad, too. What had the kiss on the cheek and the heated glances meant, if she'd said yes to a date with his brother? "Congratulations." *To me.*

His brother's dance came to a stop. "You know her better. What should I talk about on our date?"

His jaw dropped. He did know her well. Knew how she used softener on her sheets. Knew how she stretched up on her toes while thinking. Knew she'd loved her grandparents. He couldn't talk for his brother. "I won't be going on your date."

Dax's expression fell. Then, his eyebrows wiggled and he gave a jaunty smile. "We can double."

Except Reed wanted to date the same girl his brother was taking out. Sleeping with.

His heart thumped in a tortured rhythm. He hadn't had a date in forever. Why would his brother believe he could conjure one? He didn't date.

"If I had a date." Sarcasm leaked.

"Don't worry." Dax patted him on the arm. "I'll find someone for you."

You already have.

Chapter Ten

Music thrummed through Reed's brain. A juxtaposition of rhythm and lyrics. A siren's song, calling him farther and deeper. A depth he hadn't traversed in years. His fingers went from the keyboard to the scrap of paper and back. Tapping out chords, scratching out words, hearing and hearing and hearing the unique song holding him in its grasp.

It was always this way when he composed. At first, a nagging note needing to be played. Then, notes stringing together in his head. He didn't even need a piano at the beginning. The notes gathered and swelled, and his mind would burst if he didn't let the music pour out of his head through his fingers. His ears yearned to hear what his brain created. Would the composition sound as good out loud as it did in his mind?

The song was about unrequited longing and passion. About seeing and wanting. About something, or someone, out of reach. The complexity of his feelings strummed through him first in harmony and then clashing like cymbals. Awakened and unwanted desire.

Quinn.

She'd awoken feelings in him he thought he'd never experience again. Attraction and lust and just liking other people. He didn't want to hide himself away from the world. She'd awoken the music inside his mind and his heart.

His fingers shook, writing the notes on paper. He was composing. Really writing music and lyrics for the first time in years. The shaking traveled up his arms and throughout his entire body. The thrill of creating something new and artistic hummed through his bloodstream.

More than being a pianist and playing in front of hundreds of people, he'd loved the artistic aspect of creating new music. He'd gone to New York to play the piano, and learned so much and met so many interesting people. First, he'd collaborated on projects, helping compose the music. Then, he'd composed a full song. And finally, words flowed in his head along with the music. He'd become a songwriter. Even after a partner had stolen a song, pretending it was his own, Reed still heard music. The betrayal hadn't taken the music away.

One of the most devastating things about his accident was losing this ability to compose. And now it was back.

He hoped it was back forever. Fear froze his fingers on the piano. What if the music left him again? What if Quinn left Castle Ridge? What if he returned to his stagnant life?

Because he hadn't moved forward in years. Sure, he'd worked through his tough physical therapy, he'd found a new career, he'd settled.

S.E.T.T.L.E.D.

Each individual letter sank and settled in his gut. He wasn't willing to settle any longer.

Knock, knock, knock.

He swiveled toward the glass window facing Main Street. Izzy's nose pressed against the glass. Her wide eyes showed shock.

His ribcage concaved and he couldn't breathe. He'd been caught. He should've closed the blinds he'd installed on the large windows facing Main Street. Quinn had confessed to hearing him, but she didn't know his background. His sister did, and knowing his sister, she wouldn't leave.

Limping to the front door, he battled with himself. He didn't want to talk to her about playing and composing again. He didn't want to admit anything or face the real demons plaguing him. If he did his sister would realize he had hope and if he fell flat on his face or the music abandoned him again, she'd understand his devastation.

He unlocked the door and Izzy launched herself into his arms. She'd always been a hugger and always ignored his wishes to be alone. Letting her hug linger, he tried to put off the inquisition.

"You're playing again." She sang. "I spotted you through the window."

He swallowed the anxiety. "Yes."

She pulled out of his arms to stare. "Why do you sound so sad? It's wonderful." Unbuttoning her coat, she studied his expression. She squinted at the piano. "You're composing music again? Can I hear?" She must've spotted his handwritten notes.

His lungs shredded with panic. He didn't know what to say. "Yes. No." His raw emotions were part of the song. He wasn't willing to share. Limping back toward the piano, he snatched the sheets moving them out of her target range.

"Why not?"

"Because I don't want to." He wasn't ready to expose himself. What if she figured out who the song was about? She understood his process and how most of his music was related to his emotions. What if she realized the song was about Quinn? What if Dax found out? "No."

Izzy placed her hand over his on the piano. "You haven't written anything for five years." She used an it's-a-miracle voice.

In a way it was. The block in his mind had been a solid concrete wall. One no one could chisel through. And yet, Quinn had managed. She'd chiseled through his need to be alone, through his music block, and through his heart.

"When did you start playing again?"

He shrugged and tried to be vague. "A few weeks, Nosy Izzy." *A few days.*

Studying him, assessing him, his sister's green gaze lit. "Since Quinn arrived."

He sunk onto the piano bench. The want and desire he'd poured into the song tangled like mixed up sheet music with the fear and uncertainty of being no good or losing the music again. Sharing would open him up to sympathy and possibly news leaking out. He could deny, deny, deny. Except his sister was smart.

"I thought I saw something between you two, but…"

He glanced sharply in her direction. "But what?"

Izzy's face went soft, her eyes swimming with sympathy. "I was at the pub, and I saw Dax and Quinn together."

Reed's chest constricted, even though he'd known. Hell, he'd asked her for his brother. "They had a date."

Izzy's brows furrowed. "I thought I saw a spark between you and her." She sounded disappointed she'd been wrong.

Her sympathy had him jumping off the piano bench. "Ridiculous." Quinn had already slept with his brother. "Who would want to date me?" He limped toward the back of the studio. Each drag of his foot dragged on his heart.

Izzy rushed to him and grabbed his arm. "Don't you be ridiculous." Using her stern-lecturing voice, she tugged on his arm with emphasis. "So you limp. Big deal. You have so many qualities a woman would love."

He mellowed, until he realized she was his sister and had to say nice things. Flattening his lips, everything hardened. His back, his midsection, his attitude. He couldn't be weak on this point. Every time a small hope ignited about being with Quinn it was quickly doused. "Dax and Quinn are on a date."

"You're sure it's a date?" Izzy didn't want to believe him.

Reed snapped. "I know it's a date because I'm the one who asked her out for him."

"What?" Her laughter mixed with the question. "That's brilliant. Dax, the professional womanizer, doesn't know how to ask someone on a date?"

"He's getting over his break up with his ex-girlfriend." Reed crossed his arms.

Her gaze roamed him at a rapid, calculating pace. She was putting a sharp note with a flat note and figuring out the wrong composition. "So he suckered you into helping him."

He hung his head. He'd been a chump. What kind of man asks out the woman he's attracted to for his brother?

Early the next morning, Quinn sat behind the counter of her dance studio. Anxiety *arabesqued* in her stomach. Her studio opened for free classes Monday. The studio itself looked great, only a couple of small fixes. Unfortunately, the list of people signed up for the free classes was dismal.

Reed shuffled down the back set of stairs. He halted when their gazes met, and he glared. She wasn't sure what she'd done wrong.

"Morning. Everything okay?" She studied him wearing his uniform of jeans and flannel shirt. It was a style she'd begun to appreciate.

Dark shadows under his eyes. Unshaven cheeks. Messy hair. And yet, he still looked good. Marvelous, really. The roughness drew her in.

"Fine. Everything's fine." He plowed by her and

toward the other side of the counter, where a couple of lights needed to be installed.

"You seem surprised to see me." Which she didn't understand. It was her studio.

He ran fingers through his hair, messing it even more. He had that just-out-of-bed appearance, and it made her wonder how he looked in bed. Naked. His thick, carved muscles would hold his body above hers. His legs would twine with hers. When their skin touched it would erupt like a forest fire. The *arabesques* twirled faster, making her woozy.

"I thought you'd have a late night. Sleep in." His tone accused.

The *arabesques* stopped spinning, confusion making her more dizzy. "Not late at all. I'm still recovering."

His dark expression cleared. A short smirk appeared on his face before he struggled his mouth into a frown. He picked up the light fixture and stared. "Oh."

"Are you working on something in the studio today?"

He worked all day long and played piano all night. No wonder he appeared tired.

His cheeks reddened and he stared at the ground. "I was going to play the piano." He raised his head. "But since you're working…"

"I love hearing you play." She slammed her mouth, shut not wanting him to know she'd been listening during the night. She'd admitted it the one time and he'd gotten upset. Best to keep her midnight concert attendance a secret. "I mean, I'd love to hear you play again. After the first time. It would be a pleasant diversion from my nerves about the opening." In her fear of discovery, she confessed her worry.

"Nerves? What're you nervous about?" He moved to the piano and sat, seeming so confident and at home at the instrument. The exact opposite from the day they'd met when he'd kicked the piano.

"Opening show. Getting students. Making my business a success." A million other details.

His fingers tinkled lightly over the keys. The music was easy, soft and soothing.

Her tension lightened, and she leaned against the counter. Closing her eyes, she let the music calm. She'd always loved different kinds of music. Symphonic, classical, pop, and rock. Even ballet music she loved. She could lose herself dancing, forgetting about the aches and pains and politics.

"Tell me about your plans, Prima Dancing Teacher." His low voice carried across the room on the melody. He was one with the music similar to when she danced.

"Free classes start tomorrow. I have toddlers in the morning, and grade schoolers after school." She stood tall and stretched her calves and feet. On tippy-toes, she glided toward the piano, drawn by the music, drawn by him. "A few high schoolers in the evening, and even fewer adults later at night."

"Busy schedule."

The music soothed. His closeness would soothe more. She wanted to be by him, sit next to him, feel his arm muscles while he played. Swaying forward, she perched on the edge of the piano bench. She took in the heat of his body and his manly-clean scent. "Yet not enough students per session."

Glancing at her, he didn't shift away. "What will help?" He continued to play a light melody. Nothing as passionate as what he'd played last night.

He knew the right music to choose for the mood. He ran a successful business. He'd understand her questions and concerns.

"The grand opening showcase needs to be a success. A large audience who will see the fun the participants are having."

"Who have you suckered into it beside me?" His teasing grin sent butterflies flittering in her chest.

"For adults, I have Izzy and Parker, and a few others. My main business will come from kids, so I need to recruit more for my free classes."

"I can talk to a few parents I know."

The flittering changed to warmth. "Would you? You were so great yesterday in front of the studio."

Playing, his face was free of tension. He played the piano effortlessly, listening and responding without missing a beat. He played like a professional. Yet, he'd never mentioned any experience, and neither had his siblings, when she'd questioned them about Reed. In fact, it was as if the years between his childhood and his return to Castle Ridge didn't exist.

"Izzy and I were invited to a friend's house for Sunday dinner tonight. She has a daughter. And her daughter has friends."

"That would be wonderful." Warmth rose to a slow simmer. She stroked his muscled arm, wanting to communicate how he made her feel.

His fingers clattered and he stopped playing. Because of her touch? "Let me text Danielle and ask if you can join us."

"Are you sure? I don't want to be an imposition." Although it would be nice to get to know more people and make friends.

"She's family and she hosts Sunday dinners. She always asks me to bring a date."

Quinn stiffened. She pushed her lips together, trying to stop the envy. "Do you often bring dates to these dinners?"

"I rarely go. Only when Izzy nags me into it." He picked up his cell phone sitting on the other side of him.

Quinn peered over his shoulder at his phone. His texts were a stream of sentences, so much longer than one side of Dax.

"Danielle is a single mom, and tries to give her daughter a normal life. She believes a big family dinner is important, and since she has no family living in Castle Ridge, she invites us." He texted again. "All set. Dinner is at five."

"Thank you." Quinn clasped his arm, wanting to touch him one more time, feel his thick muscles, and feel the thrill she got with each contact.

"What other worries do you have?" He asked as if he wanted to lift the weight of the piano from her shoulders.

The sensation of being cared for, of being coddled, lightened her soul. The men in New York she'd dated were involved in the ballet world and thought of her as a commodity. Being seen with an up-and-coming dancer, or positioning themselves for a better role. Her few relationships burned hot and died. She'd never fallen in love. Never met the right kind of man.

She stared at Reed tinkling with the keys. Was he the right man? While she loved hearing him play, she wanted to caress him, hold him in her arms.

"We should practice our dance." Standing, she held out her hand.

His eyes widened and he yanked away. "Are you sure your ankle's strong enough?"

He wasn't concerned about her ankle. She could see it on his panicked face. Resembling a first-time solo performer in the spotlight, he was afraid.

This time, she believed he was afraid of her.

"My ankle is fine. It's wrapped for stability." She got the remote for the stereo and clicked it on. A slow, romantic song filled the room. "Are you afraid to dance?"

With me? She wanted to add.

"No." He didn't stand.

Rejection darkened her mood. Had she been wrong about the mutual attraction? "You'll be great." She stuck her hand out farther and used the sympathy card. "And you'll be helping me so much."

Grumbling, he stood. "I'm going to look like a fool."

She ignored him. Taking his hand, she pulled him to a position in front of her. "We're going to do the waltz."

"Sounds complicated." His voice rumbled with reluctance which she found endearing.

"You danced it before with me. We need to show the audience what we can do. What *you* can do."

"No, what *you* can do teaching." His confidence made it seem as if he was already proud of her.

His confidence boosted hers. She knew she could teach dancing, she'd mentored some of the younger ballerinas in the past. Now, she only had to get the students. "Put your other hand here." She moved his hand around her waist, placing his flat palm on her lower back. Her skin steamed.

"Like this?" His voice held a slight quiver.

She hid a smile. He was nervous. So was she.

Her nerves tapped in her midsection in a *rat-a-tat-tat*. Why? She'd danced with many partners. Professionally and socially. She'd taught others to dance when at a club or a party. With Reed, her hand shook, laying it on his shoulder blade. She felt the tenseness of his muscles beneath her palm. Compassion combined with determination, creating a wavering wall. He'd allowed himself to be vulnerable for her, and she wouldn't take advantage. She'd help him. She'd make him a good dancer.

They took a step. Together. Seamlessly.

As if they'd danced a lifetime together. Or danced together in another life.

Her frame fit perfectly with his tall body. As if they were made for each other. Their eyes met at the same level, their gazes connecting. As if they recognized each other's souls.

They floated across the dance floor. Staring into his deep-green orbs, her feet didn't touch the ground. She didn't count out the beat, they moved in unison to the tempo. He didn't need words or instructions. Their bodies communicated on a direct level.

A buzzing interrupted the music.

Disappointment trembled to her toes. "Sorry. It's a text." Releasing his muscular shoulder, she glanced at her phone.

"Anything important?"

"It's Dax." She sighed at the interruption. They'd attended a business reception last night, and he'd been great to have along to break the ice. He'd left the event early, and she hadn't gotten the opportunity to tell him they could only be friends.

"Then, very important." Reed dropped his hands from her body and stepped away, leaving her cold.

Reed yanked his hands off Quinn's body—the woman his brother was dating. What the hell was he thinking? They'd gone out together last night, according to his sister. Disgust curled in his stomach. He wouldn't date a woman after his brother had slept with her. Although Dax hadn't spent the night last night. Reed had been watching the driveway, and she'd walked home alone.

"What does he want?" He couldn't control the gruff quality of his voice, hating they'd been interrupted.

"Dax is going out of town for a few days." Her straightforwardness didn't sound sad or disappointed.

Was she not into his brother? She'd been upset about the skiing incident, and Reed had been surprised when she'd agreed to go out with him again. "Did you have another date scheduled after last night's?"

"Last night wasn't a date." Her you're-being-silly

tone teased. "I took him with me to the Main Street Business Association dinner. Why aren't you a member?"

Relief released the pressure. It hadn't been a date. And yet, he'd typed the text asking her out. He hadn't seen the reply. Had Dax lied about the response? Or was Quinn lying now?

"I'm not a Main Street retailer." Maybe he should join for the good of his career, and to see Quinn in a business setting.

"You should join. It's a great group, with lots of activities for retailers and the good of the community."

Reed didn't want a sales pitch about the organization right now. He was more concerned about what was going on with her and his brother. "I didn't know Dax was going out of town. Where's he going?" Concern threaded through Reed. For his brother and for Quinn. Dax had been taking multiple short, secret trips lately, and he didn't want his family to know.

"He didn't say. The message was short." Her voice pitched higher, clearly puzzled. "Which is weird."

"What do you mean?" Was something wrong with Dax?

"I told you, he acts like two different people." She stretched on her tiptoes, considering the situation. "I only agreed to go out with him, because one night he came to my window and spoke so eloquently."

The blood in Reed's veins pumped hard and then wavered. "Oh."

His words.

She liked his words. His brother had told him, and yet getting confirmation from Quinn was an aria to his soul. Maybe, just maybe she would've dated him. But how could he date a woman who'd slept with his brother?

Quinn tapped her cellphone on her chin. "When we went skiing, Dax was callous."

Reed refused to bad-mouth his brother. "He hates hospitals."

Shaking her head, she smirked. "Sometimes his texts are a song."

Uh-oh. His pulse drummed in tune with the song he was composing. Would she recognize his voice in the texts?

"Other times, he's curt and almost insensitive." Her confusion stabbed at Reed.

What he and his brother were doing was wrong. Standing on a precipice, he stared into a dark and unknown depth, feeling as if he were about to jump, or get pushed. He and his brother were tricking Quinn, and when she found out she'd hate them both.

Chapter Eleven

Nerves tightened inside Quinn similar to before a major ballet performance. Not that she was putting on a show. She would be herself, no airs or pretenses. These people would like her for who she was, and hopefully be enthusiastic about her dance studio.

Reed's easygoing presence projected calm. They were at Danielle's house for a normal Sunday dinner. People did this all the time. Just not Quinn. For years, Sunday meant a matinée performance, with rehearsal before and practice after.

The inviting home they'd entered had been welcoming. So had the people. Danielle and her daughter Brianna had greeted her with enthusiasm, and Izzy had given a hug. A real hug. Not air kisses and flattery, which was what Quinn had experienced in New York. Her eyes stung at the Norman Rockwell moment.

Moments she'd had as a child with her grandparents. This was normal and natural. Not the backstabbing ballet world, where socializing turned into a game of one-upmanship.

The central room was furnished with comfy chairs and couches with colorful pillows and lots of framed photos. The décor reminded her of her grandparents' house, only on a smaller scale. A foreign concept to the apartments she'd visited while living in the city, which were sparsely and expensively furnished.

The short spike of jealousy watching Danielle greet Reed ended as quickly as the brotherly hug. He'd said she and Brianna were family. There'd been a lot of laughter and catching up between friends. Relaxing, Quinn had sat back and watched. She'd never had such close friends. Everyone was dressed casually, comfortably. Not dressing to impress.

A home-cooked meal of baked chicken and flavored rice sat on the table. The food was served family-style, with everyone passing the dishes and helping themselves. The glass plates weren't the finest China.

"Tell us about yourself, Quinn." Their host asked, once everyone was seated at a large farmhouse table.

Under the table Quinn stretched her toes in the leather boots she'd purchased, trying to decide where to start and how much they really wanted to hear. She didn't want to bore them with details. "I used to be a ballet dancer in the New York."

"Did you and Uncle Reed meet in New York? Does the ballet dance with the symphony?" The question from the teen had her glancing from one to the other.

"Symphony?" Confusion knotted in her mind.

"The symphony and ballet are two completely different entities, Bri-Bird." Reed's chin tucked in trying to hide from the questions. "Quinn is offering free dance classes to students for the next two weeks to try out. Wouldn't you enjoy learning ballet, Brianna?"

His quick change of topic and re-directed question putting the teen in the spotlight was an aversion tactic. Could he have been involved with the symphony in New York? Quinn wanted to challenge him and make him explain. That would have to wait. She needed to focus on her studio, and getting the teen and her friends as students.

The girl's face soured. Her lips twisted together, and she kept her mouth shut. A miniature version of her mother, except with reddish hair and green eyes.

Quinn's stomach flipped and she rushed to convince. "No commitment." She tilted forward and hoped she didn't sound like she was begging. "Drop in and take a class. Invite your friends. It will be fun, I promise."

"I'm a skier." The teen slashed with her fork emphasizing her derision.

"You should give ballet a try." Danielle nodded with enthusiasm. She wanted her daughter to try dancing.

Which gave Quinn hope. Taking a sip of water, she thought of the best way to convince an athlete. "Ballet is great for your muscles. The stretching warmups will benefit your flexibility, which will help your skiing."

"My friends would make fun of me." The teen's angsty tone filled with disbelief. She set her fork down against her almost-empty glass plate.

"You won't make a fool of yourself." Her mother tried to convince. "I bet your friends would enjoy the class, too."

Quinn finished a bite, chewing on words that might convince. "Anyone can dance."

"Even me." Reed's quiet voice carried weight.

Thankfulness spread inside, warming every inch of her skin. She'd already used him as an example in other situations, and didn't want to do it again. She was happy he'd spoken up, happy he was becoming comfortable with the idea.

"You're dancing?" Izzy's high tone expressed her surprise.

Quinn had hoped his sister would be on her side.

"Good for you." Danielle was behind getting him in the spotlight. "After everything you've been through, it's good to see you're doing fun things again."

What had he been through besides the accident? More questions circled around in Quinn's head, making her dizzy. She thought she was getting to know Reed, but she'd only skimmed the surface. The prospect of learning more excited.

"He's writing music again." Izzy shot a sly glance at her brother and at Quinn.

Her head spun with more questions. He wrote music? For the symphony?

His shoulders tipped in and his expression blanked. He had a secret he didn't want known.

She wanted to help him get out of the inquisition from his sister. She also wanted to learn more about this enigmatic man. "He's a remarkable piano player."

"You're playing piano again, too?" Danielle's cheering-him-on smile struck an envious shimmy in Quinn. This other woman, who wasn't related, knew so much about him. "Are you going to leave Castle Ridge and return to the symphony?"

"What symphony?" Her confusion swirled and twirled, and the question came out as a demand.

His brows gathered in a dark thundercloud. His frown forced his defiant chin out. He shoved a forkful of rice into his mouth.

"Quinn doesn't know about your previous career?" Danielle pushed.

He placed his fisted hand on the table. "Did I tell you I ran into Luke Logan the other day?"

Izzy and her best friend froze. Both of the women's eyes went wide, and they caught each other's gazes. Their mouths dropped into perfect *O*s of surprise. Danielle's reaction was stronger. Her face paled and her body wavered. She sighted her daughter, taking a long, slow glance. A protective glance.

The awkward sudden silence caused Quinn to tense. There was more history here than she understood.

"Who's Luke Logan?" Brianna took a swallow of milk. Her innocent expression was in exact contrast to her mother's.

"An old high school friend of mine." Reed's chagrined smile showed he'd meant to cause a disruption to the conversation, and yet felt bad about it. Tossing the napkin on the table, he stood. "I'll clear the plates. Will you help, Brianna?"

The two of them gathered plates and silverware and took them to the kitchen around a counter with open shutters on top. He tweaked the teen's nose and she giggled. He was good with kids.

Quinn could picture him with children of his own. Hugging them, helping with homework, teaching them to play piano. A bright sunniness shone inside her. She could imagine her being at his side.

Izzy scooted her chair over and whispered, "Reed was the most incredible pianist at the New York Symphony."

Like a break-dance move, the entire universe shifted for Quinn. The questions in her head stopped spinning and everything clarified. She was an idiot. An angry idiot. No wonder he played with such passion. "I can't believe it."

Danielle scooted to Quinn's other side, taking part in their secret pow-wow. "He was such a marvelous player, even in high school."

She'd never had a posse of girls to hang out with. In ballet school, everyone was a competitor, and no one trusted anyone. The immediate camaraderie with these two women warmed.

"Still is great." Izzy glared at her brother. "He was playing piano in your dance studio the other night."

All the times he'd played in secret made more sense to Quinn now. "Why didn't he want me to know?" Her voice came out higher than expected because she was more hurt than expected. For some reason he didn't want to share his past with her.

His sister grazed her arm. "I hope it's okay he played your piano."

"Of course." Had she appeared shocked and Izzy had taken it to mean she didn't want him playing her piano? Quinn loved hearing him play.

Running water and laughter came from the

kitchen. Their boisterousness contrasted with the quietness at the table.

"Reed received lots of accolades. He wrote music and lyrics for Broadway while playing for the symphony. He took on way more than he should have." Izzy's tone showed concern and pride.

"And then he was in the car accident." Danielle ended on a sorrowful note.

"He told me about the accident." Quinn cared about him. More than cared. A decisiveness settled in her. She liked him, was attracted to him, and wanted to see what developed between them.

"He did?" Both women chimed.

He must not share much about himself with anyone. A lightness shined a spotlight on her decision. He'd confided in her. That must mean something.

"A limp shouldn't stop him from playing and composing." His music played in her head. "Which did he enjoy more?"

"I'm not sure." His sister's slow nod displayed her own sadness and sympathy. "Recovery took months. He didn't practice, and the symphony needed someone, so they filled his position with the stipulation when he was ready he could come back."

The image of him lying in agony in a hospital bed and struggling with physical therapy tormented her. No wonder he'd kicked the piano.

"He swore he'd never go back." Izzy's lips flattened into a grimace. "He left New York to recuperate here, and started buying buildings and remodeling things."

"He helped spruce up my house. Being in college

and working, I didn't have the time or the money to do it after my dad died." Danielle's voice went soft. She scanned the cozy great room. "Reed helped make it a real home for Brianna and me."

The dining area had the same tiled floors as the kitchen, with a painted wood counter. The older-styled cabinets had fresh paint brightening the room. This area led to a family room with thick carpet. And Reed had helped create this wonderful home.

If Quinn got together with him, how would their home take shape?

"He's remodeling a home for himself to live in, too." Izzy's tone held a wink-wink, knowing Quinn would be interested in this information.

Her wide-eyed gaze traveled the room, thinking about how he could make any place a home. He'd certainly made her comfortable in the dance studio and the tiny apartment above. The man was amazing. His talents were many. How did his new house look? Her sunny mood dampened. Once the studio was open and he moved to his house, how often would she see him?

"Where did he learn the skills?" Because he'd done a fabulous job in her studio, too.

"He did construction work in college to pay tuition and he loved working with his hands." His sister bragged on him. "Plus, the physical work of construction helped build his muscles after staying so long in the hospital."

He'd had such a prestigious musical career. The New York Symphony had agreed to give him back his position when he was ready, and yet his construction resume showed he'd been developing and remodeling buildings for over three years. Physically fit, so why not return?

Unless she had the timeline wrong. "If his only lingering issue is his limp, why doesn't he return to the symphony?"

Izzy gave her a strange expression. "He hasn't played the piano in years, until recently."

"Very recently," Danielle added.

The two women were able to communicate without words. Quinn couldn't help the thread of jealousy spinning through her. She'd never had close friends. She yearned for it. She yearned even more to find out about Reed.

"Why?"

"His love for music died. Died in the accident with his fiancée." A small, knowing smile floated on Izzy's face before she bit her lower lip. "Although it appears something or someone has brought him to life again."

Chapter Twelve

Reed's limp sounded louder walking home with Quinn later that evening. The quiet streets exaggerated the noise. Stars twinkled in the dark sky. He only noticed the cold whipping through him. From the wind and from her silence.

"Aren't you going to ask me more about my past?" The question popped out in a rush of nerves and misgiving.

Her narrowed gaze slid over him, assessing the best way to answer. "I don't understand why you want to keep your past a secret." The hurt in her tone made him hurt.

A slow, pounding ache worked through his veins. He heard the rhythm. Now he'd re-found music, he couldn't turn it off, and he couldn't decide whether that was good or bad.

Good because he felt alive. Bad because if he lost the music again, he might not survive.

Continuing to walk, they both stayed silent. He struggled to find a way to explain. He kept secrets to not expose himself and others to past pain. He didn't want sympathy or reasons for his non-productive musical mind. He knew the music had disappeared because of his guilt.

He opened his mouth once and closed it again. It wasn't Brianna's fault she'd told about the symphony. She hadn't understood the ramifications. He'd been so shocked he would've done anything to stop the conversation, even throw Luke Logan's name into the mix. Reed hung his head with shame.

When he'd left to do the dishes, he'd seen the three women whispering. Quinn in the middle had seemed so comfortable, as if she'd been friends with his sister for years. Like she belonged in Castle Ridge. Would she appreciate the house he'd bought and was remodeling? He could casually mention it to her and ask if she wanted to see the house. He could picture her in his home and in his arms.

The fantasy image yanked him back to reality. He needed to say something. The silence was killing him. He guided her to the side of the Victorian house to use the back entrance to their apartments.

"Music was part of my past and I didn't think it would ever be part of my future." He knew hearing the music was good. He was afraid of the devastation if the music disappeared.

"And now?" Her gloved hand took hold of his and he warmed, knowing the tiny confession had taken the sting out. "Do you want to go back?"

He wanted to grasp her hand tighter and pull away at the same time for fear she'd decipher the emotions running through him. "I don't know." He wasn't willing to admit how much he loved hearing the music out loud. He'd barely admitted it to himself.

A car zoomed past and he added the sound to the song creating in his brain. An owl hooted adding an emphatic beat. His limp scratched against the narrow sidewalk leading around the side of the old house.

She stayed silent, as if understanding he was not only composing music, but an explanation.

"After the accident, the music stopped playing in my head, stopped speaking to me." His doctors had told him it was temporary. His shrink had told him it was guilt. And Reed knew the guilt would never go away, so the music would never come.

Until Quinn had come into his life. The urge to play had come with her piano sitting smack-dab in the middle of the studio. The music had begun in his head as he got to know her. And the composing was his way of letting off steam about his feelings.

About Quinn.

His knees trembled confessing to himself. A confession he'd never share.

"At first I had an urge to play your piano." Instead, he'd kicked the instrument out of fear and anger of all he'd lost. "Once I sat down on the bench, chords formed in my head. Old things, new things." He ripped the knit hat off his head. "I can't turn it off."

"That's a good thing." She squeezed his hand and the action brought comfort. "Your music is beautiful."

Taking his hand out of hers, he twisted the knit cap between his fingers. He didn't want to rediscover his love of music only to lose it when he lost Quinn to some other man. Even if the man wasn't his brother, she'd find someone to love. Possibly someone from out of town. Or worse, someone from Castle Ridge, where he'd get to witness her romance.

His heart was being contorted and strangled. He wanted her to stay here forever, except seeing her with another man would torture.

The scent of fireplaces filled the air. Another owl hooted.

She raised her head and stared around. The stars lent a glow to her skin. "This is so different from New York, isn't it?"

"I hope you think it's different in a good way." He wanted her to stay in Castle Ridge forever. A slight hope he could be the reason she stayed pattered in his pulse.

"You mean you don't enjoy the smell of garbage and the constant sirens?" Her laughter tinkled and everything inside him lightened.

He wanted to reach out and grab this moment, so he could savor it for a while.

"Did you love your fiancée very much?" Her question sucker-punched.

He lost his breath and stumbled. He began to sweat. His mind churned with questions and explanations. He didn't know what to say, how to respond. The sweat chilled making him shiver. He wanted to tell Quinn his fiancée had killed any love…before he'd killed her.

One of the things he'd never shared. He sucked in, and the cold air hit the back of his throat. His family and friends believed it was lost love stopping the music in his head. It wasn't. It was condemnation, plain and simple.

"What? How?" He couldn't form a coherent sentence.

Her expression softened and she placed her hands on his shoulders, sensing his need to be held up. "Your sister told me she died in the same accident where you were injured." Quinn's tender tone oozed empathy, not accusation like his fiancée's sister.

Or the police interrogation. Or the questioning glances from acquaintances and colleagues.

Anguish crashed through his head, remembering the fight, the yelling and screaming, the ring being tossed at his head. He felt the ping of the sapphire against his forehead, and then the *clink*, as it dropped to the floor. The silence surrounding the action. The expression of fury on Elizabeth's face.

"Elizabeth and I fought that night." His voice cracked.

Quinn pulled him into a hug. Her rose scent wound around him and calmed. Her soft body comforted. She rubbed his back and made soothing noises. "All couples fight."

"Elizabeth and I were at a party and she drank too much." She always drank too much. It was one of the many things they'd fought about. "I insisted on taking her home." He shuddered, the soundtrack of the evening playing in his mind. "It was sleeting, and the road was slippery. She kept yelling and yelling."

At him. *How he couldn't break up with her. That they were perfect for each other. How she'd made his career.*

Quinn held him a little tighter, gently coaxing the confession.

"Elizabeth ordered me to pay attention to her. I

needed to concentrate on the road." His throat scratched with unshed tears. "She grabbed the wheel."

Gasping, Quinn's warm breath hit his cold cheek, making him remember he was alive, still had feelings, feelings for her. He had music, even if it had been buried for years.

"I remember the crash, the air bags deploying, and Elizabeth's bloody hand resting on my thigh." The images of the accident were so clear.

"It wasn't your fault." Quinn rubbed his back harder trying to force him to believe her words.

"She died because of me." His body iced and his voice grew cold. "That's why the music died in my head."

Leaning away from him, Quinn caught his gaze and drilled into him. "It wasn't your fault. Accidents happen. She tried to take the wheel."

The loss of Quinn's body heat sent chills racing down his spine. "Don't blame her."

She stroked his cheek and the racing chills morphed to desirous tingles. "I'm not blaming anyone, because no one is at fault."

She tilted toward him. Panic and desire shot through his body, two types of music playing at one time. Her eyes closed. His got wider. Her plush lips moved toward him.

He shouldn't kiss her.

He couldn't kiss her.

He wanted to kiss her.

His mouth descended. The magnetic pull of her lips couldn't be denied. She tasted of sunshine and lightness and a home-cooked meal. This might only be a sympathy kiss, but he was lost. Gathering her closer, he couldn't not respond. He wanted her kiss and her comfort. He wanted her to tantalize him. And boy, did she tantalize. He wanted to be aroused again, aroused like he hadn't been in over five years, aroused with an intensity only Quinn could ignite.

Even knowing this was a pity kiss, his body reacted. Fireworks exploded in his head. He threaded his fingers through Quinn's hair, caressing the back of her head, and taking control. He pressed his tongue against the seam of her lips and she welcomed him. His pulse picked up pace, pumping blood through his vessels. His manhood throbbed.

And his heart tumbled.

Quinn opened to Reed. Opened her mouth. Opened her spirit. Opened her heart.

She'd been wanting this kiss for days, and finally she initiated it. He'd been vulnerable and she needed to comfort. She'd hated seeing him upset. He must've been deeply in love with Elizabeth.

And then the kiss had changed.

He'd changed the message of contact. It had gone from comforting to passionate. And Quinn found herself wanting this kiss even more. Her tongue danced with his in the light of the moon. Poetic thoughts because of his kiss. She pressed herself against him, feeling his warmth and his hardness, and melting into him. His hands tangled in her hair, re-positioning her head so they could get closer. Thrills brushed across her body in a tease. His mouth nibbled hers as if he were a starving man. She wanted to be his meal. She wanted to fulfill his needs and let him fulfill hers.

She slinked her hands under his jacket and shirt. Her fingers brushed his waist, and sparks whooshed through her. His smooth skin was hard with muscle, carved abs and firm waist. Solid and strong. Dependable. A man with roots who you could count on. Not a flighty dancer or a building-his-reputation artistic producer. Not a user or a swindler.

He moaned. A signal of desire.

Her knees went weak and she clung to him, needing his strength. Needing him.

"I forgot how good this felt," he mumbled against her lips.

Pain radiated in her empty chest. He hadn't kissed anyone since Elizabeth. He'd been loyal to his dead fiancée for years. He must've really loved her.

Quinn should stop. Her brain said put an end to this madness. Her senses said go, go, go. He needed her. She'd initiated the kiss, and he'd responded like any man who hadn't been with a woman in years.

He leaned closer and positioned her against the side of the house. The flat surface of the wall contrasted with the hard contours of his body. Continuing the kiss, her hands moved over his shoulders and back. She didn't want to be a nameless, faceless woman, but she wanted to make him better. Make him feel good, and in the process make herself feel good. She shoved her hands farther up his back.

His fingers toyed with the edge of her jacket and she wished he'd fondle her skin. She wanted his hands on her body. When he pushed against her center and wetness pooled at the juncture between her thighs, she couldn't remember any hesitations. His kiss and his caress was so amazing it was hard to think.

She could only feel.

His hands finally found their way beneath her light jacket. His palms spread across her lower back causing shivers on her skin. She wanted more than his hands on her. She wanted his entire naked body next to hers. Flesh to flesh. She'd never felt this urgency to get close to someone so fast. If she'd been thinking clearly she'd be shocked.

She wasn't. "Let's go home."

Reed broke off the kiss. His emerald eyes widened and flashed with what appeared to be shock. His swollen lips rounded. He glared as if surprised to find he'd been kissing her and not his fiancée. "Dax."

Or thinking about his brother.

Her body sagged in disappointment.

Reed yanked his hands from under her jacket. "I shouldn't have." His voice scratched with horror. "Dax. You're dating Dax. My brother."

"Dax and I went on one date." Quinn rationalized. Reed was worried about his brother. As teens had they had a friendly competition with the girls?

He backed away, and her body slid down the side of the house. So much for him being someone she could count on. "You've made plans to go out again."

She did have plans with his brother. A follow-up meeting with someone they'd met at the business association happy hour. Business, nothing serious.

Besides, how did he know about their date? "Yes, but—"

"We shouldn't have kissed." He didn't let her explain. "Dax is my brother. Even if you aren't dating, you did date and my brother and I have a deal we don't poach—"

"Poach?" She poked a finger into Reed's pecs. "Your brother doesn't own me."

"You don't understand. You don't have siblings."

Pointing out the obvious shouldn't hurt so much. She was alone in the world. No brothers or sisters. No parents or grandparents. And apparently, no Reed.

His cruelty had her smashing her lips together. One date did not signal ownership.

His cheeks pulled in and his expression resembled the Degas painting with the terrified ballet dancer about to go on stage. "We need to forget this ever happened."

Reed's assumptions and denial of their mutual desire sliced. Anguish and embarrassment twisted inside rising to her head. Confused, she tried to figure out what was going on. Was it really because of Dax, or was Reed still in love with his dead fiancée?

He might be able to forget their passionate kiss, but could she?

How could Quinn forget the kiss when Reed's music whispered in her ear?

She rolled over in her lonely bed and stared at the ceiling. It had been past midnight when he'd started playing the piano in the dance studio. The tinkling had entered her dreams like the caress of a lover. Each vibrato hugged and heated. Each note had tantalized and teased. Each chord had stroked and fondled. And the crescendo had awoken her from a very sexual dream.

She woke up wanting Reed.

When the music stopped abruptly, she'd thrown on her robe and stepped into the hallway, hoping to talk to him. To explain Dax was only a friend. To convince Reed their kiss proved they'd be good together. He shouldn't mourn for the rest of his life. She could help him get past his loss.

His fingers pounded on the keyboard with an angry clashing of chords. Jerking, she stopped her forward progress to listen.

The song no longer sounded wanton. It sounded sharp and discordant and agonized. The beat was off. The harmony non-existent. Was he upset about the kiss they'd shared? Or was he tortured by his love for his dead fiancée?

For him not to hear music in his head since Elizabeth's death showed the depth of Reed's love. For him not to be with anyone, even a casual encounter, proved his loyalty and strength. His sister hinted he'd started playing again when Quinn had arrived. He'd been aroused by their kiss. A sign, perhaps?

She tiptoed down the stairs, unsure about her ultimate goal. Could she pry his love from a dead woman's hands? Giving him her body could lead to deeper feelings, couldn't it? Was it worth the risk? She trembled, and not from the cold. If she let him use her body without involving his emotions, the romantic encounter would only be sex. Their needs would be fulfilled, but their hearts would stay empty.

Reed's fingers slammed on the keys. The chords clashed together resembling battling dancers in the *Don Quixote* ballet. The stroke of notes struck her hard. A knife to the chest. Covering her ears, she couldn't listen to the harsh music any longer. She couldn't let Reed endure his torment alone.

On shaky legs, she continued down the stairs. She wasn't one for a casual fling. Her goal in Castle Ridge was to set down roots. Her and Reed's kiss had been fueled by lust on his part, and she needed to save herself and not get involved. Right?

Not get involved in a romantic relationship, but she couldn't let him wallow in despair.

He was emotionally unavailable. She had to accept it. She needed a friend more than a one-night stand.

Almost *en pointe*, she swished across the dance floor. The music crashed into her harder and faster the closer she got. So involved in his musical noise he didn't notice her approach. She placed a hand on the arm of his wrinkled T-shirt.

The music clashed and stopped. The harsh echoes rang through the dance studio. His head swiveled to stare as if she were an alien, when she'd believed she'd be an angel of salvation.

His mouth pulled in tight. She'd surprised him, shocked him.

Her lungs caught on a hitch. She'd done the right thing. Stopping the noise and the agony. "Are you okay?"

His face muscles tightened, seeming to control his expression. A tick pulsed in his cheek. "I'm sorry." He spoke slow and terse, again trying to hide his feelings. "Did I wake you?"

So polite. So uncomfortable. So unlike the Reed she'd come to know, who'd shared his sorrows.

"It doesn't matter." She wanted to comfort without insulting. "You sounded upset."

"No. I'm fine." His lips tightened together, like he was forcing himself not to say more.

She rubbed his arm with her knuckles. She was his buddy, his pal, nothing sexual about the contact. "You're sure?" She was sure. Sure he was upset, and talking about his dead fiancée must've started this storm.

Her fault.

"Just playing a little light concerto." The ends of his mouth lifted in a false smile. His joke fell flat.

Quinn ached for him. She moved her hand to his shoulder and squeezed. To comfort, not because she couldn't resist touching him. Sitting beside him on the piano bench, she let his warmth seep into her body, giving her strength and conviction.

"Do you want to talk about it?"

"No."

"Talking helps." She truly believed in the philosophy. If she'd had someone to discuss things out with maybe she would've quit ballet sooner, maybe she wouldn't have lost her grandparents' home.

"Quinn the psychiatrist. How come I'm the one always confessing things?" His serious tone conflicted with his agitation. He shifted on the bench to study her. "Is there no dark history in your past?"

Stretching her legs beneath the piano, she thought about her upbringing with her strict mother, the cold, sterile ballet school dormitories, the competition to become the principal ballerina. While those things had shaped her, none were important anymore. She'd truly put that life behind her. The only regret gutting her was the loss of her grandparents' house. She'd been devastated and couldn't even walk down the street in Castle Ridge where it was located.

Nerves pranced in her midsection. "I almost wasn't able to open my dance studio."

The free classes started tomorrow. The dance studio was a reality. For now. As long as she could pay the rent each month.

"Why?" He slammed the cover down on the piano, as if the keys taunted him. "You're so determined."

A laugh gurgled. She was determined because she'd never had any other choice. Her mother had pushed her to be a better dancer with extra classes, private lessons, and training at home. The scholarship for ballet school had been based on talent, so she'd had to work harder to be the best. Once in the ballet, failure wasn't an option. She had no fallback plan.

"Oh, I had my entire future planned out." She'd been so naïve. "I'd worked hard and saved enough money to start a dance studio anywhere I wanted. I was going to live my dream." Part of her dream was putting down roots and having a family. She didn't tell him that part, because she didn't want him running away as he'd done earlier this evening. If she could only have him as a friend, she'd take it. Still, she'd continue her campaign in a slow sashay of desire.

"Why did you choose Castle Ridge?"

"Fond memories of visiting my grandparents." She choked at those memories and how she'd lost part of them. "I inherited their house, so I had some place to live here."

His head angled in curiosity, and it was the first time she didn't see pain in his expression since she'd come downstairs. Maybe sharing her secrets would help him forget his misery.

"I had enough money to do a long-term lease for a dance studio, pay for renovations, and have plenty of money saved." Heat crawled up her cheeks at how stupid she'd been. "Until I dealt with an unscrupulous leasing agent."

"My leasing agent?" His eyebrows arched, and a flash of temper appeared on his face.

"No. Someone from New York who had contacts in Castle Ridge. Supposedly." She knew with certainty Reed would take care of his responsibilities. "I had leased another building before yours. Or, at least, I thought I had."

"What happened?" He placed a hand on her thigh.

The silk of her robe swished against her skin. The presence of his palm assured. She'd be sharing one of the biggest mistakes of her life with a man she wanted respect from. Her mind teased. She wanted more than respect from him. One step at a time. "The leasing agent took my very large deposit on the lease."

"First and last month?" His palm moved against her robe in a brushing gesture.

She tried not to notice how his rough hand compared to the smooth silk. She focused on her tale. "The agent said because I didn't have a track record, he needed more to obtain the lease. A full year of rent."

"That's bull." His large hand swished again and clutched her thigh.

The gesture sent a scorching spiral to her core.

The gesture was meant to console. She imagined other ways they could comfort each other. So many ways.

Start as friends.

"I know that now." Her cheeks flamed. She'd been so dumb and trusting. "I wired the money, and the agent disappeared."

His hand whipped off her thigh. Before she could mourn the loss, he'd wrapped his arm around her shoulders and tucked her head against his chest. His clean-manly scent infiltrated her senses, bringing a new sense of calm and excitement. Soothed by his touch and excited for more. She would've shared her story sooner, if she'd known he'd react this way.

Did it mean more to him? Or was he only being a nice guy?

"I didn't have enough money saved to get another lease. I'd already given up my apartment in New York. Quit my job." She sniffled, and his other arm wrapped around her. She burrowed into him, feeling cherished. "I'd planned to live in my grandparents' house. The house they left me. The house I wanted to raise my children in." The torture ripped through her picturing how it should've been. Small children with dark, curly hair, playing on the wide front porch. A loving husband. One who cherished and protected. One like Reed.

"I'm sorry." His hand massaged her back, and she melted into him.

"I had to sell my home." Sniffling again, she couldn't stop the tears from falling. "My memories."

He leaned back and wiped the wetness from her cheeks with his fingers. His compassion and understanding made her less embarrassed and more attracted. "Have you tried to find the disreputable agent?"

She nodded. She'd contacted the Better Business Bureau and the New York police. Besides taking the report, there wasn't much they could do. "That's why I love it here. People are so honest and trustworthy. No one local would lie or take advantage."

By stopping their earlier kiss, he'd proven it. She'd been upset about being a stand-in, but willing to go along for the ride. Reed had put a stop to their passion.

He shifted. "For the most part." He dropped his arms from her and reeled away.

Her stomach flipped and hung on an edge of anxiety. Had Reed lied to her about something? The lease or the dance studio? His fiancée or his feelings?

"I hate being lied to." Her muscles hardened, showing the determination she was known for. "And I hate being made a fool."

Chapter Thirteen

Early the following morning, Reed snuck into the dance studio to finish the lights before Quinn came to work. He hadn't slept well last night, with several forms of guilt choking him. He and his brother lied to Quinn with their trickery, and she hated liars. Which he totally understood after the way she'd been cheated.

He was a liar, and he coveted the woman his brother had dated. In high school, that wasn't a huge problem. In the past they'd dated plenty of each other's ex-girlfriends. Right now, with Dax so vulnerable, Reed found his needs hard to justify. Especially if Quinn only felt sympathy toward him.

Dax's ex-girlfriend, the first woman his brother had ever had a real relationship with, had hit on Reed. She'd given some lame excuse about how he was mysterious and needy. He and Dax had gotten into a huge blow-up. Reed had never encouraged the woman. He hadn't been interested in her or anyone else. When Dax had believed they were a happy couple once more, the woman had cheated on him with someone else. Hence the recent breakup, which had brought Dax to his lowest point, his most vulnerable.

Coming out of the storage area with the lights, Reed almost ran into Quinn. She backed around the corner to take a position by the front counter. Her expression rearranged from shock to welcoming, except her smile was too sunny, her eyes too bright, and her good morning too stiff.

Had her night been sleepless, too? "Morning." He purposely left the *good* off.

Tension rose between them. There was no dance music to fill the awkward silence. She'd come down the stairs when he'd been tortured and playing the piano as a friend. She wasn't lusting after him. He needed to act normal. The kiss yesterday meant nothing. He cleared his throat. "You're at work early."

Biting her lower lip, Quinn stood. She wore tights and a short, clingy, layered skirt. The top stretched across her slim waist and small breasts. She stretched to the tips of her toes—a nervous habit he'd noticed. "I'm worried about today."

First day of her free classes. He softened with sympathy, and the awkwardness disappeared. He took a step forward, planning to give her a hug. Images of their last comforting hug crescendoed in his mind. Comfort had morphed to passion. Passion to lust and lost control.

He stopped and stiffened. No friendly hug, because for him the hug would be so much more than friendly. "You'll be great."

"What if the kids don't listen? What if their mothers hate how I teach?" She sounded like a small lost girl.

"How can they not love you?" His voice rasped with the need to assure and comfort.

Everyone who met Quinn loved her. Izzy, Danielle, Brianna. Dax.

Reed's lungs tightened. He had to remember Dax.

She held out her hand, reaching for Reed, an automatic reaction. He leaned back, afraid to connect. Afraid the connection would become something more on his end.

She let her hand drop onto the counter. "I know it's silly, but I'm scared." The tremor in her voice had him tilting forward.

He wanted to reassure. There was nothing sexual about the way he placed his hand over hers on the counter. "I understand." And he did. He remembered the butterflies right before every concert. Except in his case, they'd been large bats. "Nerves can be a good thing. They heighten your performance."

"Will you stay nearby? I'll be better if you're close." Her lips pouted and her shimmering gaze begged.

He couldn't say no. "Sure."

What had started out awkward, turned into companionable silence. He worked on the lights and she organized for her first set of classes. She'd work at the computer, tie up small goody bags, and play song after song after song. Her face would pucker in concentration listening to each piece of music. She'd frown or smile and tap her feet. And look adorable doing it. She obviously loved music.

Something they had in common.

He staggered back and his heart leapt to a jumping melody. He loved music again. The antagonistic hatred was gone. There was no longer silence in his head, and he appreciated the sound. Rhythms pulsed and lyrics knocked around in his brain constantly. Even the tortured music he'd composed last night had left him with a cleansed attitude.

The bell above the door rang, and a gaggle of toddlers and parents came into the dance studio. The children's eyes were wide, either excited or scared. The parents were curious.

"Welcome." Quinn stretched on her toes, and greeted each parent with a shake of the hand and a form to be filled out.

He couldn't stop pride running through his veins. She was facing her fears, and not letting anything stop her. She'd planned and pushed forward. She'd faced adversity when she lost the original amount of money to invest in her business and found another way. She would do what it took to make the studio succeed.

A *da da da daaaaa* played in his mind. What about him and his fears? Fears hanging around him like an albatross for years. The music was inside him again. Was he willing to take the next step? To quit hiding?

Was he ready to face his fears?

"These introductory classes for the next two weeks are completely free. No obligation." Her smile appeared a little tight and strained. He could see her nervousness. "I'm hoping your children will get a taste of how fun dancing can be in a non-stressful environment."

A few parents nodded and murmured. A couple waved a greeting toward him. People he knew from school or business.

He watched, fascinated, by the way she handled the crowd. She knew the right things to say. In the past, he'd been good with crowds, and bad with management. He loved talking about music to an audience or to a classroom filled with kids. But ask him to schedule those presentations, or know where he needed to be and when, he was hopeless.

"I'll be having a grand opening showcase and party. I'd love for your children to perform, and I'd love for all of you to watch and celebrate with me. You can invite friends and family, too. The more the merrier." She laughed and it went straight to his gut.

He loved her laugh. The way it started out slow and low, and built into a joyful sound. The way it entered his ears and played in his mind like a musical trill before going to his chest and warming his heart.

After explaining the form to the parents, she gathered the kids in a circle. Each toddler introduced themselves and shared what they enjoyed about dancing.

He appreciated how once she'd explained things to the parents, she'd focused on the children. The class was for them and about them.

"Everybody on their feet and spread out." She clicked on the music. "We're going to dance off the jiggles." She shook her feet and hands in a funny way.

She beamed. She was cute and fun and good with kids.

He could imagine her running around with a trio of

her own toddlers, teaching them to dance. The kids would be athletic and musically talented because he'd teach them...*he'd teach them?*

He sucked in a sharp breath. Shaking his head, he knocked the image out of his mind. It kept returning. Because those kids he imagined of Quinn's? They were his kids, too. A yearning grew inside him. For kids, and for Quinn. The yearning clogged his throat. The wish to be a family with Quinn excited and scared. He'd promised his brother he wasn't interested. Except he was.

The toddlers shook their limbs and giggled dancing around to a merry beat.

"Everyone pretend you're a snake." She put her palms together and slithered up from a crouched position. Her hips swayed back and forth. Her shoulders dipped and rose. Her hands lifted above her head, tightening the Lycra material across her chest and emphasizing her breasts.

Desire went on high alert, and his manhood hardened. To him, she appeared more like an exotic dancer than a reptile.

Time for him to leave before he embarrassed himself. Or his lust combined with the urge to have children with Quinn became so urgent he carried her up the stairs to bed.

Exhausted and happy, Quinn relaxed in the office chair, putting her feet on the counter. The two toddler dance classes she'd taught had gone well. The kids had been cute and rambunctious with lots of enthusiasm. She couldn't wait to see how their dance for the showcase turned out.

"That went well this morning." Reed walked in, carrying a tray with sandwiches and two lemonades, and she'd never seen anything so scrumptious.

Reed and the tray of food.

He wore the same brown construction boots and tight jeans showing off his butt. His red flannel shirt was unbuttoned, revealing a tight, white T-shirt underneath, emphasizing his hard pecs.

"It did." She'd noticed he'd disappeared sometime during the first class, once she'd settled in to teaching. "I appreciate you hanging around while you could."

She appreciated a lot of things about Reed. He was dependable, and always there for her. His quiet command of a situation, his support, his sexy smile.

"No worries." He set the tray on the counter. "I made lunch. Turkey sandwiches."

"You read my mind." She ate a lot, because she burned a lot of calories dancing. Other guys she'd dated thought she didn't eat because she was thin, or thought she had dietary restrictions because she was a ballet dancer. Reed didn't treat her like a celebrity, maybe because he understood. "I'm starving."

He perched on the edge of the counter, his thigh bumping against her feet. His body heat scorched her toes, and she curled them to stop herself from reaching out to him.

Start with friendship.

Keep telling yourself that, Quinn. Her humming body wasn't listening to her mind. She couldn't stop the attraction sparking every time he was near.

And he was near. She took a big bite out of the sandwich, instead of taking a big bite of Reed. This time.

"I've taught classes for the NY ballet. Older students who had a passion for dance. This—" She waved her sandwich toward the dance floor. "—is completely different. These toddlers have never danced. I want to make it fun."

"By the laughter and smiles on the kids' faces, I say you succeeded." He toasted her with his glass of lemonade.

"Thanks." The humming slowed to a happy buzz. She took another bite and contemplated the future. She could see her studio being a success. She could see herself being happy teaching dancing in Castle Ridge, having friends close by, having Reed bring her lunch during the day.

The low croon came to a scratching halt. If she wanted to make a relationship with him occur, she'd have to make it happen. She didn't know if it was his brotherly code or his dead fiancée but something held him back.

She picked up the stereo remote and tried to click it on. "The stereo system keeps flickering out." She clicked it off and on again.

"Might be a bad connection. I can take a look at it for you."

"That would be great." Taking another bite, she watched him from lowered eyelids. He took a long swallow of lemonade, and his Adam's apple went up and down. The action fascinated. It was so manly. "I Googled you last night." Which was how she learned he was a minor celebrity.

A frightened expression crossed his face. "You did?"

Her nerves jittered. "Don't be mad."

"I'm not mad." Except, his chin tucked in, and his smile disappeared.

Wanting to discover more of his background and what other issues might be holding him back, she'd researched. "You were famous."

"Almost as famous as you." Reed set down his half-eaten sandwich. Obviously, her discussion topic had taken away his appetite. "I did some Googling of my own. Once you moved in."

"I wasn't famous." She set her own sandwich down, no longer hungry. Her curiosity had ruined both their appetites, and she was sorry. Sometimes a girl needed to know. "A faceless ballerina. You were the pianist for the symphony, you wrote beautiful music. For the symphony and Broadway."

Standing, he wheeled around and took a few steps away.

Knowing she should stop, she didn't. She wanted to know everything about him, needed to know. "How could you give it up?" What had driven him to walk away from a legendary career?

"I didn't." He swiveled toward her. His brows gathered in an angry storm. His mouth hardened, and his eyes glinted, resembling hard stones. "The music, the job left me. I deserved it."

"The accident wasn't your fault." She stood and moved toward him, needing to convince him. "Once you accept you aren't to blame, you can move forward with your career." And maybe a relationship.

"You don't know all the details." His harsh tone scraped against her spine. "I didn't tell you everything."

Ignoring the torment, she grabbed his shoulders, pressing her fingers into his arms to make her point. "I don't need to know the details. I know you. I believe in you." She wanted to convince him. Maybe if he heard it enough times he'd believe.

He shook off her touch, making her feel like a leech. His stormy expression crashed, as if thunder. He stomped out of the dance studio, leaving her standing in the middle of the floor.

Alone.

She remembered the loneliness. Emptiness. Nothingness. Quiet desperation.

Didn't matter what she believed, he didn't believe in himself. And until he did, he'd never be emotionally available.

Quinn's stomach rotated one way and then the other all afternoon. She hadn't seen Reed for the rest of the day. So much for being friends. In addition, the middle-school students would be arriving any moment, and they were going to be a tougher sell than the toddlers. She hoped a few boys came, because she wanted to teach them that dancing was manly. She wanted to break through the stereotypical vision of a male dancer.

A group of eight girls and two boys showed up. She gave the parents the general information, and started the kids in fun stretching exercises. While the toddler classes had been about movement and having fun, the middle-school classes were going to learn real dance steps.

"We're going to start with basic steps in ballet and move from there into tap and maybe hip hop." She demonstrated the ballet positions. "Follow me."

The bell rang above the door. Sara dragged her mother inside. The girl's determined expression contrasted with the mother's obstinate one.

Quinn's worry doubled, even while her spirits lightened. The girl wanted to be here. "I'm glad you came."

The girl moved slightly behind her mother. Wanting and being confident were two different things.

"To watch." The mother's stern tone told her she didn't want to be persuaded. She was here against her wishes.

The earlier lightness dampened. She needed to convince the mother to let Sara go, and convince Sara she could dance.

A couple of the kids on the dance floor snickered.

Quinn shot them a warning glance. The other kids weren't helping the situation. "There's room. Come join us."

The girl buried her head into her mother's hip.

"Okay." She wanted to try to persuade, but she also needed to pay attention to the rest of the class. "If you want to join at any time, you're welcome."

Turning her back from the door, she continued demonstrating the moves, watching each kid imitate. She spotted Reed come through the back door.

He paused and took in the class. The blood in her veins rushed at his presence.

"Second position." Automatically, she gave the instruction, and moved into the correct position.

Reed moved to the door and squatted by the girl. He said something she couldn't hear. The girl beamed. The mother appeared less sure.

What were they discussing? "Third position." She moved into the next position.

He took off his heavy construction boots and held out his hand. "Come on, Sara-Smile."

The girl slipped out of her coat and clung to his hand like a lifeline. The two of them limped onto the dance floor together.

Her heart melted with his sweetness. "You two can take a spot over there." Her voice scratched and her eyes stung.

"Everyone, let's welcome Mr. O'Donnell and Sara to class." Quinn's entire body trembled. This beautiful man made the effort to make a disabled girl comfortable. He put himself and his limp in the spotlight of teasing adolescents to help the girl. She didn't know if she could execute the next move. "Do a *plié*."

He was such a good man. Strong, caring, thoughtful.

He and Sara bent their knees and lowered, grinning at each other.

Quinn's tremulous smile forecast her emotions. She had to hold herself together in front of the class.

He smiled at the young girl. Her brilliant return smile glowed with happiness. She wanted to dance and she wanted to be accepted. Reed had accomplished both. He was a hero to the young girl.

And to Quinn.

He caught her stare and sent her a lopsided grin. A grin saying, *what else could I do?*

Other men, less sympathetic and good-natured men, would've ignored the plea in the girl's gaze. Wouldn't have risked their own pride to help a child. He did all of those things and so many more.

She thought of his attention to detail when working on her studio, his giving in when she'd convinced him to go out, even though he didn't want to, his care when she'd been injured, his comfort when she'd been nervous this morning. And his kiss.

She couldn't forget his kiss.

Her heartbeat raced ahead of the dance music. Her chest swelled. Her pulse thrummed with knowing and needing and wanting and...

...loving.

She was falling for Reed.

Chapter Fourteen

That night, Reed had showered and changed into pressed, black jeans and a soft button-down shirt, before pacing around the back hallway of the dance studio. He was early for the adult classes. He heard the laughter of the high school girls finishing their lesson. The hip hop music bounced against the wall and his nerves. He hadn't seen Quinn since saying goodbye to his dance partner in the middle-school class. While she'd talked to parents, he'd escaped out the back. He didn't want to overhear the kids or the parents discussing his performance.

Helping Sara had been his only goal. She'd faced her fears this afternoon, and would be coming back to dance. He was proud of her. Maybe he needed to face his own fears. If a twelve-year-old could push herself past the comfort zone, why couldn't he?

His phone clanged with a text message from Dax. *I haven't texted Quinn since I left town. What should I say?*

Reed throttled the phone. He'd done enough with his brother's date already. They'd lied to her, and he hoped if she ever found out she'd forgive him. *What do you want to say?*

Don't know. Need help. Typical Dax—short and to the point.

Guilt cut across Reed's frustration. Guilt for kissing Quinn and for helping his brother. He had to put a stop to the romantic consultation. Let Dax fly or bomb on his own. *Speak from your heart.*

Heart still isn't talking to me. Dax's agony from the recent breakup was understandable, but he couldn't use the excuse forever, and he couldn't use Reed.

He didn't want Quinn to be a rebound girlfriend. He'd thought Dax and Quinn would be social, help her meet people in town and help him get his groove back. Be friends and have some fun. Now that Reed knew her, he realized she wasn't looking for fun, she was looking for something deeper. Dax couldn't give her deep, not in his current state of mind. Could Reed?

He shifted his feet and listened to the voices in the studio, not really wanting to go out there. *Ask her how the free classes are going.*

Any friend would ask the question. He wasn't using poetry or words from his song to help. Plus, Dax would have to form his own sentence.

"Hi, Mr. O'Donnell." Brianna stepped out of the bathroom. She wore black leggings and a long T-shirt with a skiing design.

"Hi, Bri-Bird. How's dance class?" He'd tell Quinn if the answer was positive.

"Surprisingly fun." The teen flashed a smile. "Are you taking the adult class?"

"I am." He bowed his head. He'd hated dancing in

front of the kids and their parents today. It was going to be worse in front of friends and other adults from town. Their judgments already pounded in his mind.

"So's my mom." Brianna waved and headed onto the dance floor. "Class is almost done. Gotta go."

The music stopped a few minutes later, and the chatty girls picked up in volume. Noticing the time on his phone, he contemplated using the back exit.

The chime above the door rang and rang, people leaving and entering. Too many people. It was time. Pivoting, he headed toward the back door. Only Quinn would realize he was a no-show. No one else would expect him to dance. At the last second, he swiveled around and marched toward the studio. He'd promised Quinn he'd be there. He didn't break his promises.

She stood by the front door, greeting newcomers, handing out paperwork, and smiling. Her gracefulness and beauty took his breath away. Her head turned, as if sensing him. She stared for a second, and then her cheeks reddened and she glanced away.

Did she regret promising to be his partner tonight? He probably resembled an ogre next to the child-sized students this afternoon.

"Gather round, everyone." She waved at him. "Who needs partners?"

He dragged his foot and his bad attitude toward her in the middle of the dance floor. He should grab Danielle as a partner, leaving Quinn to dance with someone else except he wanted to hold her in his arms again. To hold her nubile body against his. Basically, to torture himself. He slammed his cell phone on the counter.

A couple of people nearby jumped, and he whispered an apology. He didn't want anyone else sensing his foul mood.

She put couples together. Izzy went with some loser named Edward. Danielle with Parker. A few other people had come together. Shifting on his feet, he stood alone on the dance floor. People probably believed he was the odd man out. He wasn't. Dancing with Quinn he should feel like the luckiest guy in the room.

"We're going to start with a simple waltz." She clicked on the music. "The steps are easy." She described the simple box step while fluidly moving across the floor.

Dread slowed his pulse. Even though they'd practiced, he'd never keep up with her. Not with his dead-weight of a foot. And as the teacher's partner, he'd be in the spotlight. Everyone would be watching.

A clanging rang above the music.

She frowned and marched to the counter. "Cell phones should be on silent during class."

Panic punctured his lungs, squeezing the air out. His phone. When he'd slammed it on the counter he'd forgotten the phone there. She might see Dax's texts on the notifications.

Reed lunged toward the phone. "It's mine."

He tripped and tipped forward. His hands stretched out, trying to block his fall. A weightless sensation tingled across his skin. He teetered in the air, and fell to the hard ground. Pain shot from contact with the floor. His shoulder took the brunt, but his pride hurt the most. Lying on his side, he was too embarrassed to attempt a funny line or a quick recovery.

Izzy hurried over. She'd hovered like a mother hen since he'd returned to Castle Ridge. "Are you all right?"

"I'll help him, Izzy. Go back to your partner." Quinn bent down with a look of concern and stroked his arm. Sparks swooshed from her fingers and up his skin reducing the pain.

The sparks did nothing to stop his mortification. "I can get up on my own."

"Are you injured?" Sympathy swam in her gaze.

He didn't want or need any more sympathy. "Just my ego." He got to his feet with only a wobble.

"Come sit on the bench." She gripped his arm, trying to lead.

He yanked away from her. "I'm not a baby." Smashing his lips together, he felt even more stupid for being mean.

"Fine." Her chin pulled in, clearly insulted. She slapped his phone into his hand and pivoted toward the class making him a bigger jerk. "Everyone, your hands should be at shoulder and lower back."

Dragging himself to the bench, he took note of any damage. No new pain. He was fine. He should've let Quinn help, even if it was only to extend her touch on his body. Which he shouldn't want or angle for. Playing with his shoelaces, he pretended the fall was his shoes' fault while he got his stupidity under control.

"Very good." Quinn held her arms up to her invisible partner. "Move to the beat. One, two, three, one, two, three."

He'd wanted to be invisible until Quinn came to town. Hide behind his job and his injury. Not go out in public. Stick to himself. He still wanted to do that, didn't he? Doubts invaded and he stretched his leg, trying to work the kinks out of his mind. He'd enjoyed spending time with Quinn, going out to dinner and eating lunch in the studio, holding her in his arms.

She'd faced her fears today. Sweet Sara had faced her fears. Why couldn't he?

"Keep moving." Quinn waltzed to him. "Are you ready to go back onto the dance floor?"

His body leapt at the opportunity. He wanted to hold her again. "No."

Angling her head, she studied him. He wanted to squirm. "I'm not sure what the big rush was to get your phone, so you tripped. Everybody trips. No big deal."

His shoulders scrunched ready to hide. "I made a fool of myself."

"If I quit every time I fell, I never would've made it through my first ballet class." She gave him a you're-being-ridiculous expression. "I saw you with Sara today. If she fell, would you have left her on the dance floor? Would you have let her quit?"

"Of course not." The young girl only needed practice and confidence.

Quinn held out her hand. "Then, let's dance." Her lips tipped into an assured-serene-challenging smile, lighting up his insides and his motivation.

Maybe that's all he needed. Practice dancing, more confidence with Quinn.

The following night more couples joined the free dance lesson. Reed didn't trip or embarrass himself. Everyone had fun. Dancing with Quinn in his arms had been wonderful. Their bodies moved in tune together like magic. They'd floated across the dance floor.

"Let's go out for drinks," his social sister suggested after class.

His immediate reaction had been a big fat no. Then, he spotted Quinn with a glimmer in her eyes and a smile on her face. She wanted to go out. She wanted to meet people and make friends.

He'd already traveled out of his comfort zone with dance class. What was one beer? "Sure."

Izzy and Danielle had been shocked. Quinn delighted.

And she was the only one who mattered.

His pulse pumped hard once, and again. Quinn mattered. What she thought of him, how they interacted. He could sing a chorus of *they were only friends*, but in his heart he knew he wanted more. Their kiss the other night had been proof.

He put on his coat and left with the other dancers. Together, they strolled to the local pub. Dazed, he kept quiet as they walked. His life had changed so much in such a short time.

The fact he was headed to a bar with a group of friends and strangers was different. Before, he only talked with Izzy and Dax. And Dax's ex-girlfriend, when she'd been forced upon Reed. And he hadn't missed it. No spotlight. No socializing. No friends.

Now, he missed the interaction. He was ready to put himself back out into the world.

Because of Quinn.

His lungs hitched.

He was in a dance class. An activity he never thought of doing. He was opening himself up to new people and new experiences.

Again, because of Quinn.

His muscles twitched.

He was playing music and composing. Nerves shivered across his skin, because he had to give credit to Quinn for that as well. And what happened if she left Castle Ridge, or dated someone else? What would happen to his music? And his life?

His stomach pitched.

He wanted to swoop her up and carry her back to the dance studio and never let her leave. And then, maybe he could kiss her again.

They entered the bar, gave their drink orders, and settled in.

Reed never thought he'd feel this way again. Lust and desire and... He stopped his thoughts, not wanting to go there, because temptation sat a barstool away.

Leaning closer, he got a sniff of her rose scent.

"I'm thinking of scrapping a building farther down on Main and starting fresh." The man sitting on her other side said. Bob had joined the free classes tonight with his wife.

One thing Reed was comfortable talking to strangers about was historic buildings and remodeling. "A lot of the buildings in town have great bones."

"Plus character," Quinn added. She'd said how she appreciated the structure of the Victorian house the dance studio had been built in.

Speaking of great bones. He smirked and she grinned. "That's true."

He lost track of the conversation for a second, losing himself in the uniqueness of her bright smile. A smile that lifted first one side of her mouth and then the other. The smile spread across her entire face, rounding her cheeks, and putting a glimmer in her gaze.

"What's true?" Bob asked, interrupting Reed's perusal of her beauty.

He focused. "It would be worth having someone appraise your building. See how solid the structure is, and see if you can gut only the insides to make it work for your purpose."

"Good idea." The man nodded in a thoughtful way. "You do that, don't you?"

"I do." Tonight wasn't about making deals. He'd always hated the hard sell. Discussing everything from work to politics to the ski season had been fun. He was enjoying himself.

Another revelation. He'd always liked the people in his hometown. Knew he'd chosen to lick his wounds in Castle Ridge for a reason. He hadn't realized it until now. Even if the music stayed, and he decided to compose, he wouldn't go back to New York.

"Can I get a card?"

He handed the man a business card. "I can give you my opinion."

The man turned to speak to his wife on the other side of him.

Quinn squeezed his arm to get his attention. "How do you do that?" She always held his attention.

"Do what?"

"You have people asking you about your business. You're not selling, and yet you make contacts."

"I wasn't selling, which is why I didn't sound like I was selling." That aspect of his business had always come naturally. He enjoyed architecture and puzzles; talking construction was easy, compared to chit chat. "I was answering a simple question."

"Answering with knowledge." Her eyes sparkled and she squeezed again. His skin ignited at her grasp, and he imagined her squeezing other parts of his body. "I need to learn to do that with the parents of my customers."

"The free classes are a great way to get started." He'd not originally agreed with giving away services, now he understood sampling. She could teach him a few marketing tricks. "Word of mouth will be good."

"The free classes won't be so great for my balance sheet." She slipped her hand from his arm, lingering with her fingers. "Speaking of which, who keeps your books?"

He wanted her fingers to linger longer. Was it a signal she wanted things to begin? Was he ready to say to hell with his brother and go for what he wanted?

Fear paralyzed and his brain short-circuited. He wasn't ready to make big, snap decisions. "I do for the most part. Musicians are good with numbers."

Her expression of surprise had him explaining more.

"I do the inputting and payments and then I have an accountant who reviews things. Why?"

"I need help setting up my books. I've always balanced my own budget and checkbook. Running a business is different."

"I can take a look." He wanted to help her, and he wanted her to succeed. More selfishly, he wanted her to stay in town, and if she was successful, she would.

"Thanks." Her phone buzzed on the bar between them. "Text from Dax."

"What does he want?" The question came out harsh.

She gazed at the message and the harshness traveled down Reed's throat to his midsection. "Dax wanted to wish me luck on my first day of free classes."

"That was yesterday." Reed knew, because he's the one who told his brother what to say *yesterday*.

"It's sweet, and it's the thought that counts."

Except it was *his* thought, not his brother's. His gut grumbled, wanting to take the credit.

"When's he coming home?" Annoying he had to ask when his own brother was coming home. Dax was an adult who didn't need to report to his family, though it would've been nice to know he was leaving town. He'd been sneaking away for a day at a time here and there.

"Do you want me to ask him?" Quinn slipped off the stool taking her phone.

"Sure." Guess he was handling both ends of the conversation. He could sit here and just talk to himself.

"I'll be back in a minute. Save my seat." She headed toward the bathroom.

"How're things going between you and Quinn?" His sister took her place at the bar.

He sent a panicked glance toward Quinn. He didn't want her to hear. She was staring at her phone, waiting for Dax's text. Everything inside soured. "There's nothing going."

His sister nudged him with her elbow. "I see how you look at her. You dance as if you're not injured, and when you move together you're so in sync."

The sourness rose, burning his throat. "Tell that to the guy she's texting."

His sister surveyed the back of the pub. "How am I supposed to tell some random guy?"

"He's not random." Reed found it difficult to breathe. "It's Dax."

"Where *is* Dax?"

Reed shrugged, trying to be casual. "Left town for a few days."

"And he's been texting Quinn the entire time?"

"Only after he texts me and asks what to text her." Reed's bitterness blew out in a quick puff of air. He shouldn't have spilled the secret, except Izzy already knew some of the details.

"What?" She set her mug on the bar with a hard slap. "So you asked Quinn on a date for Dax, and now you're telling him what to text her?"

"Shhh." He peered behind him again, checking she hadn't returned. "I shouldn't have told you."

"I love Dax, but he is self-centered." Nodding, his sister took a sip of beer. "He wouldn't even notice you have feelings for her."

"I don't." Reed wanted to shout the denial. That somehow yelling it from the rooftops would make it true. "I don't."

His sister arched a disbelieving brow and her gaze pinned him down.

He couldn't move, couldn't blink, even while his mind processed. He might be able to lie to his sister, and not very well, but he couldn't lie to himself. He did have feelings for Quinn.

A woman who made him experience things he hadn't in a long time. A woman who pushed him to be more involved and better person. A woman who brought music back into his life.

A woman he wanted but wasn't sure he should pursue.

Chapter Fifteen

Snow fell in large, heavy flakes on the other side of the dance studio window. The flakes dusted the recently-shoveled sidewalk. Several inches had piled up on the grass. Quinn wondered at the dramatic change in scenery. "I can't believe how quickly the snow piles up and how white it is."

"Snow is always white." Reed sat behind the counter with a spreadsheet and pencil, helping her set up accounts on the computer. He looked so studious, with reading glasses, and an extra pencil tucked behind his ear.

She wanted to jump this slightly-nerdy version of Reed, too.

"Not in New York." Twirling from the window to the counter, she let out a satisfied sigh. She didn't miss anything about New York. She was at home here. A completeness filled her, as if her dance card was full. This man had a lot to do with the feeling. She needed him to make the same realization.

"True." His deep laugh rumbled through her.

"There, snow turns gray or black the minute it falls to the ground."

She appreciated their shared background and a shared appreciation for the arts. She'd been a professional dancer, and he'd been a professional musician. Still could be, if he wanted. Her feet went flat on the ground. He could leave Castle Ridge and return to his profession at any time. "Do you think you'd ever go back?"

"To New York?"

"To playing at the symphony. You'd be great."

"No." His adamant tone sent a shiver through her. Maybe he was trapped in his past, unwilling to move forward, to get past whatever scarred him on the inside.

"You will play the piano in front of people again. I know you will." She put confidence in her tone and placed her hand on his, wanting to touch him, wanting him to know she was there for him, wanting him to know she cared.

They'd had fun the night before, socializing in the pub. Reed knew people, was comfortable with people. Why had he ever thought he could be a hermit?

"Thanks for the vote of confidence, but..." He slipped his hand from under hers, and she believed it was a sign. He was slipping away from her. "I don't think I could face strangers staring at me, watching me play."

It was time to be more forward, take drastic measures.

"The music has come back." She snuck down to listen to him every night. He played as if tormented for hours. The music was never as discordant as the night she'd gone down to comfort him, though. The last couple of times, it sounded like a fever flowed in his veins, bringing passion and poetry.

The music sung through her heart and throbbed in her loins.

If he could enrapture her, he could enrapture audiences. Her body tingled, remembering how the tinkling keys played to her emotions. Last night, his music had been soulful and sexual. A tease calling her name.

He tapped a pencil on the spreadsheet. "How many different columns do you want on this account?" His return to business didn't cool her desire. She wanted him, and she'd need to make the first move.

Answering, she slumped into the chair next to him, disappointed he wouldn't talk about his hidden talents, possibly his true calling.

A text message buzzed on his cellphone, sitting on the desktop.

"Excuse me." Standing, he picked up the phone and stretched his leg. He stepped toward the back of the studio.

His secretiveness bothered her. He'd acted weird when his phone had rung the first night of dance class, too. She didn't believe there was another woman in his life. Not from Dax and Izzy's comments about his socializing skills.

"Sorry about that." With red cheeks, he retook his seat and studied the spreadsheet.

Pointing her toes as she sat, she analyzed him. "Anything important?"

"No." He stared at the computer, as if wishing it would do something to distract. "Do you want the office supplies separated from the dance supplies?"

A text chimed on her cell phone.

"Sorry." Sending him an ironic shrug, she clicked on the message from Dax.

Reed shifted in his chair. He shifted again. "Who is it? Anything important?" His questions were similar to hers only seconds ago, except he asked with more intensity.

Maybe if she shared he'd share. Sharing was a start. "It was Dax. He said he won't make it home tonight because of the weather."

Reed's expression darkened. "Did you two have plans?"

Was Reed jealous? A short-lived thrill traveled through her. He'd originally pushed her to date his brother. He'd acted stand-offish and he'd kissed her. His mixed signals had her head spinning and her temper rising. Her heat level rose, too. If he was jealous, it must mean he cared.

"No. We made plans for a follow-up meeting with people from the Main Street Business Association later in the week."

"Is that all my brother said?" He twirled the pencil between his fingers.

She studied him, unsure if she should read exactly what the text said. He stared back, as if he had a vested interest in her communication with his brother.

Her shoulders sagged, not wanting to share. She needed to let Dax know they could only be friends before she seriously pursued his brother. "He wrote a bit of poetry."

"Do you enjoy Dax's—" the brother sitting beside her swallowed "—his way with words?"

Distracted by the manly movement, she shook herself out of the daze. Rereading the short verse to herself, she did like the poem. It wasn't too flowery. There was a lyrical sense to the words. Glancing at Reed, she wished it had come from him.

"Yes, I liked the poetry." She couldn't break things off with Dax over a text. She needed to tell him in person, because she didn't want any bad tension between them, not if she wanted a serious relationship with Reed.

"That's it?" His mouth gaped open.

Too vested in his brother's life.

Was that why he wouldn't pursue things with her? She'd told him she wasn't interested in Dax. After the kiss she and Reed had shared she'd thought he was attracted, and yet, he kept pushing her away. "It's not words that matter, but actions."

Lending a car was an easy thing to do. It didn't take time or effort. Reed had taken care of her when she was injured. He'd helped prepare the studio, going above and beyond his duties in the contract. He'd helped Sara and he'd danced with Quinn.

"Why do you care so much what your brother texts?"

Shrugging, he glanced away, as if he'd been caught doing something wrong. "Wondering how poetic my athletic brother could be." His acidic tone infused he didn't believe his brother could do both.

"You're a man with many talents. Composing, playing piano, construction, accounting." She wondered if his talents extended to the bedroom.

"So?"

"Dax must dance to two different beats. The first night I met him he didn't say much, until later when he came to my window. Like Romeo or Cyrano."

Reed gave her a sharp glare. "You said he was romantic. Much more Romeo." He spun the pencil around his fingers, again and again.

"Dax was sweet." At first, she'd thought he was drunk. "Most of his texts have been romantic and lyrical. Resembling a song."

Dropping the pencil, Reed grabbed for it again. "Guess Dax has picked up a few of my skills."

Angling her head, she studied him. Wariness swirled in her mind, with an edge of suspicion. "Except your brother is not like that in person."

His cheeks flushed and a short-satisfied smile flashed. Ducking his head, he shuffled the spreadsheet, hiding his expression.

Her suspicion grew. What did Reed know that she didn't? She ripped the spreadsheet out of his hands, wanting to watch his face. "I agreed to a date because of what Dax said under my window and texting."

Reed sprang to his feet and limped across the dance floor to stare out the window, as if wanting to escape. Escape from her, or her questioning? "Is no one coming for the adult dance classes tonight?"

Something was wrong, and he wanted it to stay hidden.

Distraction wouldn't work on her. Not unless she

could use his need for distraction to her advantage. She wanted to get close to him again, to have his arms around her, to have his lips on hers. Last time when he wanted to avoid her questions, he'd offered to dance. If she used the same tactic maybe she could at least get another taste of Reed.

The snow had started the night before and continued all day. Only a few people had shown up for the morning toddler classes. After-school activities were cancelled at school, and she'd cancelled the adult class for the evening. It had been the perfect time to work on her accounting program together.

"I cancelled the adult classes." Getting to her feet, she sashayed to his side. She closed the blinds on the window, and turned off most of the lights. If she was going to take what she wanted they'd need privacy. "Bri texted and said she was going skiing. I think a lot of other kids did the same."

"Most of the people in town love to ski." Was that a tinge of sadness?

She brushed his arm and felt his muscles tighten beneath, sensing his sorrow. "Do you miss skiing?"

His head started to shake in the negative direction. He stopped and pursed his lips. "Yes."

His admittance walloped inside her, vibrating in her chest and rattling her heart. His honest answer was a gift. "Maybe you'll ski again someday."

And have a relationship. With her. Her entire body shivered, anticipating the ride. Anticipating his fingers playing her as well as he played the piano.

"Maybe." He wasn't confident, and she hated his doubts.

"I bet dancing could help get you back on the slopes." She trailed her fingers around his arm and placed her hand on his shoulder, unable to resist. The shivering switched to trembling. She needed him, yet she wouldn't rush. At least, not too much. She held back a smile.

His gaze followed her fingers. "How so?"

"Dance is physical therapy." She clicked on the music with the remote. "It helps the body and the mind."

And the heart.

She grasped his other hand and held them out, with straight arms in position for the waltz. Dancing could be a warmup to making love. The touching and caresses. Bodies pressing close. Visualizing had heat pooling at her center. "Put your hand on my waist."

His eyes softened, turning a mossy green. "Quinn, I don't think—"

"We're only going to dance." At least, right now. She pressed his shoulder and smiled encouragingly. "Just dance."

Quinn's lips said *just dance* but her eyes said sex.

And Reed's sex responded, growing hard.

He couldn't stop staring at her mouth. His body drew toward her. Closer. His hand spanned her small waist and tugged her in. The music drifted around them, lifting him into a smooth and steady motion.

A dance wouldn't compromise his relationship with his brother. Although, if she found out the truth about the texting, she'd be upset. Her suspicious questions were getting too close to the truth.

Her crystal-blue eyes stared into his, and the color went deeper with desire. He'd dance with her. He'd help her with her books. He'd do anything she wanted because the attraction sparking between them came together, the individual notes having been transposed to the key of lust.

She called his lyrics poetry. She'd agreed to date Dax because of *Reed's* words. She wanted to dance with him. Not Dax. She'd stated she wasn't interested in Dax. Reed's lungs lightened, like a balloon filled with hope.

He curled their entwined hands, and brought them to his chest. His pulse thumped in tune with the music. She didn't instruct. She let her body lead him around the dance floor. And he followed willingly.

The music slowed. Their bodies drew closer. Tingles shimmered against his skin. Her breasts pressed against him. Streams of desire spiraled through his body. His hard shaft pressed against her most intimate space. She pressed back showing her interest. His entire body thrummed. With her foot between his two feet, their thighs rubbed against each other. They barely moved, holding each other close.

The closeness, the music, and her scent wove around him, creating a haze. A haze where the rest of the world didn't matter. Only the two of them.

She tilted her chin, staring into his eyes. Her body moved in a melody of desire, calling to him. Her plump lips glistened.

One taste. Surely, one taste wouldn't hurt.

When Dax was back in town, Reed would explain.

He lowered his mouth. His lips brushed against her plump ones.

Fireworks.

Their first kiss had been the same, and he'd wondered if it had been the novelty of not kissing anyone in so long. It wasn't. The fireworks exploded again, bursting in his head and igniting in his heart. He never experienced fireworks when he'd kissed his fiancée. He didn't even remember sparks.

These sparks electrified his system, shooting urgency through his veins. He dropped her hand and wrapped his arms around her waist, pressing her closer. He wanted all of her against him.

She moaned. Her lips opened, and his tongue darted inside. He needed to be inside her. To touch and taste and feel. His lips devoured, and his tongue danced in her mouth. His arms held her close, his hands moving across her back, wanting to stroke every inch.

Her slender, deft fingers toyed with the top button of his flannel shirt. She unbuttoned the first, and the next, and the next. Her hands splayed over his bare skin. His heart pounded, as if her fingers connected with the pulse of his body. The imprint of her hands tattooed against his chest.

His body flared and caught fire. She was a flame.

A forbidden flame.

Forbidden.

Chapter Sixteen

Quinn was enraptured by the kiss. A kiss so powerful and lustful and meaningful.

Reed's lips might be kissing her lips, but the connection sizzled to her soul.

The way his mouth swallowed hers. The way his hands roamed her back, trying to caress every inch of her skin. The way his body thrust against hers.

So needy. So urgent. So male.

A shiver rocked her body. Her core pressed against his shaft, and another shiver quaked through her, a mini orgasm. She needed him, wanted him with an urgency she'd never experienced.

Her tongue tangled with his in a dance, a tango. An intimate sashay.

Ecstasy thrummed through her bloodstream, pumping and throbbing and making her need more desperate.

His body stiffened. The action didn't compute in her head. She ran her hands across his shoulders and tried to push the flannel shirt off. His lips pulled off and her mouth starved.

"I can't." The torment in his tone shredded through her. Did he still have feelings for his dead fiancée?

Her ribs tightened, piercing her chest. How was she going to win him from a dead woman? A saint in his mind.

He yanked his hands from her body and she trembled from the loss. Pivoting away from her, his broad shoulders caved in dejection. He slumped onto the piano bench and held his head in his hands.

Her pulse pounded, signaling her body's desire. She wanted Reed, and she needed to convince him he wanted her, too.

She strutted toward the piano and scooted between him sitting on the bench and the instrument at her back. Placing her hands on his arms, she leaned toward him. "Why not?"

He raised his head. His eyes were blank, except for a shimmer around his pupils. Lust, and possibly something more. "We shouldn't."

"We should." She kept her tone light and positive, wanting to convince him to take this one step.

He didn't need guilt, he needed someone to help him get over his dead fiancée. He hadn't been with anyone since her death.

She pushed his flannel shirt off, revealing broad shoulders. He stiffened. Sliding her hand across his carved pecs, she relished the difference between soft skin and hard muscle. Her fingers itched with the need to get to know him.

The shimmering in his gaze brightened with desire. "I want to, but—"

"I want you." She put the honest truth out there, exposing herself to rejection. Holding her breath, she waited for his response.

He pushed her hand away, disgusted. "You slept with my brother." His harsh statement was a cold slap.

She jerked back and dropped her hands to her sides. Her skin stung and burned with temper. Irritation brewed in her stomach, while confusion twisted in her mind. Why would he think that? "No. I didn't. Did Dax tell you we slept together?"

Reed's chin dropped to a disbelieving angle. "I saw his car parked outside the morning after you went skiing. He went to your apartment the night before."

The burning and brewing bubbled into anger. She slammed her palm against his chest, and not because she wanted to touch him. "Do you think I casually have one-night stands?"

"I don't know." His bewildered and honest expression soothed. He'd seen the parked car and jumped to the wrong conclusion.

She firmed her lips. Her glare must've made him rethink his positioning, because he leaned farther back and really studied her, reassessing his original judgment.

They'd only known each other a couple of weeks. They hadn't shared everything about their pasts. Was this the reason he'd been holding back? "Dax let me borrow his car to run errands, because my car is a stick shift and I'd sprained my ankle."

Reed's jaw dropped. His expression changed from accusing to apologetic. "I'm sorry. I assumed...

I should've asked, instead of stew—"

She cut him off with a kiss.

Her lips plundered his. She sank her tongue into his mouth, a miner searching for gold. She found it. Desire tap danced on her soul. She wanted more. She wanted all of him.

Running her hands up and down his chest and abs, she couldn't get enough. She wanted to touch his body. His hands slid up her back, cradled her head, and tousled in her hair. His mouth devoured.

His finger skimmed along her butt, streaking heat to her core. She arched toward him, signaling her desire. She didn't want to take it slow, she wanted him now, before he changed his mind. Her hands went for the button of his jeans, flipped it open, and ran her hands over his hard, denim-covered shaft. He wanted her, too.

Standing, his hands spanned her waist. He picked her up and placed her on the piano. Her butt sat on the keys, creating a song of want. A song that cried out to her. His manhood pressed against her, shooting spirals of desire. He might be thinking of his dead fiancée, but for right now, for tonight, he belonged to her.

He pushed her skirt to her waist and yanked her tights down. The fabric tore, and the noise swooshed with a frantic need. His clever fingers massaged her clit like he massaged a piano keyboard. Fluent, confident, palpitating.

Her womanhood soaked with wetness. So ready.

Wetness seeped between her legs. "I want you." She wanted to be clear. She needed him to know this is what she wanted to happen, planned to happen.

"There's a condom in my purse."

He froze, and she hoped he wasn't rethinking things. "You're sure?"

"Yes." She moaned.

Hurrying across the studio to the counter, he grabbed her purse and fumbled through it. He came back carrying a small foil packet. Using his teeth, he ripped the packet open while his fingers continued to stroke her swollen nib. With one hand, he pushed his pants down. He was in a hurry, and so was she. Waves built inside her, as his fingers played her. Played her like a virtuoso.

And she wanted to sing his name.

Each stroke took her higher, closer to the edge. Her body bucked against the keys, the piano playing the rhythm of their need. Pinpoints of light glittered behind her closed eyelids. She reached for the sky.

And found heaven.

"Reed." Opening her eyes, she panted.

He was practically on top of her. His gaze blazed with his lust. His concentrated expression showed his one and only focus. "I want you."

"I want you now," she demanded needing him to fill her and satisfy her.

He plunged into her and she welcomed. His length filled her, satisfied her again. His movements were hurried and fast. There was no finesse. Only need.

The piano keys clanged and clashed. They played like he played her.

And inside she danced.

✳

Reed couldn't stop his fingers from picking out notes on the keyboard as he thought and agonized. What had he done?

Quinn slept on a couple of blankets on the wooden floor beside him. He'd grabbed the blankets from the backroom right before they'd made love a second time.

What had he done *twice*?

Her angelic expression in sleep appeared quite different from her sinful expression as they'd had sex on the piano, and again on the floor. Both expressions tugged at his heart. Her slender arm was above her head and her long, blonde hair had come undone from the topknot she always wore and splayed around her face.

A catch caught in his lungs.

He'd promised to never open himself up to a woman again. He didn't need to expose himself to more anguish. He didn't want a woman he cared about to learn his faults and deficiencies. For him, the music had always come first.

It was the main thing Elizabeth had hated. She'd come second to his music. And yet, it was because of the music she'd even cared about him. It had taken awhile for him to realize she hadn't loved him, not the real him, she'd loved his reputation and his celebrity. She'd loved attending the galas and concerts and charity fundraisers and being by his side. She'd loved controlling the business aspect of his life, because she hadn't controlled him. His thoughts, his emotions, his music.

And for him, sleeping with someone meant caring.

He didn't do one-night stands. He groaned quietly. Assuming she'd slept with Dax after she'd spent the afternoon at the hospital was stupidity on his part. Quinn wasn't the type of woman to hop in and out of bed with anyone. Everything had happened so fast. He was still in a daze.

Reed watched in fascination, as she pulled her arm down and tucked it under her head. She appeared so innocent and sweet, sleeping on the hard floor as if a child. He should sweep her into his arms and take her to a real bed, except he didn't want to wake her from slumber.

He couldn't sleep after they'd made love a second time. His body and mind were too restless. He'd pulled on his pants and moved to the piano because it called to him. Like she called to him.

Doubts about what they'd done pummeled inside his ribcage. Had she enjoyed herself, or had he gone too fast? Had she made love with him because she'd felt sorry for him? Or because she was lonely, stranded in a mountain town during a snowstorm? Or because he'd been famous at one time?

Reed plucked a finger onto a harsh key. He wanted to slam his hands down, but didn't want to wake her. He wasn't ready to talk about what had happened between them.

His fingers padded lightly on the keyboard, picking out the tune he'd been working on since they'd met. She'd brought music back into his life, and his biggest fear was she'd take it with her when she left him. He couldn't stop the thought from replaying in his brain.

"I love hearing you play." A yawn accompanied her, stretching out the last word and stoking his yearning for her.

"You only heard me play once, and not very well." He'd been so upset that night.

"I've heard you play more." She blushed and she looked even more angelic. "Almost every night when you play late."

"I'm sorry. I didn't realize the sound traveled to your apartment." Didn't realize he'd had an audience, even if it was up a staircase and through walls.

Standing, she wrapped the blanket around her naked body and disappointment buzzed in his bloodstream. "It doesn't. I open the doors and sit at the top of the stairs and listen."

His heart slipped like a glissando. A falling and falling and falling experience rushed in his chest. He'd had an audience all along. An audience of one who'd heard his tortured emotions played out on the piano. His feelings for her and his jealousy of his brother, his guilt about when his fiancée had died and how he could've done more. Should've done more.

"I especially loved one piece that had such passionate power." She appreciated his music, understood it. Understood him.

He fisted his hands, not wanting her to know everything about him. He had too much baggage.

He knew which piece she referred to, though. There was only one he'd poured passion and lust and desire into. The one he'd written about her. The urge to play the song for her, to watch her expression as she listened, couldn't be denied.

"This one?" Taking a deep breath, he placed his fingers on the keys and played the melody he was composing.

The music flowed through his veins and his body swayed to the tune. The song was about attraction and desire. The melody brought to mind fantasies of being with Quinn.

A fantasy come true.

Her blanket-covered body plopped on the bench beside him. Her warmth permeated his bare arms. He wanted to cuddle beneath the blanket with her. Continuing to play, he didn't need sheet music. He played from memory, and altered chords to suit his emotions.

She squeezed his forearm with a gentle grasp. "You must have loved your fiancée very much."

His hands crashed onto the keys. The music stopped. His fingers went numb.

His heart pounded in an off-beat rhythm. His mind went into a fugue, with crashing chords and uncompleted melodies. He racked his mind, sorting through the chaos, to find a reason why Quinn would believe the statement enough to say it twice.

A confession warped on the tip of his tongue. He hadn't answered her last time. If he told her, she might be disgusted with what he'd done. She'd assumed since he was engaged it was about love. Not sharing the truth wouldn't be fair. Not to Quinn. He needed her to know the truth, to know the real him. "I didn't love her at all."

Quinn rubbed her hand up and down his arms. The gesture meant to comfort incited instantaneous desire. "She was your fiancée. Of course, you loved her."

Quinn spoke as if that said everything. Except his relationship with Elizabeth had been complicated and twisted from the beginning. She'd discovered him and had helped his career. They were together constantly, and one thing had led to another. Everyone assumed they were a couple, including her.

And he'd been okay with it. He was too busy to date other women. Elizabeth helped him with his scheduling, made sure his tux was cleaned, and got him to the appropriate venues. When she'd pointed at a ring she'd wanted in a store, he bought it for her. It hadn't appeared to be an engagement ring, with its sapphire stone.

Everyone assumed it was. Including Elizabeth. "I never proposed."

He'd gone along with it, taken the less-resistant path because he was busy and the music played and she was there for him.

"Yet you were engaged?"

"For eleven months." Eleven agonizingly long months.

At first it hadn't been so bad. Things had continued as before. He worked and she scheduled. Then, she pressured him to set a date for the wedding. He would have eventually, but he'd had concerts to perform and music to write. Things were fine as they were, and he was in no hurry. As time passed, she'd become more demanding toward his colleagues, making him appear to be a diva. When it had been her demands. She started flying into rages and drinking too much.

"I'd known I had to break it off with her for a while. She seemed desperate. Drinking too much. Taking drugs." His gut clenched. He hadn't seen the signs at first. Or had he been too obtuse to notice? "I didn't want to make her health situation worse by breaking our engagement."

Quinn placed her hand on his thigh in a comforting gesture. "You cared for her."

"Yes." Sighing, he let his emotions about Elizabeth untangle in his head. He had feelings for Elizabeth, just not those of love. He cared about her, respected her in the beginning, counted on her. They were a good, sensible couple. He'd thought this was love. "The night of the accident, I'd had enough. She'd embarrassed me in front of the symphony director, so I broke off our engagement at a major sponsor party." His throat went dry. "She begged me to keep it quiet until after the symphony's gala."

"That was five years ago." Quinn angled her head and her brow furrowed. "The ballet performed at the gala. We might've met that night."

"I didn't stay to see the ballet." He smiled slightly, until the darkness of the night hit him like a crack of thunder.

Elizabeth hanging on him and talking obscenely loud about money and contracts, spilling a glass of red wine on the conductor's white tuxedo shirt, stumbling toward the bar and accosting more people in the process.

"Elizabeth and I left the event early. I couldn't let her drive herself home." Grasping his head in his hands, he placed his elbows on the keyboard and the discordant notes clanged.

Quinn grasped his chin in a firm hold and lifted his head to face her. "You were a good guy and wanted to take care of her." It was amazing how Quinn twisted everything to make him sound good.

"I'm no hero." The blackness on his soul darkened. He gripped her hand. "I should've called an ambulance. Instead, I took her keys and planned to drive her home and leave her at her apartment." The horror of the entire evening clashed in his head. His breath shallowed, and he found it difficult to take in air. The only thing holding him to reality was grasping Quinn's hand. "Elizabeth tried to get in my pants while I was driving. I couldn't control her. She grabbed the wheel by accident. I hit the gas instead of the brake." Sweat formed on his bare back, and yet, shivers chased down his spine. He'd shared bits and pieces of the accident, but never told Quinn the full story. "We crashed."

"Oh, my God. That's terrible." Quinn wrapped her other arm around his shoulders and pressed him against her body. The comfort she provided soothed some of the pain. "And in no way your fault."

Her strong belief in him made him stronger, made him believe there was chance at redemption. His complete confession made his hope soar with thoughts of a future. A future with Quinn.

The following evening at the adult dance class, Reed couldn't wait to hold Quinn in his arms again, even if it was only dancing. He could anticipate a different type of dance later. Her body fit snugly into him, as if she was his other half. Her warmth and goodness made him believe some of her charm would rub off on him. He enjoyed being in her presence.

Several other couples swayed to the music as the class practiced what they'd learned last time. Izzy and Edward, who had his hands a little too close to her butt. Danielle and Parker. A few other couples he knew from town.

He barely noticed them. He only had eyes for the woman he held in his arms. Her goodness came through in the way she spoke. Her caring showed in the way she instructed. Her happiness for life beamed from within.

He twirled Quinn around in a perfect circle, amazed at his dancing progress and progress in himself. "How are you feeling tonight?"

"A little sore from laying on the floor." Her gaze flickered with amusement, and she gave him a saucy smile. "And the piano."

He gave a sidelong ogle at the instrument. "I will never think of that piano in the same way again."

She laughed, and the sound drew him further in. It was one of the things he found so attractive. She found joy in many things. "In a good way, I hope. No more kicking."

"In a hot way." He twirled her again. "Who knew pianos could be so sexy?"

"Who knew piano players could be so sexy?"

Their laughter mingled like their bodies, heating each other, drawing each other closer. After last night, they'd jumped another octave into total harmony.

"Wow, Reed. You look amazing on your feet."

Danielle sidled next to them, with an uptight Parker in her arms. Her expression appeared content, not radiant. Parker wasn't the spark in her life. Or that special someone.

He glanced at Quinn, whose face glowed, as if her spark had been lit. By him. "All thanks to her."

Did he glow with everything he was experiencing? Could people tell something significant had happened between them? He didn't know what to call whatever this was. He didn't want to categorize, for fear of putting too much into what happened.

He spoke louder. "Thanks to Quinn's amazing dance instruction."

She blushed and missed a step. "Let's take a break, class."

Reluctantly, he let go of her hand, and let his other hand slide from her waist. He'd worked on his house today, missing her the entire time. The urge to speed up the remodel had overtaken him, because he wanted to show his home to her in the best possible light. A tremble ran through his body. He wanted the home to be perfect, unlike his body. In a way, compensation.

Sauntering to the area by the counter, Quinn sipped from her water bottle. He remembered those lips on him and his body rocked harder.

"How's it going?" The nudge-nudge in his sister's tone told him Izzy had her suspicions. She handed him a paper cup filled with water.

"Gooood." Did he sound too happy? "How about you?"

"Fine. Waiting on Parker to officially inform me I'll

be the next head chef at The Heights." She took a sip and gazed at him over the rim. "Have you heard from Dax?"

Reed swallowed down the water. "No." The rocking of lust halted and morphed into a quake of guilt. He'd slept with Quinn before telling Dax of his feelings. As soon as he got home, Reed would tell him about the relationship. Let his brother know Quinn belonged to him.

She moved toward him with a smile, and his skin tingled, anticipating her reaching him and coming into his arms. "Quinn said Dax's trip was delayed because of the storm."

"Quinnnnnn." Izzy eyes glinted. "What's going on between you two?"

He shut down his emotions, not ready to tell anyone about what had happened. "Nothing."

Quinn's lips flatlined. Had she heard?

"Hey." He jumped over to her, all energy and nerves. His fiancée would've thrown a tantrum if he'd denied they had a relationship. That's how he'd discovered she thought they were engaged. He grabbed Quinn's hand, trying to communicate with the connection. "What's next?"

"I was going to ask you the same question." Her eyebrows wiggled, and she flashed a teasing grin. She'd heard and wasn't mad.

He blew out a relieved breath.

"My brother is dancing marvelously." Izzy hip-checked him. "What did you do?"

"Private lessons." Quinn's teasing tone combined with a deep husk, shooting straight to his groin.

Just a laugh, a tease, or a purr from her, and he was a goner. But a happy one.

She clapped her hands to get everyone's attention. "Get back with your partners, everyone. We're going to start the second dance. It will be a tango."

He whisked her into his arms and dipped her down with a flourish. He whispered, "I'd love another private lesson tonight." His boldness surprised him. He hadn't acted with this much bravado since high school, since before his career took off.

Quinn's chuckle hit him in the groin again. He didn't know if he could make it until later tonight. He might embarrass himself right here. He was behaving like he used to. Having fun, being social, letting the music flow in his head. Quinn brought this back into his life. Maybe he could have this, and her, in his life forever.

The stereo system died, the music sputtering to a halt.

"Sorry everyone." Quinn slipped from his arms. She clicked on the remote, trying to restart the music. "There are a few kinks in the system."

"I'll take a look." Taking the remote, he moved to the stereo system housed in a shelving unit on the wall. The manual sat beside the box. He flipped through it, reading the varying reasons for the system to be erratic. Wiggling wires, he found a missed connection and reconnected it.

The music came back on. People clapped.

"The stereo system will work for now. I'll read the manual later tonight to figure out a permanent fix." He took his position at her side.

"I thought I was giving you a private lesson later tonight." Her voice oozed with sex and something more.

"You sure can, Private Dancer." He couldn't wait for class to end.

Chapter Seventeen

Candlelight shimmered and scented the bedroom with a floral smell. The bed was fitted with sexy, silk sheets. Sheets Reed couldn't wait to slide around on. A bottle of wine chilled on the nightstand, two glasses side by side. Classical crossover music played on small speakers. Quinn had set the mood for romance.

A pang shredded through him that he couldn't identify. Fear or anticipation? Rolling his shoulders, he knew he anticipated the sex. It was the romance that had him worried.

Quinn posed at the doorway leading from the bathroom, wearing the same peach camisole and shortie-shorts she'd worn the first night. The night she'd gotten soaked helping him with the leak and his lust had reared its head.

My, how their relationship had changed.

From antagonistic to friends. From friends to lovers. From lovers to…

He froze. His thoughts tornadoed, spinning and spinning until he forced them to stop. He didn't want to analyze what they had or were to each other. He just wanted to love her body, make her feel good, persuade her to orgasm. Last night, both times had been rushed. Tonight, he'd take his time. Savor and sample.

Her long hair hung past her shoulders brushing the top of her breasts. The thin spaghetti straps of the camisole could be easily torn off. The skimpy outfit tucked in, emphasizing her slim waist and long, slender legs.

Taking her all in, his head spun again. "Wow."

"You're overdressed." She strolled toward him, tempting and desirous.

After class, he'd hurried back to his apartment across the hall and thrown the stereo system manual on his coffee table, too much in a hurry to read the boring technical information. He'd brushed his teeth and put on more deodorant and aftershave. He'd grabbed one, no three, condoms, having high hopes for the night.

When he'd bought the extra-large box of condoms at the convenience store, the male clerk had given him a high-five. He was doing what any normal male would do. He was normal.

His spirits rose even higher and he teased, "Do you want to undress me or shall I?" He flicked the first button on his shirt.

"Oh, I want to watch." She perched on the bed. Crossing her dancer's legs, she smiled a secretive, sexy smile. A smile saying she awaited the pleasure of the evening.

With nimble fingers, he undid the buttons on his

shirt. He might want to make love slow, but he wanted to get naked fast.

"Slower." Her order caused his motions to stop. He wasn't used to talking and teasing and tantalizing while having sex. With Elizabeth it had been a scheduled appointment, and they'd lost any spontaneity and fun. "I want to anticipate the unveiling of such a fine specimen of manhood."

His chest rose and his cock twitched, rearing to go. She thought he was a fine specimen? From construction he had nice arms and broad shoulders. And from constant physical therapy his waist was narrow and his thighs muscular. Since the accident, he'd never considered himself good-looking. He was too big and brawny.

While Quinn was slender and petite. Last night he'd worried about crushing her delicate frame. Until he realized how strong she was. She didn't possess an ounce of fat. Her flexible legs had twisted into incredible positions he'd only dreamed about. His shaft hardened and grew.

"Why'd you stop?" Her demanding question brought him out of his fantasy and back to the moment.

Except every second of tonight was a fantasy.

He flicked the rest of the buttons and tugged off his shirt, pretending to dry his back, sliding the material back and forth and flexing his muscles. During sex with Elizabeth, he'd gone through the motions, his mind sometimes wandering back to the music.

Quinn's pupils dilated, and her eyes softened with desire. Her mouth opened slightly as if already tasting him.

Feeling silly and turned on, he tossed the shirt in her direction. When she stretched to catch it, her breasts jiggled, and he noted the nipples through the fabric. A thrill spiraled through him. His striptease was working.

He straightened and shot her what he hoped was a sexy grin. He unsnapped the button on his jeans and teased the zipper down, back up, down again. He held a laugh in until she licked her lips, her gaze glued to his manhood jutting out from his boxers. The laugh escaped in a slow sizzle.

"Are you always this slow of an undresser?" The teasing question edged with impatience. She wanted him naked.

His shaft surged. He wanted both of them naked, and him on top of her. Except good things came to those who waited. He wanted to please and pleasure her, first.

"You told me to go slow. You don't like?" He twirled around, similar to how she often did in the studio. Bending, he wiggled his jeans over his hips.

"Oh, I like. I'd just like it a little faster." The breathless mewl she made had his pulse picking up pace.

"Fast was last night." He yanked the jeans and kicked them off from around his feet. His long socks and underwear were the only thing left. The socks, covering his mangled ankle, wouldn't come off. "Tonight is about slow."

She leaned back on the bed with a come-hither expression. Her perky breasts tipped up in the air. She uncrossed her legs, giving him a glimpse of paradise. "How slow can you go?"

"I can go all night." The brag was optimistic. The way she devoured him with her eyes, he could *go* at any moment.

"Then, let's get started." She flopped back onto the bed, her body displayed for him.

Only him.

Possessiveness grabbed onto him. He couldn't let her go. He was in lo—

Lust.

He was in lust, *dammit*. If he fell in love, he might think of devastating loss, and if he thought about losing Quinn, he'd freeze at this important moment. He didn't want to lose Quinn tonight. He'd think about tomorrow and the future another day.

Stripping off his boxers, he joined her on the bed. He lay beside her and snuck a hand inside the peach camisole. His hand thumbed her nipple, pleased when it pointed higher. "Where do you want me to start?"

"There's good." She ended on a moan as he fondled her.

His cock hardened to a rod. "Second position?" He'd learned a few things from her. "Or as we called it as teens, second base."

"You should take my camisole off." Her coy-suggestiveness pleased him.

"Should I?" He dropped his mouth on her breast through the silky material. His tongue laved first one, and then the other, breast. "Do you still want the camisole off?"

"Yessss." She hissed.

"Too bad." His shaft throbbed at the sexy sounds

she made. "The texture of the material is so soft." He pinched her nipple and her body jolted. "So sensual." His hand slid to her waistline and grazed the skin peeking between the top and bottom. "So wet." His hand went lower, between her legs.

Her body pushed against his hand. She squirmed. "Please, Reed."

His movements paused, dragging out the sexual tension. "Please, Reed, what?"

"Please, touch me." Her words nearly undid him.

Through the silk, he caressed her most sensitive spot. Wetness pooled on the material throwing off the muskiness of sex. The sparks she must be feeling ignited an answering spark inside him.

He had to taste her.

Dragging off the silk shorts, he tossed them in the air. They landed around the bottle of wine they'd not had an opportunity to drink. They were both already drunk with their lust.

Raising her long, flexible, amazing legs, he draped them over his shoulders, positioning his mouth at her entrance. His tongue laved the delicate, swollen nib, and she tasted like sweet marmalade.

At first touch, her butt raised off the bed. "Oooooh."

Her purr curled through him, lighting an urgent fire. He reined himself back, because he'd promised slow. "My turn for commands. Say my name."

"Reeeeeed." She stretched his name out and it ended on a high note.

The fire flamed, engulfing him in an inferno. "A

divisi is when musical parts are split or divided. When you say my name, I will lick."

"What?" Her wispy tone suggested she was coming out of a desirous haze.

"You set the tempo by saying my name." He tasted her. "Say my name."

"Reed."

Flaring, he licked and sucked in control of her. Needing her to want him as badly as he wanted her. "Say it."

"Reed."

The heat ignited to an inferno. He sucked. "Again."

"Reed." She panted. "Reed." Her voice grew higher. Her body jerked and swayed with the movement of his tongue and mouth.

His cock urged release with his own wetness, his body responding to her taste and her call. And his possession.

"Reed, Reed, Reed."

Every time she said his name he licked and sucked and fire scorched inside him. He felt her nub swell and fill with need. She pushed her clit against him, wanting more and faster. His tongue was getting a workout.

"Reed, Reeeeed, Reeeeeed!" She screamed his name. Her body bucked, and spasmed, and rocked. "Oh, Reed."

The fire incinerated, and power exploded through him. He'd done that. Made her scream his name. Made her come. Made her feel good.

Peeking up, he watched her expression. Her skin glowed. Her mouth opened slightly and she panted.

The muscles on her face relaxed. Her lips turned up in the most beatific smile.

The smile was the final ovation.

Quinn's orgasm continued to rock her body. She lay back on the bed, experiencing the aftereffects. Her body was languid. Her mind mush. But her heart…

Her heart stepped in an unfamiliar dance.

His emerald eyes stared from between her legs. She should've been embarrassed at the position, instead she felt satisfaction and fulfillment and need.

Always the need. "Reed."

"You want more?" His pleased chuckle made her giddy.

"You're awfully pleased with yourself." She rubbed his thick, dark hair.

"I'm awfully pleased with you." He helped her remove her legs from his shoulders and he crawled up her body and gave her a kiss on the mouth. "You are amazing."

Her inner glow brightened. He played her body like she was an instrument attuned to only him. "You make me amazing."

And it was true. Similar to an apprentice with a principal dancer, he'd mastered her. Made her experience things she never had before, made her the best she could be. He did the same in everyday life. She was a better teacher and a better businessperson because of him.

The soft gleam in his eyes showed his pleasure at pleasing her. The mischievous glint told her he wasn't done with her yet. The glow intensified, restarting her desire. She wasn't done with him yet, either.

After putting on a condom, he poised above her, his hands taking the weight of his body. His legs were positioned between hers, and his tip twitched at her entrance. Wetness pooled between her legs and her need spiked.

His gaze bore into hers. "I want to make you feel amazing again."

His tip nudged and a new spasm shocked her body. His manhood slid into her, filling her, making her more complete, more satisfied, more whole.

He moved in a slow tempo, each thrust had her clenching around him wanting to keep him inside, wanting to please him like he'd pleased her. Tiny spasms quaked, growing stronger and stronger.

Her fingers traced the muscles on his back. Strong, carved shoulder blades, muscular waist, hardness everywhere. He was so much bigger than her, she should've been worried or threatened. Instead, she felt protected and revered.

He picked up the tempo, his movements faster and his body straining. She loved how she could make him feel this way, which made her feel good. Pleasure reciprocity. He slid back and forth, caressing her already-excited clit. His body tightened and went rigid. He shot to the stars.

The quakes became a full blown earthquake. Clinging to him, she flew right along with him. To the stars and back. Now and forever.

Forever.

The word conga-ed in her chest. She wanted forever with Reed. He centered her and brought her home. He was her home. She loved him.

Truly loved Reed.

The word tattooed on her heart in a *tap-tap-tap* dance. Her pulse tripped the light fantastic. The realization larger than her earlier orgasm. Excited and afraid. Joyous and wary. Reed was a wounded bear. Would he run and hibernate if she confessed?

The realization she was falling had hit her earlier. Tonight with his teasing and playfulness, with his caring and caressing, with his tenderness, she knew for sure. She loved Reed and wanted to spend the rest of her life with him.

He collapsed on top of her and then slid to her side keeping his arm around her middle. Keeping her safe.

But was her love safe? Did they have a future together, or was she only the woman who'd gotten him past the fear of socializing with the opposite sex? The woman who'd helped him forget his dead fiancée for a little while?

Chapter Eighteen

Stretching in bed the following morning, Quinn reveled in the heat of Reed's naked body sleeping next to her. It was a chilly, late fall morning and yet the blankets and sheets were smashed at the bottom of the bed. She didn't need another source of warmth.

The scent of sex, burnt candles, and Reed's unique manly smell blended in a sultry tango. She felt languid and slow, and didn't really want to get out of bed. She did want a chance to study the man she loved. Slowly moving into a sitting position, she scanned his body.

He slept on his back with his hands tucked behind his head, an Adonis waiting to be awakened. Black curly hair swirled around his peaceful face. His tender expression displayed none of his regular tension or anxiety. She hoped she'd contributed to the look.

His strong mouth was open slightly, and she was tempted to give him a good-morning kiss. The skin on his arms and legs was darker than the midsection of his body. He must work outside in shorts and short-sleeved shirts in the summer. She couldn't wait to see that. Strong neck led to broad shoulders and carved pecs. A smattering of dark hair led from his chest, past his abs, to where his cock lay between his legs.

Lust heated her, remembering how he'd made her come alive last night.

Her gaze continued its path down muscular thighs and strong calves. And stopped at his sock-covered feet. He'd made love and slept with his socks on. Her pulse quickened because she instinctively knew why.

His scarred ankle.

She grasped the edge of the material between her fingers and tugged the sock off. She drew in a sharp breath. He must've suffered so much pain.

The reddish skin was raised around the entire ankle and heel of the foot. Multiple white slashes mottled the thicker skin. Ragged edges surrounded each of the scars. She couldn't tell if the scars were from the accident or surgeries afterward. The ankle wasn't formed correctly and the angle where it attached to the foot wasn't ninety degrees.

Empathy pains ripped through her own feet and ankles. Feet she'd abused with decades of toe shoes and *en pointe* dancing. She remembered her agony. And yet, the pain he experienced must've been a hundred times worse. She wanted to kiss and make it feel better.

Bending at the waist, she placed a kiss at the junction of a particularly nasty scar.

"What're you doing?" His stone-cold voice snapped her back to sitting position. His expression went from sleepy-shock to anger, as if he'd been awakened suddenly from a good dream. He snatched his foot and tucked it beneath his other calf.

She wrapped her hand around his ankle and tried to pull it from hiding. "I'm kissing your scars to make them better." She kept her tone light, using a Mom-kissing-an-owie tone.

He struggled to keep his foot hidden. "Don't. It's ugly."

She yanked his foot out and bent to kiss the scarred ankle again. "The scars show character." She kissed again. "And strength." She kissed again. "And bravery." She kissed one more time, wanting to prove she wasn't grossed out.

His foot jerked. "Stop. My feet are ticklish."

"I'm kissing your ankle." She placed her lips down again and used her tongue to swirl a pattern on his skin. An answering pattern of desire shimmied inside of her.

"You're touching my feet."

"So I need to kiss higher?" Her voice dropped to a husky level. She lowered her head and kissed his calf. "Or higher still?" She licked a trail from his calf to his knee.

The muscles in his calf tightened. "There are no scars on my knees."

"No?" She raised her head and sent him a grin. "How about your thigh?" She wriggled up his body, leaving tracks of small kisses up his leg. Her body tingled with each graze of her mouth on his skin. Exciting him, exciting her.

His breathing shallowed and his legs flopped open,

giving her room to maneuver. "I think other parts of my body need your ministrations."

His heavy-lidded eyes and his slightly open mouth expressed his lust.

"Do they?" She waited, wanting him to wonder, would she or wouldn't she?

He shifted and his cock caught her attention. Already it was bigger and rock hard.

A sense of awe filled her. She'd done that. With a look and a caress and a suggestive tease. She'd aroused men before. With Reed it was different, because she loved him and wanted to imprint herself on his soul. Was he ready for a serious relationship?

Her fingers cruised up his shaft. So soft, so smooth, so different than the rest of his body.

He moaned and she wondered how he tasted.

She slid her hand down to his balls and to the top of his cock. His member twitched and grew. Power, womanly power, charged through her body and excited. She was the one leading this dance with the man she planned to be her last partner.

"Do you want my kiss now?" She positioned her mouth above his head and blew.

His mouth dropped open and his sultry-green eyes closed. The muscles on his face tightened and his lust raised her desire. "Yes." He spoke in ragged tones.

She tasted him. Just a quick lick.

"Oh, man." The words were more of a grunt.

"I'm not a man," she teased.

"I know. I know. I know." His body rose and his voice went higher.

Her mouth wrapped around his wet tip. She slid

her tongue up and down enjoying the sensation and control. She could stop at any time. She didn't want to stop. She wanted to please him as he'd pleased her last night. Anticipation quivered across her spine. Her hand went to his balls and gave a squeeze.

His legs flexed and tightened.

Seeing his body stretched out in ecstasy caused her own body to react. Moisture pooled in at the juncture of her thighs. Her mouth went up and down, and her bones liquefied. His excitement spurred her excitement. She moved faster. He grabbed her hair and threaded his fingers through the strands.

His entire body went taut and bucked. He shouted her name, "Quinn!"

Reed didn't want to leave the paradise of Quinn's bed. Holding her close, he felt the beat of her heart. He smelled her rose scent mixed with the muskiness of sex. He wanted to snuggle with her and stay in bed all day. Music played in his head, adding to his pleasure, and also adding to the song he was composing about his emotions for Quinn. The piece wasn't quite done, just as their relationship wasn't completely defined.

He dropped a kiss on the top of her head, needing to communicate his love. His inner voice sung like a tenor. His chest clutched tight and released.

He loved Quinn.

His mind and body stilled. His heart punched, then punched again.

He'd vowed to never love, to never even have a relationship again. And yet, with Quinn, it was different. He'd never loved Elizabeth, and he'd felt horrible about her death. He'd been even more devastated by the loss of his music. Quinn had brought the music back into his life.

She snuggled closer to his body, as if sensing his mind's panic and withdrawal. Her warm body heated him from the inside. He loved being with her, making love or talking. Her blonde hair splayed around her head, resembling an angel's halo. Her mouth pouted in a just-been-devoured moue. Her eyelashes fluttered and settled, implying she only needed to be closer to him.

His body thawed and he calmed, although his pulse sped with the knowledge of his love. He could trust her with his love. He could trust her.

Even though they'd only known each other for a few weeks, she'd brought him out from his cave. Made him feel again. Made him hear music and want to play and compose. He'd shared his terrible secrets and he knew she wouldn't tell anyone. She'd been sympathetic to his internal torture, empathized with his scars and limp, wanted to help him improve and get better. Become whole.

She stretched beside him and her eyes blinked several times before opening. A molasses-slow smile spread on her face and heated him. "After a fantastic night, why are you frowning?" She wrapped her arm around his neck and brought him in for a kiss.

It had been a great night and a great early morning. And it was going to be an even better day. No, a lifetime with her. He couldn't profess his love now. She had classes and he had a song to finish. And then there was his brother.

"Just thinking." Maybe once the song was complete he could play it for her and tell her of his love.

"About?" She kissed him again, and his thoughts flew out of his head.

All he could think of was her lips on his, her body pressed against him. "Now? About you." He murmured against her mouth, and deepened the kiss with his tongue.

A chiming interrupted.

She broke off the kiss and glanced at the phone on the bedside table. "Remind me to turn off my phone when we're in bed."

His cock sprung to life, thinking about the next time they'd be in bed together and giving him hope for the future. Their future. "Whoever it is, they're persistent."

Her phone continued to chime.

"Too persistent." Her frustrated tone was adorable.

He wanted to continue the kiss, even though music poured through his mind and he wanted to capture the chords while fresh. The realization blasted an entire orchestra in his mind. "I should go, anyhow. Plus, don't you have toddlers coming to dance?"

She kissed him on the corner of his mouth. "I could forget about dancing if I can stay in your arms."

"I'd never want you to forget or give up your passion."

Her gaze brightened, and a huge smile lit her face, realizing what he meant. "You are wonderful. I'd never want you to give up your passion, either." She dropped a kiss on his mouth.

It wasn't a come-hither kiss, more of a kiss of gratitude and likeability. And he hoped more.

Nerves jangled in his stomach, similar to the constant chiming of her phone. What if she didn't feel the same? He had to keep things light. He wasn't ready to confess his love. It was too soon. "If you keep kissing me, I'll forget you need to dance and we'll do a more intimate rhumba right here in this bed."

"You are so poetic. No wonder you're a composer." Her chin angled and she considered him. "You need to write these words down and put them into a song. Become a composer again."

He warmed, because he'd started the process, and couldn't wait to get back to the keyboard he'd dug out of the garage. "Maybe I will."

Maybe he wouldn't. He didn't want to share his music with anyone except her. He didn't want to disappoint her right now with negativity.

She climbed out of bed and strutted toward the bathroom. His cock protested. He shouldn't have hurried her out of bed so quickly.

He forced himself to move. "I should go back to my place and shower." And write.

Since being with Quinn he couldn't turn off the music. The melody was in his head as he worked his construction jobs, with him when he danced with her, and with him as they performed a more intimate dance. She'd tapped into his creative side, bringing it back to life with her joy and her caring. With her intelligence and her warmth.

A shiver of apprehension slid down his spine. If she left him, would the music leave him too? He realized he couldn't doom a relationship before it started. He loved her and he hoped she cared for him. He needed to finish his song expressing his true feelings, and plan on spending the rest of his life with her.

After throwing on his clothes, Reed crossed the hall to his apartment. The door was unlocked. He opened the door and the smell of cooking eggs greeted him. Dax stood in the tiny kitchen, making breakfast.

Reed's initial surprise dropped into dread. He needed to tell his brother about himself and Quinn.

"Glad you made yourself at home." He shut the door with a bang.

Dax dropped by his apartment all the time. Both he and Izzy had keys. Usually the dropping by wasn't a surprise, though, because Reed was always home.

"You were up and away early this morning." His brother wore a knit beanie, hiding his long hair. His eyes appeared bloodshot and shadowed. "Want some eggs?"

His brother had assumed Reed had left the apartment early instead of being out all night. Yet, Dax's appearance suggested he hadn't slept. Immediate sympathy clogged Reed's lungs. "Sure."

He spotted his music sheets on the coffee table. Panic jolted his limbs. Quinn's song. He glanced at his brother and back at the papers. Had his brother seen the sheets? Seen her name at the top? The jolting buzzed his brain. Read them?

His emotions bled into every chord and key. His thoughts about her flowed in every word. He poured his love into the song, even before realizing he was in love.

Shuffling to the coffee table, he snatched up the papers and tucked the telling white sheets into the first thing he spotted. The stereo-system repair manual. "I need to clean my apartment."

"Your place is always spotless." Dax's place was always a mess.

Blowing out a breath, Reed moved to the small kitchen and poured himself a cup of coffee, glad to have a mundane motion to put his nerves at rest. "Where have you been the last few days?"

"Utah." Dax mumbled and ducked his head.

Reed's shoulders dropped. Where Flirty-Phoebe lived. This woman had his brother wrapped around her finger. Their on-again, off-again relationship had Dax swinging like a yo-yo. "How did it go?"

His cheeks went red and he yanked his hat off. "It didn't."

Reed's sorrow increased, because he now knew real love. How it lifted you higher and made everything right with your world. He clapped his brother on the back. "I'm sorry."

His brother saluted him with his flirtatious-smarmy smirk. A smirk saying he was about fun and didn't take much seriously. "Which is why I texted Quinn this morning and asked her out."

Quinn read Dax's texts with wariness. His words were pure poetry speaking of love in a lyrical fashion. If the text had come from Reed she'd be ecstatic. Frowning, she realized he'd never spoken any words of love, or even like.

She barely knew Dax. There was no possible way he felt the words he'd texted. His mind seemed to be somewhere else. As was hers. She'd hinted they could only be friends. He wasn't taking the hint. She needed to speak straight and tell them nothing could ever happen between them.

She turned on the stereo system before her first class. No sound came out. She needed to have an expert repair the system, not have Reed jerry-rig it together. Glancing at her watch, she'd have enough time to run up to his apartment to grab the system manual, and a quick kiss, and call the warranty number on the manual before class started.

Dashing up the stairs, she couldn't believe how much she anticipated seeing Reed again. She'd been with him less than an hour ago, and already missed him. She wanted to know he was going to be there at the end of every day. That they'd eat dinner together and talk about their day. That he'd help her and she'd support him. That they'd make love every night.

After knocking and being told to come in, she opened the door. "I've only got a second to grab the stereo manual and give you a quick ki—"

Dax slouched against the counter separating the small kitchen from the main living area. A couch and coffee table separated them. "A quick answer to my question?"

"Dax." The lightness inside her evaporated, and her feet slid to a halt. She twisted her fingers together in a nervous dance. "What're you doing here? Where's Reed?"

Had he told Dax about their relationship? And if he

did, what had Reed told his brother? Because she knew their connection was more than a friendly affair.

"He's in the shower." Dax paced toward her on the hunt. "Did you get my texts?" He ran a finger down her bare arm.

And she felt nothing but a friendly touch, a brotherly touch. "Um, yes. I did." Swallowing, she tried to figure out a way to let him down gently without causing a rift between him and his brother. Obviously, Reed hadn't said anything about their love affair.

"Well?" Dax's green orbs, so similar to his brother's, rounded with hopefulness, and what appeared to be a flash of desperation.

"I'm super busy right now." She jerked her arm away and picked up the stereo system manual to distract. "Got a class starting in a couple of minutes." She'd have a room full of expectant toddlers and mothers in less than five minutes. It wouldn't be fair to blurt out the truth and hurry downstairs. She wouldn't dump and dash. Not that she was dumping. The two of them didn't have any type of relationship. They'd had one date. Plus, she didn't know what to tell him about her and Reed's relationship. They hadn't defined it yet. "I needed this manual."

Dax put his hands on her neck and moved his fingers in a massaging motion. "You need to relax. I can help you."

"She said she was in a hurry." Reed's curt tone cut across the room.

He stood in the hallway, only wearing a short, gray towel wrapped around his waist. His dark hair dripped water. His eyes stormed.

She took in his glorious body. She'd seen him naked before. In her bed. Laying on a blanket in the dance studio. On the piano. But this hulking, strong, menacing man appeared to be protecting his territory.

Her.

Her knees weakened and her bones went to mush. The urge to rush into his arms almost overtook her.

"Quit being such bear." Dax kept his hands on her neck. Either he didn't notice his brother's possessive voice or he didn't care. "I was massaging the tension from her neck."

"Don't." Reed's warning shot out.

She didn't want to see the two brothers fighting because of her. "It's no big deal, Reed." Backing away, she tucked the manual to her side. Guilt weighted her body down. She'd dated Dax and slept with his brother. She needed to clear up the mess and confusion, just not at this moment. "I really need to talk to you, Dax. Can we meet later?"

Reed's eyes widened and his chin tucked in. He shook his head. He didn't want her talking to his brother about them.

Why? Because he didn't want anyone to know about them? Or because he didn't want his brother upset?

"How about drinks?" Dax used his sexy-charming tone, a tone that must've worked on tons of women. Not her.

She glanced at Reed begging for assistance. She didn't know his brother's entire story, and she didn't know what to say about her and Reed.

"No drinks." Reed's expression firmed and he

stepped farther into the small living room. "No dating. No Quinn."

Dax yanked his hands off her, and spun around to glare at his big brother.

She got queasy. She didn't enjoy being fought over. She did love how Reed defended her. "No fighting, boys."

"No worries." Reed sent a short smile that was supposed to assure. It didn't. "We're going to have a chat."

About her.

"You have a class. You should go." He pointed at the door.

Dax's gaze widened, staring between the two of them, possibly putting everything together. Putting them together.

Her concern doubled. "Are you sure?" She glanced at the clock on the wall. She was already late. "I really think I should stay. Talk to—"

"Go. I'll handle this." Reed's confident tone told her the two brothers needed to work this out between them. He was protecting her. Her being present wouldn't help the situation. She'd explain to Dax later.

Reed was sure he could handle things, and she was sure about him.

Chapter Nineteen

"What the hell?" Dax resembled an upset child. "Why'd you scare Quinn off with your surly attitude?"

Jealousy pumped through Reed. His brother had had his hands on Quinn. He couldn't stand by and watch.

His brother stalked toward him. "She was about to say yes to a date."

"No, she wasn't, Dax the Pretender." Reed sounded absolute, even though inside he trembled. This conversation was not going to be easy, especially since he didn't know how Quinn felt about him.

His brother stepped into his space. "How would you know, brother? You haven't been around a woman since the stone age."

The insult sliced through his midsection. His brother didn't know about his relationship with Quinn.

Could he qualify what they had a relationship? He wanted to. Did she? They'd only known each other days and made love four times. He'd been wrong about Elizabeth loving him. She hadn't. She only wanted to use him and his celebrity. He could be wrong about Quinn.

Even if he was wrong, Quinn deserved more than a one-sided flirtation with his brother. "You were just with your ex, and now you're sniffing around Quinn."

"Me and my ex are finished." How many times had Dax made the pronouncement? "And Quinn is special."

Temper crashed into agreement in Reed's veins. She was special. "You can't use her to get over your ex." He wouldn't allow it.

"You're jealous." Dax's expression turned contemplative. His gaze flashed, as if a light had been a clicked on. "She eyed you like she wanted to strip the towel off of you, bro."

Reed's lust stirred. He would've loved for Quinn to undress him and have her way. When he'd walked out of the bathroom and heard her voice he'd been drawn to her, hoping she'd changed her mind about teaching class and wanting to spend the day with him.

Until he'd noticed his brother's hands on her.

Tugging at the towel, he pivoted away, wanting to get dressed before having a serious conversation. "Let me get dressed and we can talk."

"What's going on between you two?" Dax grabbed his shoulder and spun him around. "You two have had sex!"

Horror drained the blood from Reed's head. He couldn't believe he was so transparent. "No." He jerked the hand holding him off. Because they hadn't only had sex. They'd made love, at least on his side.

"Don't deny it, bro." A knowing expression smeared across Dax's face. A smarminess.

Reed braced himself for his brother's smack talk.

"You had sex with Quinn." His brother's grin reminded him of high school and talking about whose pants they'd gotten into at a dance. "Was she good?"

The questions were gnats at his ear. The buzzing stung, and he reacted. He took a wild swing at his brother. His knuckles connected with his brother's cheek, and Dax flew onto the couch and flopped back against the cushions. He grabbed his cheek.

"Sorry." Reed was the older brother and needed to help, not hurt his brother. The talk was supposed to be calm and rational, not hormones and jealousy.

"Oh, man." Dax rubbed his cheek. A teasing twinkle returned to his eyes. He didn't appear upset about the situation. "You've got it bad."

"Shut up." Reed knew he had it bad. He didn't need it pointed out.

His brother shook his head. "I can't believe my big brother has really fallen hard."

Sinking onto the couch, he held his head in his hands. His heart pounded with the gravity of his fall. He'd fallen in love with Quinn, and yet, she'd said letting his brother massage her neck was *no big deal*. As if having another man's hands on her was okay. What did that mean for their relationship, moving forward? Did she have *it bad* for him?

Quinn tried to explain the problem to the stereo technician on the phone at lunch during the day. How the music kept stopping and the wires were loose. When he asked her to get the model number, she pulled the manual from where she'd left it on the counter. Loose white pages fluttered to the ground.

After providing the information and scheduling a service call, she hung up the phone and picked up the papers.

Her name was penciled at the top.

For Quinn.

Followed by staff lines with handwritten notations of chords and keys she couldn't read. But she knew enough to know this was a song. Her soul hummed to the music. Reed had composed a song for her. She scoured the pages. Words, beautiful and lyrical poetry sang to her. He wrote of loss and renewed hope. Of dreams for the future. He spoke of desire and forever and the hold on his heart.

Her! She squealed inside.

An inner tune thrummed in her bloodstream. This was the most beautiful thing she'd ever read. Parts seemed familiar. He must've said them to her during one of their passionate lovemaking sessions. This song was his declaration.

Her happiness overflowed. Joy spread through her body, creating warmth and happiness. Their love was mutual. They might not have spoken the words, yet she sensed his emotions in the song. Felt his love.

Hugging herself, she tapped her toes in excitement. She couldn't wait to see him, to share her love for him. With him.

She frowned. He'd taken care of speaking to his brother for her, and she wanted to do something for him. To show her love and her belief in him.

Glancing at the papers she held in her hands, a frizzle went up her spine. The song was amazing. Would he take her word for it, or would an expert opinion be better? He'd written the song for her. She could prove her support for him by sending the song to a music producer friend, and if he loved it, tell Reed. If the music producer didn't like the song, which she found impossible to comprehend, Reed would never know.

She could do this for him. To support him and show she believed in him. To give him a little push. To help him achieve dreams of a musical career.

Scanning the pages, she composed a quick email. She had connections in the music industry in New York. She understood his fear of performing in front of audiences, but his music needed to be heard. She attached the song, her song, to the email.

And pushed send.

Reed scoured the top of the coffee table, searching for his sheet music. While working on a construction job most of the day, he'd made notations of changes he wanted to make to the chorus of Quinn's song. He still needed a good title. *For Quinn* didn't express what he wanted to say.

The stereo manual was gone. No one had been in is apartment since his brother left this morning. Picking up his cell phone, he called his brother. "When you were here this morning, did you see sheet music laying around?"

"Musical sheet music?" Dax sounded stunned, so Izzy must not have shared the gossip Reed was playing and composing again.

Swallowing, he took another small step in his recovery and admitted the truth. "Yes."

"I thought those were random scribblings."

"So, you saw my song?" Pulling information from his brother resembled pulling tiny, rusty nails out of recycled wood.

"You're writing music again?"

He'd tried to hide the evidence when he'd strutted into his apartment and found Dax cooking. One small step led to bigger ones. Reed's physical recovery had gone the same way. "Yes."

"Wow! Quinn's really done a number on you." Was that disgust or envy in his tone?

Reed didn't care. He loved Quinn and his entire world would know soon enough. "If by a number you mean she's good for me, then yes. Yes, she is good for me." Everything inside him lightened at sharing his emotions. "I'm hearing music in my head again. I'm composing."

"You're doing more than dancing with Quinn." If a voice could be suggestively wiggling eyebrows, Dax's was.

Reed didn't want to deal with his brother's immaturity. He wanted answers. "I shoved the sheets into a manual this morning."

"A stereo manual?"

Niggles of anxiety worked their way through him. How would his brother know the specifics? "Yes. Why?"

The line went silent.

His lungs constricted. He hadn't made a copy. What if the sheets were lost?

Sucking in a breath, he couldn't get enough air. Terror at someone else finding the musical sheets screamed inside him. He wasn't ready for anyone to see his latest attempt at writing and making music. What if what he thought was good was actually terrible?

His temples pounded out a beat of tension. "Why, Dax?"

"Because a stereo manual is what Quinn came by to pick up this morning."

The pounding in Reed's temples clashed together like cymbals on both sides of his head. The noise shattered in his chest. He wasn't ready to share his feelings with Quinn. And he certainly didn't want her learning of his love by reading sheet music. He'd imagined a candlelit dinner, maybe at his house, a fire in the fireplace. Romantic and cozy.

And together.

He didn't want her finding the sheet music and reading the lyrics alone. He wanted to watch her expression as he played the melody and sang the words. He wanted to experience her reaction and hopefully the way she expressed her love in return.

Chapter Twenty

Quinn's phone buzzed with another text from Dax: *Did you need the stereo manual this morning because it's broken? If so, did you need my help?*

She responded with a quick no before her thumb accidently scrolled through his earlier text from this morning. His poetic words jumped out.

Words sounding vaguely familiar.

She tapped her phone against the counter. Why would Dax's words be familiar? Why would he be asking to help with the stereo? She'd picked up the manual from Reed's apartment this morning, while Dax was there. He'd seen her take the manual, so he must've surmised she had a problem.

Flipping through the pages, she stopped at the sheet music tucked inside. Read the lyrics. Spotted Dax's earlier text and read his words.

Words identical to the lyrics on Reed's music sheet.

Shock reverberated in her body, zinging around her ribs and up her spine. How was that possible? Dax sometimes sounded like Reed through his texts, but to come up with the same thing word for word would be impossible. Maybe they'd worked together on the song. Except Reed was the only composer.

Her mind swirled with other possibilities, except for the one obvious one. The one option she didn't want to believe. The brothers wouldn't be so cruel. Would they?

Her heart throbbed a beat of its own. A hurt, angry, foolish beat. A beat so off-rhythm she was surprised she didn't pass out. The two brothers had tricked her. Things started to add up into the complete equation.

From Dax's sweet words the first night when she'd stood by the window, to his poetic texts—all had been written by Reed. Even though Dax was a handsome guy, it was the words that wooed her. Reed's words. Why would he do such a thing?

He'd been quiet in the beginning. Not exactly shy, but withdrawn. Afraid to talk to her and other people. Recently he'd confided so many things to her, shared his past. A steam of confusion clouded her judgment. Why wouldn't he confess this happened and stop?

The steam billowed into temper. She'd commented on how Dax could be poetic and lyrical, resembling a composer one minute and short and to the point the next. She'd recognized something was odd, giving Reed the perfect opportunity to tell her. He hadn't.

With his reticence to be social, she could sort of forgive him in the beginning. But now? If Reed liked her, why would he help his brother get a date with her? Anguish tapped across her midsection. He was attracted to her. They were sleeping together, and she'd believed he felt something more. She certainly felt something for him.

Why would they be deceptive? Why would *Reed* lie by omission? The tapping became more rapid, more painful, more angry. She hated being lied to, and having her trust broken. That's how she'd lost her grandparents' house and lost her heritage.

The pain radiated outward in waves of gall and frustration. She'd been fooled by the investor, and now she'd been fooled by Reed. The two brothers must be laughing behind her back. Dax had never been really persistent. His attention seemed to wax and wane. He was a player, and this could be a game to him. But Reed?

Why continue this cruel game after they'd made love? She sucked in a breath and coughed. Was having sex the winning factor? She found it hard to believe he'd be so mean and immature. Her mind spun with bewilderment. Her pulse pounded, similar to performing pirouette after pirouette. She'd vowed never to be tricked by dishonest words again, and yet, both Dax and Reed had lied.

"Everything okay?" Izzy stood at the front door of the dance studio.

Quinn had been so deep in her furious thoughts she hadn't heard the door chime. She throttled the manual she held.

"You look like you want to kill someone." Izzy's friendly-not-prying tone had Quinn trying to control herself. She shouldn't jump to conclusions.

These were her friend's brothers she was pissed at. Well, pissed at Dax. Hurt by Reed. She set the manual down and smoothed out the edges with a little too much pressure. "Are your two brothers competitive with each other?"

"Always." Izzy dropped her chin. The question didn't surprise.

"About women?"

"There was this one girl who Reed had a crush on forever. He finally got the nerve to ask her to a dance, only to find Dax had swooped in and kissed her in the hallway." Izzy's eyes glinted with concern, realizing why Quinn had asked. "That was in high school, though."

Her head spun like performing a series of rapid turns on *demi-pointe*, twirling faster and faster until she couldn't tell dizziness from anger. They competed for women. They lied. They used each other's words and actions. They fooled her.

The bigger question: did Reed mean the words he wrote? Her body sagged, because the words had been so strong emotionally. And if he meant the words, why share them with his brother this morning?

Izzy grabbed her hand. "Did one of my brothers screw up?"

"Both of them." Trying to control the anger and hurt, Quinn forged a plan to make Dax and Reed regret what they'd done. She'd find a way to share her displeasure. "I'm not a prize to be won."

Reed's blood thrummed, taking the stairs too fast for a guy with a bum leg. Nerves jumped off his skin. He hoped to sneak behind the counter, grab the manual and the music sheets, and get out without being noticed. Quinn should be teaching classes until her short dinner break before the adult classes tonight.

Skirting the backroom and bathroom, he stopped short at the edge of the floor.

Quinn stood in front of the counter, talking to a student. Her body leaned against the counter in a casual pose, and he remembered some of the poses he'd seen her in this morning. His body reacted with an internal flare of heat. Her hair was in the usual tight bun. His fingers itched to take the bun down and run his fingers through the strands. She hugged the girl and his body tilted forward, wanting his own hug.

The student left, and Quinn swiveled and spotted him. She frowned, not welcomed. His anxiety ramped up. Her gaze narrowed and shot arrows at his heart, making it shiver. Something was wrong. Had she seen the sheet music? And if she had, what did she think? If she realized he spoke of his real emotions, he'd expected a different greeting.

The anxiety twisted in his stomach.

He didn't move to kiss her, and neither did she. "Is something wrong?"

"Wrong?" Her voice was shrill, straining his eardrums. "Nothing's wrong." She twirled away and picked up her phone. "I received the sweetest text from Dax."

Reed clutched the counter. The arrow she'd shot earlier infiltrated his heart and oozed green. "Sweet?"

Her smile appeared stiff around the edges. "I won't bore you with the lyrical details but, as I said earlier, your brother has quite the way with words."

He hadn't helped his brother text anything new, and Dax didn't do lyrical. And the song, Quinn's song was missing. "Dax?"

"Yes, Dax." She danced out of Reed's reach.

He re-gripped the counter, trying to control his blood pressure from spiking. She thought his brother was sweet after they'd made love? Had last night and this morning meant nothing? She'd slept with Reed, not his brother. Dax wouldn't continue to pursue her knowing how Reed felt. So why was Quinn tormenting him?

Clutching the counter tighter, he fought against the need to take her in his arms and punish her with a kiss. "What about us?" More of a demand than a question.

"What about us?" She flipped a few strands of loose hair, playing the part of a tease.

He didn't believe she was a tease, and yet her not-so-innocent jibe stabbed. "What about last night?" *And this morning.*

"Last night?" She tapped her long finger against her chin, as if she couldn't quite remember. Which was ridiculous. How could she forget? "Oh. Last night was nice."

Nausea rose, and he went lightheaded. Was this a joke? In a panic, he scanned the room trying to comprehend what was happening. "Nice?"

She nodded, a glint of amusement or temper flashing in her eyes. "Yes, nice."

Images of the caressing and kissing and positions swooshed in his head. Last night had been incredible. The best night of his life. His head spun. Obviously it hadn't been the best night of her life. "Maybe it would be nicer with Dax."

"Maybe it would." Her flippancy had an edge of hardness.

A hardness cut into Reed, and he bled. He'd been used. What he thought was the most amazing, magical, perfect experience of his life had meant nothing to her. The bleeding spewed out of him in ugly words. "If you enjoy Dax's words and his body so much, maybe you should dance with him for the opening showcase."

"Should I text Dax and ask him, or will you do that *for* me?" Her super-innocent tone told Reed she wasn't so innocent. Her lips pursed in an injured moue. "You know, like you text for Dax."

Reed's gut clenched. Blood raced in his veins. "I can explain—"

"Let me read you his last text from this morning. It resembled a song." She paused and glowered with shining eyes. Tears. "Or I bet you could tell me what he wrote, because you wrote it for him."

Shit. She knew. She knew what he'd done. How he'd lied and pretended and was a total jerk.

Panic slashed through him. He stumbled backward. "I didn't—"

"You didn't help Dax compose texts?" She held her phone out in evidence. Evidence or a bomb.

Terror froze Reed. He couldn't look at the phone. He knew some of the things he'd helped his brother text. If he couldn't find a way to get her to forgive him, he'd lose her. He'd fallen in love for real this time, and if he lost her he'd lose everything.

He focused on the words on her phone. His raw emotional words glared back. The bomb exploded blasting shrapnel in his skin, each piece poking and stinging and bleeding. Bleeding out his love for Quinn.

On her phone, texted by his brother, were the lyrics from the song he'd composed for Quinn. Dax must've found the sheet music before Reed had returned to the apartment. He must've used the lyrics to text Quinn. And Quinn found the sheet music in the stereo manual.

The pieces fell into place. Unlike the pieces of his heart. "I did, but not tod—"

"You know I hate dishonesty. You know I hate being deceived." She scowled, her anger palpable. "You know I hate liars."

Each sentence was a punch. She must hate him. Desperation clawed in his lungs. He grasped at straws or the final notes in a song. "I can explain."

She slammed the phone on the counter. The noise echoed in his head. "I don't want any more sweet-talk, or lyrical poetry. I should've realized it was a trick. A competition between you and your brother."

The desperation choked and he couldn't breathe. "I was only trying to help him."

Her lips scrunched in distaste. "Help him try to sleep with me, too?"

"No. I wouldn't do that." He reached for her hand and she snatched it away a signal she wouldn't forgive easily. A signal their relationship could be done. "What we have is…"

Her head cocked, listening to him, but when he

trailed off she asked, "What were you trying to do to me?"

The pain in her voice pressed against his chest. In the beginning, he'd been trying to win her for his brother, to help his brother with confidence issues. Except it was his own confidence that was lacking. He hadn't admitted his own attraction and his own need for her. Not to himself and not to her. He'd been hiding his feelings and his love. And because of that, he'd ruined their budding relationship and broken her heart.

That evening, Reed perched at the edge of the stairs, peeking into the dance studio minutes before the adult classes were to start. A class where he was Quinn's partner.

Not Dax. Not anyone else.

Which is how it should be. Reed realized she'd been upset and he shouldn't have made excuses. He should've apologized and begged for forgiveness instead of retreating to his apartment. Except retreat had been his specialty for years, and it was a hard habit to break.

He needed to apologize and tell her he'd never deceive her again. She was the best thing in his life and he wouldn't lose her because of a misunderstanding and a mistake. His mistake.

He was going to march into class, sweep her into his arms, and apologize. He never should've helped his brother and once he'd started seeing Quinn he should've told her about his deception. He'd never deceive or lie to her again.

The chimes above the front door rang and Dax strolled into the studio. Reed's body tensed. He needed to have a long talk with his little brother about taking things. Dax should've told him he'd texted the lyrics to Quinn this morning.

Dax grinned and Quinn greeted him with a hug

A hug?

Reed's pulse pitter-pattered in a confused pattern. She'd ripped into him and gives his brother a hug?

Dax's offense had been worse. He'd stolen the lyrics this morning without asking when they'd been lying on the coffee table.

She placed his hands on her waist and held the other one out, teaching him a dance. The same dance Reed and Quinn were supposed to perform together in the showcase. She was replacing him.

In the dance and in her heart.

Chapter Twenty-One

Quinn wanted to do an angry dance, not the calm waltz the adult class had been practicing for the showcase. Her body was tight and stiff. Her instructions and corrections were more clipped than courteous.

She'd been furious with Reed. Furious he'd lied. Furious he'd played Cyrano for his brother. Now her fury was spent, and she knew they needed to talk. Except Dax danced with her, not Reed. Her choice. She'd texted Dax back and asked him to be her partner in dance class tonight.

His lanky body moved with an easy rhythm, not the strong support she was used to with Reed. Dax smiled and laughed too often, suggesting his entire life had been a party. His hand in hers felt wrong.

While everything about Reed felt right.

She wanted everything to be right again. "Okay, class." She dropped her hands from her temporary dance partner and stepped into the center of the dance floor. "We only have five nights to practice before the opening day showcase. You all look wonderful. This is going to be great."

Izzy tugged on her arm. "Where's Reed? What I said earlier didn't upset you, did it?"

"Yes. And no." Quinn stretched on her toes. She needed to work things out with Reed without sisterly, or brotherly, interference. "It will be fine." She turned the music back up. "Let's do the entire routine one more time before calling it a night."

Five minutes more and she could find Reed and explain. They'd work it out. She knew it. When she first realized their trickery, she'd been furious. She deserved an explanation from Reed and an apology. Then, she'd forget and move on. She didn't hold grudges.

"The stereo is working fine now." Dax came to her side and pulled her into his arms for the final dance. "What was Izzy bothering you about? You looked upset."

Worried more than anything. She wanted to talk to Reed and hold him in her arms. Kiss him and have the best make-up sex ever.

"Quinn?" Dax pushed.

"I really didn't want to discuss this during class. I know what you and Reed did." Dax probably considered what he'd done a small prank. Reed should've known better. They'd spent so much time together, he knew her and understood her fears. He should've told her what had happened and promised to stop. They both should've told Dax about their relationship at the first possible moment.

He missed a step. "Did?"

She scowled. "The texts Reed wrote for you. I know."

Dax blushed and examined his feet doing a simple maneuver. "Sorry. I wanted to impress you, and Reed has a way with words."

A way with his body, too. She warmed all over. "It was deceitful and wrong. He shouldn't have helped."

Dax tilted his head and studied her. "You're not mad at me? Only Reed."

Both brothers were to blame. Reed's deception was more personal. He knew her past. He'd made love to her. He'd hurt her.

"That's why my brother isn't here tonight dancing. You two had a fight." When Dax wasn't being self-absorbed he was actually smart. "You're attracted to my brother."

She took a misstep. What exactly had Reed said to his brother this morning?

"You know, I pushed Reed into helping me." Sounding earnest, Dax performed a flourish. "The night at your window I was drunk. My brother picked me up from the pub and brought me here to sleep at his apartment. I started shouting at your window."

She'd wondered why his voice had changed.

"You came out and I fell to the ground. I was slurring my words and messing up what I wanted to say." He twirled her around. Her head spun for a completely different reason. "Reed was trying to help his little brother."

She snorted. "I can't imagine you need help with women."

"Normally, I don't." Dax quieted. "I've been in a slump. My ex-girlfriend keeps giving me the runaround.

She misses me and then she tells me she doesn't want to hear from me again."

His sadness had her sympathizing and possibly understanding why his brother had helped. "You really cared about her."

"I did."

And what about Reed? Her heart cried. He'd sworn off women completely since his fiancée's death. Until she'd danced into his life and pushed him into a relationship. A relationship he might not have been ready for. Her thoughts ground against each other. The fit with Dax wasn't natural like with Reed. Even though he had a limp, they moved together as if they were made for each other.

Had their fight caused him to retreat into his dark hole? If she'd pushed him too hard into a relationship he wasn't ready for, had she lost him forever?

Reed pounded on the small electronic keyboard he'd moved from the garage to his apartment, trying to play over the noise from the dance studio. He didn't want to hear the dance music and be reminded his brother danced in Quinn's arms.

She'd smiled at Dax. Danced with him. Forgiven him.

Reed's fingers slammed against the black and white keys. Life wasn't black and white, and he didn't understand why she could forgive his brother and not him.

The texts she'd received today from Dax had come from the song Reed had written. For Quinn. About his feelings for her. His brother must've found the sheet music in his apartment this morning and used the words to woo her.

He'd confronted Dax on the phone today when he'd discovered the music sheets were missing. He'd said he'd only seen the sheet on top which had been the last page Reed had worked on, so it didn't have Quinn's name at the top. Dax had told him he'd thought the song was old because Reed didn't write music anymore.

Which was true, until it wasn't. He should've told his brother about the recent changes in his life. His playing. His composing. His Quinn.

New wounds sliced inside Reed, leaving him vulnerable and exposed. He wasn't ready to share his feelings with her or anybody else. He used music to sort through his emotions. Once he had things figured out he planned to tell her.

And others who needed to be told.

He didn't want to taunt his little brother by flaunting his relationship with Quinn. Although Dax had seemed more amused than upset this morning when he'd told him to leave her alone. His brother had been flirting for fun. It had never been anything serious.

Not like what Reed felt for her.

Pain spread across his chest in a panicky rhythm. If she'd found the lyrics, what had she thought? How could she yell at him after reading his singing love letter? The pain struck a note of finality. Unless, she didn't care for him. Or she'd hated the song.

Someone banged on his door.

He didn't want to answer. Didn't want to talk to anyone.

A key scratched in the lock. Only Dax and Izzy had keys to his apartment. Unless they'd given Quinn a key.

Reed held his breath and watched the entrance.

The door opened and Izzy stood there.

He let out the breath in a long, slow whistle. "It's only you."

"Don't sound so thrilled, big brother." Izzy invaded his apartment. "Why weren't you at dance class tonight?"

Her question stabbed. "Quinn didn't want me there."

"I wondered if you two had a fight. What's up?"

The insides of his stomach twisted. Quinn was already mad he'd overshared with Dax. "She found out I was helping Dax text her."

Reed had expected an I-told-you-so expression, but only got sympathy. "I'm sorry."

"She acted as if I'd betrayed her, yet she danced with Dax." The twisting in Reed's stomach knotted tighter. "She forgave Dax."

"You hurt her more deeply because she cares more about you." Izzy brought him into a hug. "Not Dax."

The realization struck like a perfect treble. That's why Quinn had been angry, why she'd teased and tortured, because she'd been upset by his actions. He hadn't gotten the chance to explain he'd stopped helping his brother before their relationship had developed. He understood honesty and openness was the most important key in a relationship, but he hadn't put it into action. Similar to his past. He'd gone along with Elizabeth's plans and said nothing. With Quinn, he needed to perform a trio: apology, explanation, and share his feelings.

Izzy leaned back out of the hug. Her eyebrows raised in a challenge. "So what're you going to do about it?"

After his sister left, and with her thoughts ringing in his head, he slipped out the back door and into his garage. Before he could lay everything in the open with Quinn he needed to confront and accept his past. To face one more demon. The demon the symphony's conductor had delivered to Castle Ridge when Reed had been in hospital.

He scrutinized the black tarp covered in dust concealing the large object taking up most of the space in the garage. Expecting sickness and anxiety, he was surprised when only his muscles tightened. His body wasn't as shocked with his plan as his head. He gripped the edges of the tarp. The smoothness of the plastic contrasted with his rough fingertips. He whipped off the heavy tarp to reveal what had once been the love of his life.

The black grand piano gleamed in the harsh fluorescent light from the ceiling of the garage. The smooth finish appeared the same. He lifted the top and studied the mechanics underneath.

Just as he'd referred to Quinn's piano as his nemesis on the day it arrived, this piano had been an albatross around his neck. He'd carried the weight of the instrument with him, being so close physically and yet so far away emotionally. This was the piano he'd sat at for hours, days, really, composing.

Using his hand, he brushed the dust off the bench and took a seat. He shimmied into position. The wood felt solid, familiar. This piano had been his lover more than his fiancée. He'd spent more time with it, caressed it more, played with it more. This time would be different. He wouldn't let music take over every aspect of his life again.

He'd go to Quinn and lay his feelings on the line. Tell her everything and share all of his emotions. He wanted to have a clear conscience, a whole heart, and no weight from his past dragging him down. If he ever did decide to start composing again, and with the music in his head he might go crazy if he didn't, his relationship with her would come first. And composing did not mean publishing or selling his songs. He'd do it for himself and for her. No one else needed to know about his music.

He stretched out his arms and wiggled his fingers. The black keys didn't shine and the white keys had grooves from his fingers. From overuse. He cringed, thinking about how the piano was going to sound after sitting in the cold garage for years.

Playing this piano would be different than playing the small electronic one his parents had sent him when he'd been recovering. He'd never used it until the other day. The electronic keyboard had been buried in his garage, too. Buried like his heart.

Now his heart and his music had been freed by Quinn.

He was determined to soothe her anger. He'd beg and plead for forgiveness.

He placed his fingers in home position on the keys

and was surprised his new, ugly fingers fit in the grooves. A sense of satisfaction and completeness filled him. His hands were home at this piano, similar to how he was at home in Castle Ridge with Quinn. He picked out a couple of notes and the off-key noise pained his ears. The noise was a complaining mistress, nagging about how he'd been gone too long.

The piano wasn't his mistress anymore, Quinn was. Or, he hoped she'd be. He hoped she'd be more than a mistress. Once she'd forgiven him, he'd sweep her off her feet and into a romantic marriage proposal.

Picking out a scale, he recognized certain attributes from his piano. Even out of tune, the piano sounded familiar. With some love and attention, she'd be as good as new. He could move the piano into his new house when it was ready. He'd convince Quinn to move in, too.

With hope soaring, his fingers glided across the keyboard. The possibilities for the future, his future, their future, played in his soul.

Quinn had pounded on Reed's apartment door. No answer.

She'd called his cell phone. No response.

She'd even texted his brother and sister to ask where he might be. No idea.

Frustrated, she flopped onto her lonely bed and glanced out the back window.

A light was on in the detached garage. A glimmer lit her mind. With hurried steps, she went down the stairs and out the back door. She put her hand on the garage doorknob and turned.

The large tarp was gone, and beneath it stood a black grand piano. The dusty piano had scratches on its legs and was bigger than the one she owned. Professional and well-loved. That's not what her eyes were drawn to.

From his seat on the bench, Reed's fingers flew across the keyboard. His curly, dark hair flopped in front of his face with the movement of his hands. His expression appeared vulnerable, and he poured his agony into the song. Her heartstrings tethered to him.

The melody changed and slowed. Went from anguished to a tune she recognized from sitting on the stairs night after night listening. "Is that my song?"

His fingers stilled. His chest moved up and down. "Yes."

The song was amazing. Hearing the music and knowing the lyrics hit her hard. She couldn't believe she'd argued over something so beautiful. Her throat went dry. "It's beautiful."

Stretching to her toes, she stayed by the doorway. He'd been in the wrong. And even though she'd struck back with unkindness, he needed to apologize. To accept responsibility.

He lifted his head and stared. She could get lost in those emerald orbs.

"I'm sorry I helped my brother in the beginning." His tender expression and round, sorrowful eyes tugged. "Once I realized something was developing between us I stopped. I should've told you right away what I'd done."

He must've read her mind. His forthright and honest apology was a spring shower, cleansing and enlightening. Unable to hold onto her anger, she rushed to the piano bench and sat beside him. She'd missed his scent, and his warmth in dance class and in bed. She loved the sensation of him at her side or in her arms. Of him always being there for her.

"I didn't give Dax the music sheets with your song." Reed's voice held a plea. His expression begged for forgiveness. "The sheets were lying on my coffee table this morning."

Her rigid stance from this morning had already softened and his words melted her to mush. She wanted to forgive. And she wanted to forget, to move past their argument. "I was so upset about being fooled. I should've asked you, not been cruel."

From this point forward, if she doubted him she'd ask.

"Dax must've texted you before I told him about our relationship." Reed took hold of her hand and their fingers intertwined automatically, as if they were meant to be together.

Her heart soothed and swelled with hope. "What did you tell him about us?"

She knew what she wanted Reed to say—that they were a couple, that this was more than dating, that it could lead to something permanent.

He lifted their entwined hands and kissed her knuckles. "I told him we were together."

Her shoulders dipped. She'd take *together* for now because the lyrics in the song said so much more, told her so much more about his emotions. "The lyrics are amazing."

"Thank you for forgiving me and for being my inspiration."

She liked being his inspiration.

He turned to her and placed his mouth on hers in the slightest movement of a kiss. A yearning grew inside her for him and only him. She teased her tongue along the seam of his mouth, needing to taste him.

"I wasn't ready to share the song with anyone yet," he murmured against her mouth.

A twinge of guilt doubled in her midsection. His fiancée Elizabeth had gone behind his back and messed with his career. Quinn wasn't messing with his career, though, she was giving him a push in the right direction by emailing the song. Music executives were busy. By the time her friend got around to reading the email, she and Reed would be in sync about his future.

About their future.

"Are you ready to share the lyrics with me now?" She untucked his shirt and ran her hands up his strong back. Her fingers electrified with contact.

"With you? Yes." His mouth whispered on the corner of hers. Kissing her neck and behind her ears, he slipped his hands under her shirt and cupped a breast.

The electricity spread a sizzling shock through her system. "I'd love to hear you whisper the chorus while we make love."

Imagining the words of desire being blown into her

ear as if she was an instrument and Reed the musician, she groaned. He was a musician. A virtuoso with the piano and his songs. A virtuoso with her body.

"Quinn-tessential."

She sighed at the meaningful nickname.

He pushed open her blouse and kissed a trail from her neck to her chest. "I trust you." He nipped a nipple between his teeth and she stopped thinking and imagining. She only felt. "I trust you with my words and with my heart."

Reed installed new lighting in the lobby of Castle Ridge Lodge. He'd done a lot of work for the lodge, and yet the owner wouldn't even consider a bid from him to remodel the restaurant kitchen. The man wasn't taking local bids.

He wouldn't let that get him down. Things with Quinn were going spectacularly. They spent every free moment together talking, laughing, dancing, making love. His music had returned, and with it, his spirit. He trusted her and believed in her. She'd become the other half of his soul, making his life complete.

The other night they'd attended the Castle Ridge Snow Festival. The local event celebrated the ski season before the tourists arrived. He and Quinn had strolled hand-in-hand through the festival. He'd introduced her to old friends he hadn't spoken to since his return, and she'd handed out brochures for her studio.

He might've been introducing her, but he was the one being reintroduced into society. His strut past the booths and carnival rides picked up pace. He liked being out in public with Quinn. Liked the recognition and camaraderie. Liked getting to know his old friends and neighbors again.

"I can't believe how crowded this event is. I didn't realize how many people actually lived in Castle Ridge." Quinn's smile never left her face. Her happiness brightened his world.

"Between the people in town and the people who live in the surrounding backcountry, we're a good-sized area." A perfect size. He'd always thought of Castle Ridge as small. He realized now it was perfect. The population, the location, the local attitude. He was happy here. "Add the skiers from down the mountain, and the people who come from all over the world to ski, and our size triples."

"Probably why we never met as kids." Her voice quieted. "I was only a visitor staying with my grandparents for a week or two."

"You said their house was on Pearl Street, right?"

She hadn't shared much about the place, just how devastated she'd been when she'd had to sell. His house could be on the same block.

Her smile faded. "That's right. It was several blocks from Main Street, because the house had been built on a larger lot."

He should show Quinn his house. How he planned to restore the home to its former glory. How maybe someday they could.... He shook off the thought unsure of where she believed their relationship was going. He knew what he wanted but he didn't want to rush. They'd only known each other three weeks.

She spun in front of him and gave him a kiss. "How about a ride on the Ferris wheel?"

"You won't get cold?" His concern for her overtook everything else.

Giggling, she wrapped her arms around his waist. "We'll cuddle and you'll keep me warm."

His body heated and he agreed. Then, he'd bring her home and get her even hotter.

Buzz. Buzz.

His phone ringing brought him back to the present. The light he was working on was only partially attached, and he couldn't let go. His hands were full. "Can you tell me if it's Quinn calling?"

Danielle sat behind the reception desk reading a college textbook and grabbed his phone off the counter. "It's a New York number."

"Would you mind answering for me?"

"Sure." She picked up his phone. "Hello. Reed O'Donnell's phone. May I ask who's calling?" Totally professional, she paused and listened. "Hold on a sec." She placed her hand over the mouthpiece of the phone. "It's a Mr. Stewart."

"Never heard of him." He screwed in the next bolt for the light. "Do you mind asking what it's regarding?"

"No problem. I'm not busy this morning." She was always willing to help a friend. "Reed is in the middle of something. May I ask what this is regarding?" Her serene-professional expression changed. She smashed her lips together a couple of times, and sent him an unsteady glance.

Must be bad news. More curious than upset, he knew nothing could ruin his day.

"Um, sure. I'll tell him. Hold on." Her voice was stiff, uncertain. She covered the phone again and squeezed it in her hand. "Reed. This man says he's a music executive. He received a copy of your song called *For Quinn*, and wants to buy it."

What his friend said blurred together and then slowly, word by word, the sentences processed and re-formed in his head. How could someone from New York have seen his song?

His mind kaleidoscoped with different options. Dax was the only other person who'd seen the song. He hadn't recognized what the music sheets he'd copied from actually were. He didn't know anyone in the music industry. And he hadn't known what had happened to the sheets after Reed had shoved them in the stereo manual.

The music of joy symphonizing in his head changed into a tone cluster...or a clusterfuck. His ribcage tightened, and punctured his lungs. He couldn't breathe. Couldn't stand. His entire body trembled.

His arms were dead weight. His hands dropped. The light fixture crashed to the ground and shattered.

Shattered like his trust.

Chapter Twenty-Two

Reed's heart lay on the floor broken like the light fixture. There was only a single possible way a music executive had gotten the one song he'd composed. And it wasn't from his brother.

Quinn.

He hadn't planned to send his song out into the cruel, harsh world. Not his baby. The words and chords were for her ears only. For her pleasure. He hadn't pitched a song in a long time and hadn't planned on doing it again.

The sensations vibrated bringing back the time when his partner had stolen his music and passed it off as his own. The betrayal was just as sharp. Sharper this time because he'd trusted the person doing the theft.

"Reed, are you okay?" The concern in Danielle's tone didn't comfort.

Nothing could comfort. He slouched against the ladder and gaped at the glass pieces lying on the carpeted floor of the lobby, feeling the same way.

Smashed and broken into hundreds of pieces. He'd trusted Quinn. Trusted her with his music and with his love. If she betrayed one she could easily betray the other.

"Mr. O'Donnell will have to call you back. Can I get a number?" He heard Danielle's voice through a haze. Saw her move around the reception counter and toward him in a fog.

A fog of disappointment and fractured dreams.

"Climb down, Reed." Placing her hands on the ladder, she coaxed him. "Everything's going to be okay."

He took one rung of the ladder going down, down, down. Just like his hopes. Sinking into the oblivion of betrayal.

"Come here." She opened her arms and he went into them. Her short stature didn't compare to Quinn's height, but Danielle's honesty and dependableness were worth a lot.

A spike struck his empty chest. The torment wove between his ribs.

Elizabeth hadn't loved him. She'd loved his celebrity. He'd believed Quinn loved him for himself. His new self. The one who lived in Castle Ridge and did construction and heard music in his head and played piano only for her.

Not for anyone else.

She'd asked about him playing for the New York Symphony again and pushed him about composing.

He didn't want to be a professional pianist, and his new music wasn't ready to be analyzed and reviewed. Why would she send it off without his permission? Without even an acknowledgement?

His shattered heart froze. Cold anger hardened everything inside him. He was a glacier. Did Quinn only want a relationship with him because he might be famous again someday? Was she as addicted to celebrity as Elizabeth?

Danielle patted his back. "Did you injure yourself when the light fixture fell?"

"No." He choked. He hadn't hurt himself physically.

"Good." She continued to pat his back. He barely felt the touch with the rapid rushing of his pulse. "The light can be replaced."

A light could be replaced. Not his broken heart.

"So, you wrote a new song?"

"A ballad." To his love.

A numbness seeped through his bloodstream and hardened his veins into ice. An ex-love who'd betrayed his trust and shared a gift she'd had no right to exploit.

"That's wonderful." Danielle's voice shook, unsure where to take this conversation. "I take it you didn't send it to the music executive."

"No." His tone was frigid.

"Who did?"

"Quinn." He spat the betrayer's name.

After all they'd done together and shared. After the dancing and him playing the piano for her. He'd told her the song was only for her. After the lovemaking and the promises, she'd gone behind his back and betrayed him.

✳

Reed had charged out of the lodge with a promise to pay for the light fixture. He'd jumped in his truck and careened through town. His subconscious drove him to turn right and left. He ended up on Pearl Street and pulled into the driveway. Staring blindly through the windshield at the house he'd believed would become a home, he tapped his fingers on the steering wheel to an inner angry beat. Being at his home should've soothed him. It didn't. A crescendo of notes clashed in his head.

He was too infuriated. Too embittered. Too lost.

Jumping out of the truck, he slammed the door and stomped up the front porch. A front porch made for relaxing evenings and visiting with neighbors. He wouldn't have any of it now, because he wouldn't sit out here, he didn't care to meet the other people who lived on the street. He'd go back into his cave.

Quinn had made him believe in himself again. Believe he could make music and he could love and be loved. By breaking his trust, she'd broken that belief. She wanted him to be famous, or make more money, or have celebrity, so it would shine on her. He should never have come out of his self-imposed exile.

It was safer. No love, then no hurt. No music, then no rejection.

He shoved the key in the door and tromped inside, glad he'd never told Quinn about the house. Glad he hadn't brought her here and shown her around. Glad her presence would never taint the hardwood floors or the large living space meant for a family.

His head pounded with furious, unessential notes. Unessential because he didn't plan to ever play or write them down. To his amazement, the music hadn't stopped, even though he was broken and shattered. He hadn't gone mute. The music played on and on and on in his mind.

A blessing or a curse?

Even without Quinn, he'd hear the agony of the music in his head forever. The agony of lost love, of betrayal, of abuse of trust.

The noise echoed in his chest, shouting and clanging and causing chaos. Before when the music wouldn't stop, the sound had been calm and less noisy. Not filled with fury. Because Quinn had caused this firestorm in his head and in his heart. The only way to calm the fury was to never see her again. He trembled. *Never see her again.* The best choice. The only choice.

He gripped the wooden banister and slid his hand over the smooth surface he'd spent hours sanding. With the holiday season approaching, he'd pictured Quinn helping him decorate for the first time, starting their own traditions.

There'd be no traditions. No baking or decorating. No fun.

Hobbling toward the fireplace, he rested his forehead against the hearth, letting the cold hardness of the stone cool his ire. The imagined cold nights cozying up by the fire with Quinn sputtered out. His chest emptied to nothingness. His head banged on in a slow, slow rhythm.

The tune might be a death march, but it was music. The music hadn't died. The music flourished with an agonized, tortured melody. A melody that would haunt him.

Unless maybe he figured it out by playing and writing it down. He couldn't listen to the terrible noise in his head getting louder and louder. If he composed and wrote the notes, maybe the beats wouldn't drive him insane. And then he'd burn the music sheets so no one else saw them, or claimed them as their own, or sent them off to music executives.

Back at the Victorian house on Main Street, he ignored the pull toward the dance studio and went up the back stairs. He didn't want to see Quinn. He had nothing to say. The music in his head would speak for him. It would flow out in the anguish and heart break.

The song would sit on sheet music, useless except to exorcise his demons and kindle his fireplace.

Opening his apartment door, he found Izzy and Dax sitting on his couch. Both sat with their arms crossed and identical expressions of unease. Understanding he was being attacked by a loving army, Reed hunkered his shoulders and waited for the blows to fall.

"I'm guessing you heard." He didn't even need to elaborate.

"Where have you been? Danielle said you left the lodge hours ago. She told me about the music executive." Izzy rushed forward and put her arms around him, trying to comfort. "I tried to call you a million times."

Over her shoulder, he glowered at his brother. He needed to write music, to pour his emotions into a tune. He didn't need to be questioned and consoled.

Okay, the hug from his sister was nice. He was thankful he had a close family.

"Don't look at me, bro." Dax stood and held up his

hands. His expression exhibited anxiety. "You worried both of us. What exactly happened?"

Stepping out of his sister's arms, Reed stood tall. He wasn't ready to share the details. "Quinn betrayed my trust. End of story. End of relationship."

"Danielle gave me this." Izzy held out a piece of lodge stationery with a name and number. "She said this is the music executive who—"

Reed grabbed the paper and ripped it into shreds, similar to his future. "Quinn had no right."

"Have you talked to her?" His sister bent to pick up the littered pieces of paper. Could she put the note back together?

A small, tiny spark ignited. Anticipation or excitement? Did he want her to put the name and number into legible form? Was he interested?

No, no, no. He'd never be interested in that world again. Not even if that was the only reason Quinn was interested in him. In the past, he'd been so wrapped up in his music he hadn't noticed anything else happening around him. He didn't want to become a music-zombie again. He wanted to be aware and involved.

If only his life was as easy to pick up as the pieces of paper. "Don't plan to talk to Quinn, ever." He yanked the small electronic keyboard off the shelf.

"You can't avoid her." His brother's matter-of-fact tone annoyed. "You practically live together."

Panic pulsed. He glanced at the apartment door and back at his brother. Quinn lived across the hall. She could knock at any time. "I'm halfway through remodeling my house. I can move there."

"With no heat or electricity?" Izzy pointed out the pitfalls.

"You're Quinn's landlord." Dax pointed out the obvious.

An obvious thing Reed hadn't thought of, because he'd been too tormented.

"I'll appoint you my proxy." Ironic, since now his brother would be speaking for him. "You can talk to her for me like I helped you talk to her."

"You can't throw that back in my face." Dax's objections didn't sway Reed.

"I just did." He waved at his siblings, impatient to get moving. "Now, get out. Both of you. I have music to write and an apartment to pack."

And a woman to avoid. Because forgetting her would be impossible.

"Will you be living with Mr. O'Donnell, now he's moving into his house?" The teenage girl, one of Brianna's friends, asked, as she put on her coat, getting ready to leave dance class.

Quinn shook her head, unsure if she heard correctly. "Excuse me?"

The girl continued buttoning her coat, unaware she'd dropped a bombshell. "Mr. O'Donnell's been moving boxes and stuff into his house on my street all afternoon."

The words slowly penetrated her brain. The entire town knew Quinn and Reed were a couple. It was a small town. She should've expected it. "He's moving into his house?"

"I'm sorry. That was rude." The girl blushed, clearly embarrassed. "I shouldn't have asked if you'd be moving in, too, except you'd be a fun neighbor."

The girl knew more about her lover than she did. "He didn't mention anything about moving. How do you know?" She'd heard noises from his apartment all night. Every time she'd knocked she'd been ignored.

"He's going to be my neighbor on Pearl Street."

The street name hit Quinn, as if she were kicked in the gut. The same street as her grandparents. She didn't even hear the girl say goodbye, or the door chimes tinkle. She was too numb. Reed was moving out of his apartment upstairs without telling her.

Without thought, she grabbed her coat, turned off the lights, and locked the door. She bolted the few blocks toward Pearl Street. She needed to talk to Reed, find out what was really going on, and why he hadn't opened the door to her last night.

Since returning to Castle Ridge she'd avoided this street, didn't need reminding of what she'd lost. She'd failed her grandparents and her legacy. Veering down the street, she counted down the houses to her grandparents' old house and searched for Reed's truck in the different driveways. She spotted both. At the same location.

Her numbness sizzled across her skin, resembling electric shocks. Her feet rooted to the ground.

She stood in front of the Craftsman home she'd visited hundreds of times as a child. Some of her happiest memories lived in this house. The wide veranda where she'd drunk lemonade with her grandfather and played hopscotch. The porch swing where her grandmother had read her books. The large windows she'd stare out of, watching snowflakes fall.

"I can't believe Reed never told me he owned this house." Her voice swung into a high, happy note. It was serendipitous. He owned *her* house. Why hadn't he shown the house to her? Taken her there? She could once again visit, and maybe live in the beautifully constructed home with the man she loved.

"You're getting ahead of yourself." She tried to control her happiness. Reed and her had a relationship, and were building toward something more. She sensed it deep in her bones. She loved him and he loved her. They just hadn't spoken the words yet.

The house needed repairs. It had been empty for years while she lived in New York. She'd paid a management company to take care of it. By the peeling paint and rotting wood they hadn't done a very good job. There were aspects of new construction, though. The door had been replaced with stained-glass-window door. New windows had been fitted for the upstairs.

In her mind, she could picture the house in its glory. A big, square veranda covered by a sloping tiled roof. Clean, large windows to view the many trees out front—trees needing trimming. Wood shutters decorated the upper story windows. A two-car garage attached to the side where Reed's truck was halfway unloaded.

They hadn't made specific plans for last night, but they'd been spending every free minute with each other, and every night. Last night was the first time she'd slept alone for a week.

She missed him.

He must've been busy with packing and moving.

Excitement tripped over trepidation, causing her lungs to catch as she continued up the wide front steps leading to the front door. After knocking, she tiptoed inside the open door, feeling like a trespasser, even knowing Reed would welcome her. Their relationship had evolved so quickly he'd forgotten to tell her about moving day. That was all.

She stepped into the entryway and immediately felt at home, because this had been the one home she'd known. Her mother had moved from apartment to apartment around New York, and Quinn had lived in the dance school residence halls before being old enough to rent an apartment. None of those places had ever held her heart like her grandparents' house.

She stood on the entryway landing, which opened to an open-floor plan to keep families connected. No furniture. Piles of lumber and construction equipment sat in the living room. Scratched wooden floors showed lots of use. A stone fireplace to keep her and Reed warm on those long, winter nights. The inside of her chest flittered. She could see herself living here with Reed. Coming home after a day's work and sharing a meal. Working on house projects together. Decorating each and every room, including a baby's room.

Reed tromped into the main living area carrying a large cardboard box. His limp was less noticeable since he'd started dancing. She'd helped in his recovery, and she couldn't stop a smile. His messy hair curled more than normal, as if he hadn't combed it today, and he looked adorable. Sweat dribbled down his cheek, reminding her of his slickness while they were making love. He must've been working extra hard.

She took all of him in. She'd missed him. Missed his presence and his voice and his smile.

Wheeling around, his gaze locked on hers. The green orbs brightened, flashed, and then dulled.

Her heart thumped, and dropped into her stomach. Unease clutched around her neck. Why did he seem angry? Why hadn't he told her about moving? They were building a relationship. Why wouldn't he want her to know? Anxiety clogged her throat, making her mouth go dry. She couldn't breathe.

He pinched up his face and yelled, "What the hell are you doing here?"

Chapter Twenty-Three

Reed's body quivered with rage and lust and remorse. The tremors had started in his toes and traveled up his body, making him lose control. He hadn't meant to shout at Quinn, he rarely shouted. He hadn't meant to ever talk to her again. And here she was standing in his house, making him hurt and need at the same time.

Anger at his neediness had him tossing down the box. "What're you doing here?"

He didn't swear, only asked a polite question because he had control. Of himself, of his body, of his emotions. Even though he trembled from head to toe. Even though she made him crazy. Even though he should've known he couldn't walk away from her. Not with her determination.

Quinn's cheeks whitened and she wavered near the door. She clutched the banister around the door landing. Her chest moved up and down and he shouldn't have noticed. He wasn't interested in her distrustful ways. "This was my grandparents' house."

His turn to waver with dizziness. The last thing he expected.

"This is *my* house." *And he didn't want her here.*

He planted his feet on the hardwood floors, standing on one side of the room, while she stood on the far side. Not far enough. He'd bought this old house at an auction about six months ago. Slowly, he'd been fixing the home up, making it livable. The old house had been empty for years. The previous owners had been elderly and passed it on to an ungrateful heir who lived in New York.

Realization kicked and his abs clenched. Could she be the ungrateful heir?

She'd never acted ungrateful, she only talked fondly of her grandparents. He knew they'd lived on Pearl Street. But here, in this house?

"I told you I had to sell the house to pay for the dance studio." She stepped down the entryway steps, further invading his home. She scanned the entire living space. "It's why I rented the apartment above the studio at the last minute. When I'd originally made my plans, I thought I'd be living here."

Her words struck him. "You won't be living here."

He had to get through her thick head. And his thick heart.

If he couldn't trust Quinn, he couldn't love her. He'd learned the lesson long ago, in a different place and time.

She moved stiffly into the center of the living room. She must've been stunned to discover he'd bought her grandparents' place. He'd been attracted to the strong bones of the older home and planned to flip the house.

While repairing the roof and polishing the wood shelves, he'd fallen in love with the home.

White-faced, she moved to a wide, empty space by the bay windows, moving so fast he didn't have time to block her way. It was as if she hadn't heard him.

Her expression softened, and her eyes glazed in a trance. "When I was a kid, my grandmother had the piano sitting right here, and I'd dance around while she played."

His stomach twisted, shooting pain through every major organ. Her grandmother's piano. Her piano. The piano in her studio where they'd made love the first time.

The spot she referred to would be perfect for his grand piano, the one now occupying the garage. The windows would provide enough light to play, and yet the instrument would be shielded from the harsh rays of the sun. From that position in the open floor plan the acoustics would be perfect sending the tinkling chords of the piano throughout the large room.

Everything inside him hardened. His limbs, his core, his backbone. He'd never place his piano there because he'd see the child Quinn with blonde ringlets dancing around and laughing. The image would haunt.

"You should go." His voice was less forceful, even though he needed her to leave.

He didn't want her visit contaminating his new home. He didn't want to live here and think about her. It was why he'd moved out of the apartment so quickly. That and the too-close proximity. Shivering, he tried to shake off his empathy for her and what she'd lost. He hadn't known she'd already been in this house multiple times.

She focused those clear, blue eyes at him. Eyes beseeching and questioning. "I don't understand what's going on. We should talk." She wandered to the fireplace and trailed a finger across the top of the hearth.

The heart of the home.

Every muscle and tendon tightened. "Please leave." *Now.* Before he begged her to stay.

"Why are you mad at me?" She studied him, moving forward and getting too close. Close enough he saw the tiny black flecks in her eyes that sparkled when she orgasmed. Her chin angled and she got a confused expression. "What have I done?"

Did she believe he was so desperate for love he'd let her get away with breaking his trust?

"You know." He used a harsh tone, desperate to get through to her. And himself.

He couldn't forgive her. He'd let Elizabeth get away with lying and twisting the facts and doing things behind his back. She'd used him and his career. He would not let Quinn get away with it, too. She would only stay if he became famous by writing songs. She didn't love this small-town, construction worker version of himself. She wanted more out of him, from him.

Quinn stretched onto her toes holding onto the fireplace as if it was a ballet barre. "If I knew, why would I come here expecting a big welcome or a surprise?"

"A surprise?" The question shot out of him in a surprise of his own.

She hung her head and color finally returned to her cheeks. Too much color. "This is stupid, but when I saw your truck in the driveway, *this driveway*, I thought maybe you knew how special this home was and bought it for me."

Shock she'd even think such a thing rocked through him, and he stumbled backward. A warm sensation calmed his quaking body, because if she'd thought he bought the house for her, she must have deep feelings for him, dreamed of them being together.

Or was it another way for her to take advantage of him? Push him into playing, try to sell his music, expect him to buy a house for her. Similar to Elizabeth and her engagement ring.

"I bought this house before I even knew you." He squashed Quinn's dreams like she'd squashed him.

The questions seemed to double on her expression. Prowling toward him, she ran her fingers up his arm. He stiffened, forcing the blood pumping to his cock to stop. "And now you do know me, and—"

He grabbed her hands and tossed them away. "Stop." Her contamination was complete. Contamination of his house and his body. He couldn't let her convince him with sex. His heart might be breaking but he wouldn't let her know. Hardening every vulnerable part of his body, he forced himself to be tough. "I don't ever want to see you again."

She staggered back, as if she'd taken a direct punch. Her ocean-blue eyes rounded and then narrowed with hurt. She crossed her arms. "You're not even going to tell me why you're mad?"

He'd taken a punch, as if it was his fault she'd betrayed him. He couldn't feel sorry for her. His anger scorched inside him. "Were you ever going to tell me about your music executive friend who wanted to buy my song? The song I'd written exclusively for you?"

Her mouth dropped open, and she stepped back. Her gaze flashed with guilt. "How did you find out?"

He could write a song about the way guilt was written all over her face.

No. No more songs about Quinn.

Her non-denial stoked the flame higher. "Does it matter? I did find out." The flame flared, burning in his chest and creating a firestorm of fury. "Found out you lied and went behind my back. Found out you weren't trustworthy."

She flinched. Torment crossed her face. She held her hand toward him, reaching for understanding. He stepped away. "Reed, listen. I was going to tell you. First, I thought I'd send it to my friend and see what he thought. If he hated it, you'd never know —"

"It's lying." His tongue flicked with the fire. Elizabeth had cancelled concerts at the last minute because he was *sick*. Really, she'd wanted a weekend at the beach. She'd never told him until after the fact.

"If the music executive loved the song, you'd realize how talented you are. And if you wanted, you'd have a major music deal again." Quinn pleaded for understanding.

"I don't want a music deal. I don't want to write music." He wanted to stomp his foot to emphasize the untruth. He did want to write music; even now, a melody played in his head. A melody of anger and love and distrust. "I don't want anyone to hear my music."

The last statement was true. Except for Quinn, he wasn't ready for anyone to hear, and didn't know if he ever would be because if he became famous everything about his life would change. He wasn't ready for change.

"The song is beautiful." Her tone beseeched. She again reached out to him. When he didn't respond she let her hand drop to her side. "The world needs to hear your amazing talent."

"No." He sounded firm. Inside, he quaked with the idea. Fear or excitement? He couldn't tell. Maybe a bit of both.

"I sent the song off for you." She paused and made sure he was listening. "Because I care about you." Her voice cracked. "Because I love you."

The fire seared the declaration into his soul. She loved him? He found the word hard to comprehend. How could she love him, when she'd betrayed him?

She. Loved. Him. A short spurt of joy cooled his anger. Why did she love him? Wariness steamed in his veins. Did she love him for what he could do for her if he became a composer again? By sending out his song without asking, she'd proved her level of loyalty.

Shaking his head, he rejected what she said. Rejected her. "I can never forgive you for what you've done."

"Don't forgive me." Her voice turned harsh. She placed her hands on her hips in a combative stance. "You need to forgive yourself for the past."

"You don't know everything about my past." He

fisted his hands at his sides. "Elizabeth went behind my back. She lied. She stole."

Elizabeth broke him, not his heart. Because he realized now he never really loved her. His feelings paled in comparison to what he felt for Quinn. He was breaking his own heart this time, even though she claimed to love him. Better for him to end it before he was totally suckered in, before she could break him even more.

"The world needs more music written by Reed O'Donnell." She spoke like a prophet which rubbed him the wrong way and caused him to lash out.

She didn't understand the world of professional music. How cutthroat the business was, how quickly you needed to create, how you could be hot one moment and stone cold the next. He'd held everything in his hands, and now he had...nothing. "Too bad. The world never did anything for me."

"How can you say such things? You've lived an amazing life. Have a wonderful brother and sister. Started a second career you love. Live in this wonderful town." She swung her arms around, encompassing all he possessed.

He hated that she made sense.

He wasn't ready to accept anything she said. He'd committed to Elizabeth too soon. He'd lost her in a tragic accident where he'd suffered physical and emotional injury. He'd lost the music. "Leave my house, Quinn. I don't want to see you again."

Because his will was weakening. He wanted to yank her into his arms and kiss her senseless. He wanted to hear her claim of love again.

She staggered back again, and he wanted to catch her. Her expression fell, and her eyes pooled with tears. Swiping at her face, she headed for the door. Headed out of his life forever. She took one step and the next. Each move stomped on his heart.

Swinging around at the last second, she tossed him a regretful expression. "You deserve to be heard."

You deserve to be heard.

Reed pffft at the idea hours later. Quinn hadn't claimed to love him again. She hadn't said she couldn't live without him. It was about his song and how he could be successful. How she wanted him to be successful. In his mind he knew he was being selfish, but he wanted her to love him for him.

He slumped on the entryway step of his house in the last spot he'd seen Quinn. The home was quiet, yet he heard echoes of their argument. He'd lost his motivation to unpack. He'd lost her. He'd lost everything.

Desolation and agony echoed in his empty chest.

You deserve to be heard.

Why would anyone want to hear what he had to say? Hear his music?

He'd been successful before. So had a lot of other people. There were hundreds, possibly thousands, of one-hit wonders.

Of course, *he* heard his music constantly. Since Quinn, the melodies wouldn't stop playing in his head. He needed to write them down and put lyrics to the tune before his mind would stop churning with his thoughts and emotions.

Grabbing his hair with both hands, he let his head drop between his knees. He'd finally believed he could love and be loved. For himself. Not for his talent and his music. Because Elizabeth had never loved him. She'd loved what he could do for her. She'd loved being part of his entourage and his girlfriend. She loved taking control of his life and screwing things up.

He'd believed Quinn was different. Except she'd sent his song off to a complete stranger. A stranger who would demand more songs. Demand more of him. He'd lose the joy of creating. And for what? So he could make more money and Quinn could be taken care of in grand style.

A shiver wracked his body. He didn't want to live in a grand style. He wanted to live here, in this house, in Castle Ridge.

She'd said she wanted to live here, too, an inner voice taunted.

Supposedly, she loved Castle Ridge, and didn't yearn for the bright lights of New York. She'd loved this home and been devastated when she'd lost it. He knew that was true.

Why would she send the song off to some stranger? Why wouldn't she ask first?

He would've said no. He probably never would've shared a song again. He would've been stubborn.

Stubbornness had kept him from playing the piano for the past few years. Stubbornness and fear. He'd had the ability and the full range of motion in his fingers. But if he couldn't hear music in his head, why would he want to play?

Another shiver wracked him. Playing in front of strangers again? Sharing his music with the world? He hated the fact he yearned to compose. He'd expected after tossing Quinn out the door the music would abandon him. If anything, the noise in his head became louder, screaming for attention. Screaming for him to put his emotions into notes and chords and lyrics.

Getting to his feet, he trudged to his truck and pulled out the small electronic keyboard. He grabbed his construction notebook from the front seat and brought both of them into the house.

Glancing around, he scanned the large open space. He kept stopping at the spot where Quinn's grandmother's piano had sat. If he was going to push himself, force himself to discover who he was now and what he wanted, he needed to go all the way.

Setting the keyboard in the spot where Quinn's grandmother's piano had sat at one time, he rattled his fingers on the keys, picking out the most effective chords.

He composed and he healed.

Stretching his stiff limbs, he got up and prowled around the lonely house. A house that had spoken to him when he bought it and he'd decided to keep the home for himself. To see Quinn here, loving the same place, had helped him heal even more.

Letting the music speak to him, his subconscious counseled and organized his thoughts like notes in an arrangement. Organized and processed his feelings for Quinn.

She hadn't meant to deceive him. He realized that

now. She'd been trying to help. She believed in him and his music.

He had to believe in himself.

The day had gone dark. House lights went on across the street. All he had was a heavy-duty flashlight and the light of his love to compose by. His fingers moved faster on the keyboard. He sketched the notes down on paper, with words to match. Normally, it took him days, sometimes weeks, to compose a single song. This afternoon and tonight, he'd written as fast as she danced across a stage. She'd sent his music off in secret so he wouldn't worry, or if he was rejected he wouldn't be aware. His heart softened. She'd been thinking of him. Not herself.

She'd been right about a lot of things. How he should be heard again, because he had something to say. How he did have a lot to be thankful for. He only hoped it wasn't too late to salvage what they had together. He loved her, and now knew he deserved her love.

Hope filled his emptiness. His music spoke of hope and love and happiness for the future. This afternoon, she'd confessed she'd loved him. He had to believe that was still true.

Chapter Twenty-Four

Stretching onto her toes, Quinn twisted her hands together, viewing the crowd gathered to watch and participate in her grand opening showcase at the dance studio. The reception area was crowded with rented plastic chairs filled with people. There was Izzy and Dax. And Danielle and Brianna. And a host of people she'd met and become friends with in the past few weeks.

There was no Reed.

Quinn's lungs squeezed. Tears prickled. She refused to cry. This was supposed to be a triumphant night.

Izzy had counseled on his stubbornness. Dax had over-explained his absence. Quinn knew Reed hated her, and would never forgive. She hadn't known about how his fiancée had deceived him and messed with his career. Quinn had sent the song out of love, out of a need to protect and yet cherish his gift.

Without realizing it, she'd crossed his line about deception. She'd ruined the best relationship she'd ever had. Would ever have. Her lungs constricted again. With or without Reed, the show must go on.

"Thank you for coming to our Opening Dance Extravaganza. I'm Quinn Petrov, and I've had the pleasure of teaching students of all ages for the past two weeks." Her gaze touched on the people she'd become close to. Living in Castle Ridge without Reed by her side would be tough, but worth it. She loved the town and she loved the people in it. "If my students can do this in two weeks, imagine what your dancing skills will be after a month or two months."

The audience laughed, knowing a sales pitch when they heard one.

"Let's start with our youngest students." Making sure the kids were in their places, she clicked the music on. "They'll be doing a short ballet sequence."

The toddlers went through basic positions, each one a bit off-rhythm. They *pliéd*, and *relevéd*, and *sauté d*. The last, a small jump, was greeted with applause. Quinn's mind wasn't with them. She watched through a haze of misery, reminding her of when she'd first heard Reed play the piano. He'd sounded tortured and miserable.

Clapping interrupted her thoughts. The toddlers were done.

"Weren't they sweet?" She glanced at the audience again. Still no Reed. The obstinate man had taken years to forgive himself for his fiancée's death, why would he forgive her in two days?

He should've let her explain her side. She'd sent the song off for him, not against him. She hadn't known how damaged he'd been by Elizabeth's tricks. Because he hadn't told her.

She stomped her foot. "Next, we have our grade-school and middle-school students."

The next group of kids filed onto the dance floor. Sara limped in at the back. She reminded Quinn of when Reed first started dancing. His limp had improved, and so had Sara's. Quinn also remembered how sweet he'd been to the child.

Her throat dried at the image of her and him, together in his house, with their children. His song had expressed his love, and yet, with one mistake, he'd thrown her love away, not even willing to discuss.

More clapping. She needed to pay attention to her show. This was important to her future, because she didn't have a future with Reed.

The middle school kids were next, and with the usual assortment of girls were three boys. She couldn't help but be proud of the accomplishment. When they were done, she clapped extra loud for the co-ed group.

"Up next is the high school students."

The smaller kids scattered back into the audience and the high school girls spread out across the dance floor, including Brianna.

Quinn clicked the remote. No music played.

Her blood pressure spiked, taking her out of the numbness she'd lived with since her argument with Reed. The stereo system repair guy had come and couldn't replicate the problem. Of course she could, on the day of her showcase.

She clicked the remote again and again. "Excuse me for a second."

She hurried to the system on the wall console and

pushed the power button off and on again. Nothing. The manual slipped off the top and fell to the floor. Freezing, she stared at the black-and-white manual where she'd found Reed's song. The song he'd composed for her, and she'd carelessly scanned and emailed to a friend. Not carelessly. She'd sent the song out of love and respect. She punched the power button harder.

"Something wrong?" A deep, male voice rumbled through her.

A beloved voice.

She raised her head.

Reed stood beside her in nice slacks and a dress shirt. His handsome face gave a short, tremulous smile. His gaze glimmered with something other than disgust. Could it be love?

Her heart hitched and raced at a rapid pace. She'd believed he'd loved her. He'd written a love song for her.

"Everything's wrong." And she meant more than with the music. Everything was wrong without him.

"Can I help?" He leaned toward her with eagerness.

Hope soared, fluttering in her chest. "Will you help? Help me always?" She whispered the last part, aware of their audience.

"Always." His serious tone bespoke volumes, spoke more than the lyrics in his song. His eyes bored into hers, making a solemn vow.

"I'm sorry I sent out your song."

"I'm not. It forced me to make some decisions." His green orbs softened with seriousness. "I thought you were pushing me back into the New York life."

"I risked everything to be successful here. I love Castle Ridge."

"Me, too." He held out his arms and she rushed into them, coming home.

Because home wasn't a place for her, it was a person. Reed.

His lips claimed hers and joy lit through her bloodstream giving her hope wings. The kiss was a promise.

He'd been suffering, too. His past had affected his perspective. And hopefully now, things were in proper order. She'd learned more about him in the day they'd been apart, learned more about herself. He needed time to process; his music came from his soul, and was a precious gift. A gift she shouldn't have passed along until he was ready.

Clapping broke out from the crowd. Loud, piercing whistles and catcalls. Heat scorched her cheeks, but it was a good embarrassment, a happy embarrassment. They were happy for her and Reed. Knowing they'd have a lifetime to sort things out, she broke off the kiss and pointed at the stereo. "I've got to finish the showcase."

He grinned broadly, and started fiddling with the wires. The air crackled and then went out completely. "I don't think I can fix this."

"We can fix us, right?" She rubbed a finger across her just-kissed lips.

He nodded and tried again with the stereo. Nothing happened.

"Sorry, everyone. One more minute." Stretching on her toes, she clasped her hands together. This was her showcase. The event was the first step in making her dance studio a success. She turned to the one person she counted on. Reed. "What am I going to do?"

"I might not be able to fix the stereo, but I can make music." Swiveling, he started in the direction of the piano. "And I know the songs."

Startled, she grabbed his sleeve. "No. You don't have to." She didn't want to force him to do anything he wasn't ready for. She'd rather suffer the loss of business, than have him play piano for an audience.

Reed scanned the audience of mostly friends. Nerves tripped in his stomach, but nothing like the paralyzing fear he'd first had after the accident. The only stranger in the audience was the music executive he'd picked up from the airport. The reason he was late.

The executive's number had been in Reed's recent call list on his phone. He'd hesitated before placing the call. He was willing to hear what the man said and then make a decision. A decision he planned to make with Quinn by his side.

He knew the song the high schoolers were dancing to from memory. He also knew the song the adults were performing. He could do this. He would do this. For Quinn.

"I can perform. I want to perform." He also needed to do it for himself, to prove how much he'd grown. To show he'd forgiven himself.

The confidence pumping through him didn't quite make it to his feet and fingers. The audience's attention followed him with each step he took across the dance floor.

He sat at the piano and placed his fingers on the keys. Scanning the audience, his gaze lighted on Izzy and Dax's expectant expressions. He connected with Quinn, who had her head held high, as if willing him fearlessness. His hands stopped shaking. Nodding at her, he set his fingers down.

"Sorry about the delay. We've had some trouble with our stereo system. I'm happy to announce we have world-renowned pianist Reed O'Donnell to accompany the rest of our dancers."

He really wasn't world-renowned anymore, and didn't want to be. He'd be happy composing and constructing and building a life with Quinn.

The audience clapped. Dax whistled. Izzy stood on her feet.

With calm fingers, he began to play. Peering over the piano, he connected with Quinn again. Her look boosted him. He could do this.

For her. For him. For their future.

The high school dance blurred past him. All he heard was the music, the joyfulness in his heart.

"Now for the adults." Quinn moved beside him and asked, "Do you mind if I dance with Dax, so you can play?"

Reed straightened his spine. He knew he had nothing to be jealous of. "As long as you'll dance with me later. In private."

Her face glowed. Her smile broadened and brightened his insides. "I'll dance with you for the rest of our lives."

He floated through the final song. His fingers whizzed over the keyboard. His shoulders swayed through the tune.

The audience applauded the end of the dance.

"Thank you everyone for participating and attending. We have snacks to celebrate." Quinn glided toward the piano. "Let's give an extra round of applause for Reed O'Donnell, for providing the music."

Standing, he bowed. "To celebrate Quinn's opening I have a gift for her."

She placed a hand on her chest. Her gaze widened in surprise and softened with love.

Love.

A tingle went from the top of his head to his feet. He wiggled his toes. Any doubt cleared from his mind. Quinn loved him. And with her love, he could accomplish anything.

The audience oohed and aahed.

His love gushed, surrounding his heart. "I love you, Quinn."

She cupped his chin, her fingers holding his face like a cherished object. "I love you, too. With all my heart."

"This is the gift." Stretching his fingers, he cleared his mind and connected his gaze to hers. Staring into her eyes, he began to play. Quinn's song. Formerly entitled *For Quinn*. Now, *Quinn-tessential*. Because she was essential to him.

Everyone else in the room ceased to exist. It was only him and her. Him declaring his love for her with his music.

✳

The champagne popped in celebration of the dance studio opening, and Reed celebrated their love. Izzy and Dax hugged him, both happy Reed was out of his shell and could play music in front of people again. Danielle and Brianna congratulated him.

Quinn worked the crowd, signing up people for paid classes. She was going to do great in Castle Ridge.

Her friend, the music executive, shook his hand. "I loved the song on paper and I loved it more hearing it live. I want to buy the song from you, and talk about other songs in the future."

"I don't want to perform. I only want to compose." Reed didn't want to leave Castle Ridge, or Quinn. He could continue his remodel business and write. With her by his side.

She sidled up next to him. "Wonderful news. How does it feel to be a composer again?"

"It's good." He could write at his leisure, putting the music in his head on paper. He could play his piano and Quinn would listen. He'd be happy living a whole life.

Sara tugged on his pant leg. "You didn't dance Mr. O'Donnell." She sounded disappointed.

He bent to her level. "I'm sorry. I needed to play the music."

"Dance now." The girl crossed her arms and glared.

"Um, there's no music, sweetie." Quinn tried to appease.

"I'll sing." Dax showed his support for Reed and Quinn's relationship.

"Me, too." Izzy raised her hand.

"And me." Both Danielle and Brianna joined the chorus.

A few other people joined in with the humming.

Reed's chest swelled with love for his family and friends. With his love for this woman. "Can I have this dance, Quinn-tessential?"

Quinn placed her hand in his. "For the rest of my life."

*Read on for excerpts from other books
in the Castle Ridge series.*

Dear Reader,

I hope you enjoyed *The Romance Dance*. If you enjoyed the book, please consider leaving a review at your place of purchase. Word of mouth is crucial for any author to succeed so she can continue bringing you more stories you love.

And don't forget to join my newsletter for a free book. You'll also get the latest book news, sales, and contest information. You can join at www.allieburton.com

Allie

Excerpt from

The Christmas Match

A Castle Ridge Small Town Romance, Book 2

by ALLIE BURTON

The season for second chances.

After heartache at a young age, single mother Danielle Marstrand has finally found her place in her hometown. A good job, a good home, a great daughter—nothing can sway her from her course until Luke Logan returns to their small Colorado mountain ski town.

Champion skier Luke Logan is ready to return home to Castle Ridge, even if he's not quite sure the town's ready to welcome him. Especially his high school sweetheart Danielle. Nursing an injury that nearly ended his career, Luke's struggling to get back more than his range of motion...he's hoping returning to where his career began might help reignite the passion he's lost. But instead of discovering his passion for skiing he discovered the daughter he never knew he had.

Hurt that Danielle never told him about Brianna, Luke is determined to know his child. Danielle's reluctant to allow Luke in, fearing he'll just leave again, but she's willing to compromise when Luke suggests fake dating with Brianna tagging along. Why then, does a kiss for show feel oh so real?

In this classic reunion story, love finds a second chance.

EXCERPT:

"You're single. I'm single. You've changed. I've changed. You asked to meet *me*." His voice rose in accusation. "Nothing smarmy about that."

Her eyebrows rose. "Every time a woman asks you to meet does it mean having sex?"

"Pretty much." His cockiness caused the wine to burn in her chest.

Disgust made it travel the wrong direction. "Not with me."

His eyes blinked. For a second she thought she'd seen hurt on his expression, but then the suave-macho guy she'd seen in interviews on TV made his reappearance. "Then what do I owe this... pleasure?"

His hesitation told her he meant the opposite of pleasure, but again the imagined images of the two of them together burned. Her entire body felt as if she sat in the fire, not next to the fireplace. She blew out a breath and focused on what she came to do.

Tell Luke. Tell Luke. Tell Luke.

The room seemed to close in on them. The few people in the dining area were normal people having normal conversations. They weren't about to change someone's life. They weren't about to alter their own reality. And their daughter's.

The fire roared louder. The flames spurted higher, taunting. Other people's laughter spiked through her head. The clanging dishes echoed and burst in her brain.

She blew out a slow breath, knowing she just needed to spit it out. "I need to tell you something and I want a promise you won't yell or make a scene."

"I promise." His snippiness set the wrong tone.

Nerves scraped in her stomach making the wine go sour. Nausea rumbled and burned up her chest. She felt as if she was going to heave on the table. She pinched her lips together and then forced her mouth to open. To speak.

Nothing came out.

"I haven't seen you in thirteen years. There's nothing you could say that would make me angry." He grabbed his mug and took a long pull.

She froze at his statement and his casual action. *He didn't believe anything she said mattered?* Her iced body cracked and heated. Fissures formed with her fury. *He didn't think she mattered?* Her brain popped and her veins burst in a torrent. *He probably wouldn't think their daughter mattered either.* Her hands curled into cold claws. She wanted to scrape the annoying expression off his handsome face.

Instead, she scooped up her coat and lunged out of the booth. "Oh!"

To hell with him.

"Well?" His impatient tone yanked her to a stop, goaded her.

Her heart thumped once. Deviousness had her swirling back around. So, he didn't think anything she said would affect him, did he? She was going to give him the shock of his life.

She took a step forward, leaned toward him, and whispered, "Brianna is your daughter."

Excerpt from

The Flirtation Game

A Castle Ridge Small Town Romance, Book 3

by ALLIE BURTON

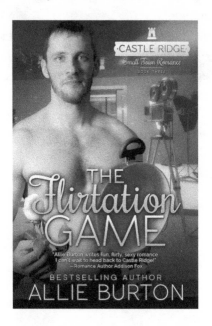

Love isn't all that's cooking.

After a scandal in Hollywood, celebrity chef Michael Marstrand accepts a position to be head chef at Castle Ridge Lodge and star in a television program about re-opening a five-star restaurant. He believes returning to his hometown to help the struggling restaurant will earn him public relations points and help an old friend. What he doesn't know is the sous chef expected to be named head chef and the television series is a reality show called *Kitchen Catastrophe*.

Sous Chef Isabel O'Donnell returned from vacation to discover the restaurant kitchen remodeled and a new head chef. With contracts already signed, she has no choice but to work for Chef Michael, a man she'd had a crush on since middle school. A man who'd stolen her job.

With the hidden cameras rolling, Michael tries to make the day-to-day routine boring so *Kitchen Catastrophe* will never be shown, but an interfering producer introduces a bridezilla and an employee who causes trouble. Add the simmering attraction between Michael and Isabel and the reality show has everything: drama, fights, and sex.

In this best friend's brother conflict, will a fake flirtation produce the perfect recipe or enflame desire?

EXCERPT:

Michael stepped away from Isabel and straightened his shirt. A shirt she hadn't even realized she'd messed.

She ran her fingers through her hair, trying to pull herself together. She was going to be head chef; she couldn't be caught making out in the kitchen. Not only was it unsanitary, it was unprofessional.

Parker, the lodge owner, observed the two of them, a glint of confusion on his face. His perfectly-coiffed hair appeared tame compared to the man she just kissed.

"What do you need?" Michael's voice sounded normal. He obviously had more control over his libido.

Her skin cooled. Maybe he wasn't as attracted to her.

"Good. You two are getting reacquainted." Parker wrung his hands together. He seemed more together than on New Year's Eve, but still jumpy.

Why would he be nervous of either one of them? In high school, Michael and Parker had been best friends. Now, they acted like strangers.

Michael's face was a complete mask. What was he hiding?

"I'm glad you're going to be okay with this decision, Isabel." Parker's shoulders relaxed.

She tilted her head, trying to figure his puzzling words out. "What decision?"

"Now that Chef Françoise has retired, I'll be announcing the new head chef."

Her chest pounded. She stood straighter, and pulled back her shoulders. This was it. Parker was going to tell her the head chef position belonged to her.

He waved his hand in a vague fashion. "The press release with head shots will go out today."

Air caught in her lungs. "I didn't take new photos."

Michael jerked beside her. He gaped at her with raised eyebrows and tightened facial muscles. "What?"

"No need for the sous chef to take head shots." Parker avoided her gaze like a guilty man.

"But...but." The catch in her chest morphed into a

fissure, a fissure cracking and widening with each of her panicked thoughts. "I'm the new head chef."

Michael's shoulders hunched, and he took a step back, as if he'd taken a punch to his midsection. Except she was the one who'd taken the punch, because something was wrong. Parker acted nervous. Michael shocked.

She sucked in a sharp, jagged breath, ignoring the pain. "Chef Françoise promised me the position."

Michael's skin had gone white as a chef's coat. His round eyes had dimmed of color. "What?"

Parker's expression softened, except for his pinched mouth. "I'm sorry, Isabel. I thought Michael told you. I thought that's why you two were talking in the kitchen together."

Her breath spasmed, sending alarms throughout her body. Her gaze switched back and forth, between Michael and Parker. "Told me? Told me what?"

Parker touched her arm. "The new head chef at the Castle Ridge Lodge is celebrity chef Michael Marstrand."

Excerpt from

The Playboy Switch

A Castle Ridge Small Town Romance, Book 4

by ALLIE BURTON

Instructed in fun. Schooled in love.

After almost dying in an avalanche, Dax O'Donnell makes a promise to himself: get serious about life and his career. His playboy ways might be fun, but he needs to plan for his future. Applying to paramedic school has always been a dream, but is he smart enough to succeed?

Lexi Henderson has loved Dax since joining the ski patrol team at Castle Ridge Resort. Knowing he's a playboy, she's kept her distance, but when he's rescued from an avalanche she kisses him and sparks both of their desires. But he thinks she has a boyfriend—another playboy, and she keeps a major secret. Or two.

Dax suggests *fun lessons* to turn Lexi's quiet and rigid attitude around. But when fun turns to passion, he must ask, is she willing to make the playboy switch?

In this secret identity tale, love overcomes secrets and lies.

EXCERPT:

"That guy will break your heart." Dax eased up next to her with a drink, but no woman in hand. His carefree expression was gone and the light had dimmed from his green gaze.

"Will he?" She was curious to see where this was going. He must not realize Ryder was her brother and would never hurt her. Not like others in her past.

"Ryder Croft is a playboy with no serious career or goals."

She glared. Her brother loved coaching the kids on his ski team. Sure, he was a little lost when it came to a career. Dax had no right to judge. "Really?"

"Croft is a gazillionaire." Dax sounded as if his beer went sour. "If I had as much money, I'd quit my job and ski around the world."

"Sounds as if you want to be just like him." His sour tone filled her mouth with a bitterness that burned down her throat. He was jealous of Ryder's wealth, not because he'd been dancing with her. Dax reminded her of her ex-fiancé Andrew who had only been interested in her money and her family's connections. Pursing her lips, she tried to control her annoyance. "You don't care about your job?"

She had a passion for saving people which is why she'd joined the ski patrol and become a paramedic. She didn't want anyone else to unnecessarily lose their life on the mountain. The invention she'd been working on and trying to get developed would help her mission.

"I care about my job. I don't want to see you get hurt." He took her hand and patted it like she was a cowering puppy. "Croft's a playboy."

"And you can say this because you have the greatest dating record?" Overplaying her sarcasm, she let her pessimism come out in her voice. She'd always been attracted to Dax, yet kept her distance knowing his true personality. "You're a playboy."

His eyes morphed into chipped emeralds. He gripped her hand tighter and pulled her against him. "Then go out with me instead."

The whispered words sent a tingle down her spine.

She'd longed to hear a declaration from Dax. A sexual tease or an invitation. Except this was a declaration of competition because he was jealous of her brother. The moment he learned about her background, she wouldn't know if he liked her or her money. Plus, what exactly was he asking for? A date or a night in bed?

Stopping the tingles before they reached her heart, she forced a sappily sweet smirk. "So I should dump Ryder and start dating you, doing a playboy switch?"

Excerpt from

The Billionaire's Ploy

A Castle Ridge Small Town Romance, Book 5

by ALLIE BURTON

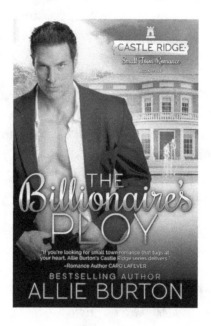

All's fair in love and business.

Billionaire Jackson Croft refuses to let anything interfere with his merger and marriage plans. His merger. His brother's marriage. When Emory Barrington returns to Castle Ridge and catches his younger brother's attention, Jackson needs to take drastic steps to stop the flirtation. Even if it means using himself as bait.

As a child Emory was infatuated with the younger Croft brother, so when he invites her to a party she can't resist. Until Jackson interrupts their dance, tries to bribe her, and then steals a kiss. A kiss that vibrates to her soul.

To make up for the attempted bribe, Jackson offers her a job decorating his Denver penthouse. She's just starting her interior design firm and can't turn the business away even if it means working closely with the billionaire. The project turnaround is fast and the attraction between Emory and Jackson grows faster. She believes she sees the real man beneath the façade, but when she learns of his double-dealing her heart can't take the betrayal.

In this take off on the *Sabrina* story, can deception lead to love?

EXCERPT:

"The party is tonight. You should come." Ryder's invitation had Emory's stomach clutching.

All of her teenage fantasies about attending one of the Croft events burst into an explosion of light. Joy shot through her entire body setting off tingles of excitement. *Ryder Croft invited me, Emory Reese Barrington, to a Croft party.*

Geez, quit acting like a child. She shouldn't be impressed. She'd been to lots of fancy parties in Spain. She was a special guest at a Vizconde's party. Her thoughts soured. One of many of his special guests.

"You're inviting me to your sister's wedding reception? Isn't it a bit late to RSVP?" Except he wasn't inviting Emory, he didn't know who he spoke to.

"There will be hundreds. One more person won't be noticed." He took her hand and rubbed his thumb against her skin. "We could dance."

She practically swooned. Clutching the coat tighter between her hand, she imagined holding Ryder in her arms while they danced, of him walking her through the elaborate gardens like she'd seen him do with other girls, of him kissing her.

Ryder would be disappointed when he found out her name, but for now, for this one moment in time, she could be special to him. "I'd love to."

"Great." An uneasiness slid into his gaze and she wondered if he was picturing the woman he'd planned to propose to. He turned away and opened the trunk taking out her suitcase.

"Hello, Emory." An even deeper masculine voice rumbled.

In a panic, she pivoted around at the greeting. Her fantasy to pretend for a little while longer died by two words from the scary, older brother. She'd hoped Ryder wouldn't learn who she was until tonight at the party. When she was dressed up and looking her best.

She straightened her shoulders. It was too late now. "Hello, Jackson."

Wearing a suit and tie on a Saturday afternoon, he strolled from his boring sedan parked ahead of them. His brown hair had been slicked back from his forehead in perfect grooming. A couple of new lines had formed on his forehead. Because he never had fun, his only interest being the family business.

"Emory?" Ryder raised his brown eyebrows into high arches. He hadn't figured out who she was after spending thirty minutes in her company.

Her spirits lowered. Had she been so unnoticeable

as a kid? Jackson had recognized her immediately.

Jackson signed off on a clipboard a worker gave him, barely glancing at her. "How was Barcelona?"

She angled her chin surprised not only that he remembered where she'd gone, but that she'd been gone at all. Their paths didn't cross frequently in the past, on purpose. She'd avoided him and his scary and overbearing attitude. "Good."

The work experience had been great. The personal life not so much. But she wasn't going to go into detail. Not with Jackson.

"Emory?" Ryder's jaw dropped.

"Your mother is going to be glad you're home." Jackson looked at her and then at his brother. His gaze went quizzical. "Good to see you," he said before heading up the stairs and through the front door.

"Emory?" Ryder shook his head as if trying to get her name straight.

Disappointment speared through her chest. Her fantasy had ended sooner than expected. They weren't even going to have drinks together. "I suppose your invitation to the party has been withdrawn now you know who I am."

"No." He shook his head again still appearing shocked. "No. Of course not."

She raised her brows. "Are you sure? Do you still want to dance with the housekeeper's daughter?"

He waved a hand in front of his face and his expression cleared. His gaze roved over again as if assessing her shape. "This is the twenty-first century."

Her stomach squirmed with misgiving. That wasn't really an answer to her question.

The Heartbreak Contract
A Castle Ridge Small Town Romance, Book 6

by ALLIE BURTON

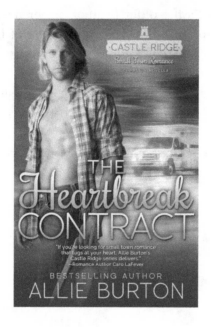

Love on the dotted line.

Self-made sports and entertainment agent Vivienne Tucker knows no one in the frozen town of Castle Ridge is going to melt her heart. No one can. She's been on her own for too long and while her skin might appear soft, she's as tough as nails.

Paul Bradford is a devoted family man to his younger siblings, whose heart and life belong to the town he grew up in. He's not used to taking time for himself or relationships, but after an anonymous one-night stand, he can't forget the ice queen who heated at his touch and ignited a passion he thought he'd lost. Until the next day when he spies her kissing someone else.

Vivienne never expected to see Paul again until she discovers he's the older brother of her newest client. An older brother who doesn't approve of her client's career choice. An older brother who stirs up desire she's tried so hard to forget.

When her client is involved in a possibly career-ending accident, Vivienne and Paul must put aside their differences and work together. But what if working together makes them both re-think the heartbreak contract they'd agreed upon?

COMING SOON IN THE CASTLE RIDGE SERIES!
The Marriage Merger
The Runaway Royal

If you love young adult romance with fantasy and adventure, try Allie Burton's two young adult series FREE!

About

Atlantis Riptide
Lost Daughters of Atlantis, Book 1

by ALLIE BURTON

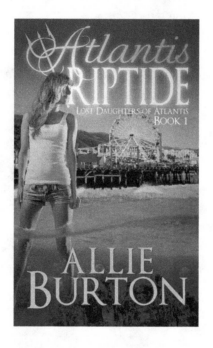

When a girl runs away from the circus...

For all her sixteen years, Pearl Poseidon has been a fish out of water. A freak on display for her adoptive parents' profit. Running away from her horrible life, she craves one thing—anonymity. But when she saves a small boy from drowning she exposes herself and her mutant abilities to Chase, a budding investigative reporter.

Now, he has questions. And so do the police.

Once Pearl discovers her secret identity, she learns she's part of a larger war between battling Atlanteans. A battle that will decide who rules the oceans. A battle raging between evil and her true family. Will she find a way to use her powers in time to save a kingdom she never knew existed?

This is the start of a young adult fantasy action adventure novel series. "Free sweet summer young adult paranormal with death-defying underwater rescues."
– Reviewer

Soul Slam
Soul Warriors, Book 1

by ALLIE BURTON

An ancient Egyptian amulet.
A pharaoh's soul inside demanding she obey.
A double cross that ends with a curse.

On her first heist to steal an ancient Egyptian amulet, sixteen-year-old Olivia inadvertently receives the soul of King Tut...and the deadly curse that comes with it. And Olivia's not alone at the museum.

A member of a secret society, Xander believes it's

his place to inherit King Tut's soul and justly rule. He knows nothing about the society's evil plan to control the world or the curse. Now, he must deal with the female thief who stole the amulet.

When the two teens find themselves up against the secret society, they reluctantly join forces and must figure out how to end the curse before it turns deadly. On the run and unable to touch because of the curse, Olivia and Xander develop a connection during their quest.

As the mystery surrounding the amulet unfolds, Olivia and Xander fall for each other. But is love enough to save them and the world from destruction?

"If you are a fan of Rick Riordan books about a quest with love and history thrown in…this is for you!"
– Hooked In A Book Review

Other Books by Allie Burton

CASTLE RIDGE SMALL TOWN ROMANCE SERIES
The Romance Dance
The Christmas Match
The Flirtation Game
The Playboy Switch
The Billionaire's Ploy
The Heartbreak Contract
The Marriage Merger (*coming soon*)
The Runaway Royal (*coming soon*)

LOST DAUGHTERS OF ATLANTIS SERIES
Atlantis Riptide
Atlantis Red Tide
Atlantis Rising Tide
Atlantis Tide Breaker
Atlantis Dark Tides
Atlantis Twisting Tides
Atlantis Glacial Tides

SOUL WARRIORS SERIES
Soul Slam
Tut's Trumpet
Peace Piper
Cleo's Curse

Find all of Allie's books on her website.
http://www.allieburton.com/books.html

Acknowledgements

Switching from young adult to contemporary romance has been an exciting journey. I want to thank those who encouraged me to make the change, who helped me distinguish the differences between writing first person young adult and third person romance, and who assisted me with the learning curve of writing something different. Through the process, I have grown as a person and as a writer.

Thanks to my developmental editor, Caro LaFever, who pushed me to dig deeper into the character's emotions, careers, and backstories. Who also read each of the Castle Ridge books twice! Thanks to Addison Fox, for her encouragement and critiques. Her knowledge of the romance genre is undeniable. And thanks to Tanya Saari, my proofreader, without her I'd have commas in all the wrong places.

Finally, thanks to my husband, who is the hero in my own romance.

Allie Burton has always been a reader and writer. She wrote her first novel at the age of twelve when she was stranded at a hospital by a snowstorm. Receiving her first romance from her grandmother, she fell in love with the genre. As an adult, she read young adult books with her own teens and was excited to find something fresh and new. Now, she writes both.

Having so many jobs as a teen and adult became great research material for the stories she writes. She has been everything from a bike police officer to a professional mascot escort to an advertising executive. She has lived on three continents and in four states and has studied art, fashion design, and marine biology.

Allie is a member of the Society of Children's Book Writers & Illustrators and Romance Writers of America. She loves to ski, golf, and run. Currently, she lives in Colorado with her husband and two children.

CONNECT WITH ALLIE ONLINE:
www.allieburton.com
www.twitter.com/Allie_Burton
www.Facebook.com/AllieBurtonAuthor
www.wattpad.com/AllieBurton